PRAISE FOR LESLEY KAGEN

The Mutual Admiration Society

"Lesley Kagen's latest gem . . . takes readers on a fabulous adventure to discover whether or not a murder has been committed in the local cemetery. With the hilarious Finley sisters at the helm, nothing can go wrong—or can it? Spunky, fun, and entirely charming. Both a mystery and a coming-of-age story that's sure to delight!"

—Mary Kubica, *New York Times* bestselling author of *Don't You Cry*

"A captivating tale that is woven together with sharp wit and heartbreaking honesty."

—Heather Gudenkauf, *New York Times* bestselling author of *Missing Pieces*

"With its gloriously quirky kid's-eye view of grief, mental illness, and strange happenings in a nineteen-fifties neighborhood, this heartwarming story is sure to delight fans of *The Curious Incident of the Dog in the Night-Time*."

—Barbara Claypole White, bestselling author of *The Perfect Son*

"Fact: You will fall in love with eleven-year-old Tessie Finley and her sister Birdie. Proof: Lesley Kagen's novel *The Mutual Admiration Society*, where Tessie Finley sets out to solve a mystery in true Nancy Drew fashion. Except Nancy D your heartstrings like Les

will not want to put down, and Kagen is a master storyteller who will keep you hovering between laughing and crying the whole way."
—Cassie Selleck, bestselling author of *The Pecan Man*

The Resurrection of Tess Blessing

"How wonderful it is to spend time inside Lesley Kagen's creative mind. In *The Resurrection of Tess Blessing*, Kagen deftly illustrates her gift for blending the serious and the funny, the light and the dark. With a touch of magical realism, she once again creates a story that's as hopeful as it is poignant. As a reader, I feel safe in her hands."
—Diane Chamberlain, international bestselling author of *Pretending to Dance*

"Kagen's talent shines in this wholly original and richly imagined story where unbearable heartache is softened with humor and a touch of magic."
—Beth Hoffman, *New York Times* bestselling author of *Looking for Me*

"Read *The Resurrection of Tess Blessing*, but don't read it in public because it'll yank the emotions out of you. You'll laugh, you'll cry, and by the end you'll be Tess Blessing's best friend."
—Cathy Lamb, bestselling author of *What I Remember Most*

"Lesley Kagen at her finest, magically weaving together a tale of poignant regrets, powerful aspirations, and forgotten dreams through Tess, a woman who is really a bit of each of us. By traveling this journey with Tess, we are shaken, uplifted and transformed."
—Pam Jenoff, bestselling author of *The Winter Guest*

"Confronting her own mortality, Tess Blessing, a lifelong list maker, tackles the only To-Do list that matters: healing fractured relationships, and empowering the children she fears she will leave behind. Poignant, funny, and searingly wise, *The Resurrection of Tess Blessing* will stay with you long after you turn the last page."

— Patry Francis, bestselling author of *The Orphans of Race Point*

"Helmed by the most interesting narrator I've read in ages. She and her gifted author, Lesley Kagen, lead us through heartbreaking, humorous, compassionate twists and turns until we find ourselves on the other side, wiser but also, appropriately, resurrected and blessed. It is a journey I was delighted to take."

— Laurie Frankel, bestselling author of *Goodbye for Now*

"I was hooked from the get-go. Tess Blessing's story is quietly inspiring. With faith, hope, grace, and humor she shows us how to keep moving forward in the face of fear, uncertainty, and pain . . . Put one foot in front of the other and call in your oldest friend."

— Julia Pandl, bestselling author of *Memoir of the Sunday Brunch*

"Tess's emotional journey makes for compelling reading . . . a richly detailed, deeply resonant story of a woman of incredible strength."

— *Kirkus Reviews*

"Told with abounding humor and wit, *The Resurrection of Tess Blessing* is an engaging page-turner that women everywhere will relate to . . . an intimate and uplifting character sketch of a middle-aged woman's life journey, filled with the unexpected twists and turns and sage wisdom that come with the passage of time."

— *Shepherd Express*

The Undertaking of Tess

"A tender yet bighearted coming-of-age story filled with heartbreak, secrets, and humorous observations of the convoluted adult world through which two young sisters must navigate."

—Beth Hoffman, *New York Times* bestselling author of
Looking for Me and *Saving CeeCee Honeycutt*

"A bittersweet coming-of-age-in-the-fifties story that'll have you crying one minute and laughing out loud the next. Kagen's ability to capture children's deepest emotions never fails to impress."

—Bonnie Shimko, award-winning author of *Stony Lonesome Road*

Mare's Nest

"From page one, *Mare's Nest* reached out and grabbed me. A true-to-life tale that is artful and lovely and smart."

—Lauren Fox, bestselling author of *Friends Like Us*

"*Mare's Nest* is a fascinating and heartfelt look at the intricacies of the mother-daughter bond, along with that often inexplicable, yet oh-so-powerful girl/horse obsession. I couldn't put it down and neither will you."

—Theresa Weir, *New York Times* bestselling author of
The Orchard

Good Graces

"A beautifully written story . . . You will weep for and cheer on the O'Malley sisters . . . [and] immediately miss them once the last page is turned."

—Heather Gudenkauf, *New York Times* bestselling author of
Missing Pieces

"*Good Graces* deftly dwells in '60s Milwaukee. Through her preteen narrator, Sally O'Malley, [Kagen] evokes the joys, sorrows and complexities of growing up."

—Milwaukee Journal Sentinel

"Kagen does a remarkable of balancing the goofiness of being an eleven-year-old with the sinister plot elements, creating a suspenseful yarn that still retains an air of genuine innocence."

—Publishers Weekly

"For all the praise garnered for *Whistling in the Dark*, *Good Graces* more than lives up to its predecessor."

—School Library Journal

Tomorrow River

Outstanding Achievement Award from the Wisconsin Library Association

Shelf Awareness's Top Ten Books of the Year

"[A] stellar third novel . . . Kagen not only delivers a spellbinding story but also takes a deep look into the mores, values, and shams of a small Southern community in an era of change."

—Publishers Weekly (Starred Review)

"Packed with warmth, wit, intelligence, images savory enough to taste—and deep dark places that are all the more terrible for being surrounded by so much brightness."

—Tana French, New York Times bestselling author of
The Trespasser

"The first person narration is chirpy, determined and upbeat . . . Shenny steals the show with her brave, funny, and often disturbing patter as she tries to rescue herself and her sister from problems she won't acknowledge."
—*Mystery Scene Magazine*

"The charming genuine voice of Shenny . . . is impossible to resist."
—*Milwaukee Magazine*

"An excellent, moving story, very well written, and one that will linger in your thoughts long after you've finished it."
—*Historical Novels Review*

Land of a Hundred Wonders

Great Lakes Book Award nominee

"Kagen's winsome second novel offers laughter and bittersweet sighs."
—*Publishers Weekly*

"A truly enjoyable read from cover to cover . . . Miss Kagen's moving portrayal of a unique woman finding her way in a time of change will touch your heart."
—Garth Stein, *New York Times* bestselling author of *The Art of Racing in the Rain*

"I've been a Lesley Kagen fan ever since I read her beautifully rendered debut, *Whistling in the Dark*. Set against the backdrop of the small-town south of the 1970s, *Land of a Hundred Wonders* is by turns sensitive and rowdy, peopled with larger-than-life characters who are sure to make their own tender path into your heart."
—Joshilyn Jackson, *New York Times* bestselling author of *The Opposite of Everyone*

"Gibby hooks the audience from the onset and keeps our empathy throughout . . . Her commentary along with a strong support cast make for a delightful historical regional investigative tale. [Gibby] is a 'shoe-in' to gain reader admiration for her can-do lifestyle."

—*Mystery Gazette*

Whistling in the Dark

MIDWEST BOOKSELLERS ASSOCIATION CHOICE BOOK AWARD

FINALIST FOR THE GREAT LAKES BOOKSELLER AWARD

NEW YORK TIMES BESTSELLER

"Bittersweet and beautifully rendered, *Whistling in the Dark* is the story of two young sisters and a summer jam-packed with disillusionment and discovery. With the unrelenting optimism that only children could bring . . . these girls triumph. So does Kagen. *Whistling in the Dark* shines. Don't miss it."

—Sara Gruen, *New York Times* bestselling author of *Water for Elephants*

"One of the summer's hot reads."

—*Chicago Tribune*

"The loss of innocence can be as dramatic as the loss of a parent or the discovery that what's perceived to be truth can actually be a big fat lie, as shown in Kagen's compassionate debut, a coming-of-age thriller set in Milwaukee during the summer of 1959."

—*Publishers Weekly*

"Delightful . . . gritty and smart, profane and poetic."

—*Milwaukee Magazine*

The

Mutual
Admiration
Society

OTHER TITLES BY LESLEY KAGEN

The
Mutual
Admiration
Society

A NOVEL

LESLEY KAGEN

LAKE UNION
PUBLISHING

Published by Lake Union Publishing, Seattle

www.apub.com

Amazon, the Amazon logo, and Lake Union Publishing are trademarks of Amazon.com, Inc., or its affiliates.

ISBN-13: 9781503941038
ISBN-10: 1503941035

Cover design by Rachel Adam

Printed in the United States of America

For the always and forever loves of my life,
Casey and Riley
Charlie and Hadley

1

PARTY POOPER

I, Theresa Marie "Tessie" Finley, hereby confess that on the night of October 17th, 1959, instead of keeping my ears to the ground and my eyes peeled for suspicious goings-on in our neighborhood, the way I swore to do on the Holy Bible, I screwed up really bad.

For cripessakes, any president of a blackmail and detecting society worth their salt would've at least poked their head outta their bedroom window at 12:07 a.m. to see who was hollering their head off in the cemetery behind their house, "I'm warning you! Watch yourself! You're treading on dangerous ground!" But what did *I* do? I acted like some dumb schmoe who doesn't know the score.

According to Chapter One in what has to be the best book ever written on the subject, *Modern Detection*, a private investigator is never supposed to "assume" they know something without having proof *and* they're also never supposed to "let emotions cloud their judgment."

But the minute I heard that hollering over at Holy Cross, I'm ashamed to say, instead of really listening to the voice barging through our bedroom window so I could figure out who it was—I am an ace at that sort of thing—I right away "assumed" that it was Mr. Howard Howard, because every once in a while (mostly after he's been hitting the schnapps bottle), he staggers over to the cemetery in the wee hours to collapse in a heap on his wife's grave to bawl his eyes out and threaten God that He better give his Mrs. back ASAP or else. And if *that* wasn't bad enough, I also let my emotions cloud my judgment, because Mr. Howard Howard and me, we have that in common.

I could be an expert witness on sad madness. If Mr. Perry Mason called me to the stand, I'd step right up, swear to tell the whole truth and nothin' but, and testify in that court of law how when the missing sadness comes out of nowhere to kick me where it hurts, I'd say and do almost *anything* to make the pain stop. And how when I start remembering the smell of the Pabst Blue Ribbon beer sloshing around on the bottom of the white motorboat, the cracking sound my father's head made when it hit the motor, and the taste of the lake water that splashed into my laughing mouth after he fell overboard, I can switch real fast into the off position of God's and my on-again, off-again relationship, too.

So, when I first heard the yelling in the cemetery, I thought, *Give 'em hell, Mister Howard Howard. Let HIM do a little sowing of what HE reaped for once and see how HE likes it,* and I went back to doing what I always do in the middle of the night—besides slipping my hand under my sister's heinie every once in a while to make sure she hadn't wet the bed, working on my lists, shadowboxing, practicing my impressions, and a couple of sure-fire jokes that I think will get the crowd going—I breathed in deep and got ready to launch into the "Favorite Things" song that I'm going to perform for the talent portion of Miss America someday in honor of my father.

But when a high-pitched scream, also coming out of the cemetery, interrupted "Raindrops on roses . . . ," a couple of ideas hit me over the head like a "bright copper kettle." *Mister Howard Howard's voice is much gruffer than the one I'd heard yell, "I'm warning you! Watch yourself!*

You're treading on dangerous ground!" And that screeching? Even though it sounded kinda familiar, that couldn't have belonged to him, neither. That had to have come out of a mouth wearing lipstick.

And thanks to a certain librarian, I knew exactly what I had to do next.

You wouldn't think by the looks of the gray-eyed brunette that she'd have a brain in her head, but boy, oh, boy, the famous saying that I bet is thrown around the Finney Library on North Ave. more than anywhere else, "You can't judge a book by its cover," is so true.

Last month, when that pretty librarian Miss Peshong found me loitering around my favorite aisle, she smiled, nodded at the stack of mysteries in my arms, and said, "Judging by the books you've been reading for the Billy the Bookworm contest, Tessie, I've been wondering if you're interested in becoming a real-life Nancy Drew when you grow up."

Of course, I breathed in deep, smiled back, and told her, "That's a bright idea. I'll think about that," even though it wasn't and I wouldn't. The only reason I was interested in reading those books was so I could learn more about *doing* crimes, not *solving* them. But I liked that Miss Peshong had given my future some thought and that she always smelled like baby powder even though she didn't have a baby and she kept a pink lace handkerchief in her blouse sleeve in case a kid accidentally started crying when she saw a dad and his daughter checking books out together, so I felt sorta cruddy about fibbing to her, but only a little, because believe me, honesty is *not* always the best policy. If I'd told the librarian the truth, which was that I thought her idea stunk up the joint because when I grew up I was going to keep being exactly what I already was—an eavesdropper, liar, shoplifter, cat burglar, poison-pen writer extraordinaire, and top-notch blackmailer—because she goes to Mass at St. Catherine's Church, the same way most everybody around here does, I'm pretty sure that'd get around the neighborhood in nothing flat.

"Yes. Solving mysteries is an interesting line of work that I think you'd be very well suited for, Tessie," Miss Peshong said with a wink as she pulled a thick, black book with gold writing off the shelf I was standing next to. "Perhaps this will help set you on your path."

I told her, "Thank you," even though my knees buckled under the weight of *Modern Detection* and I had 0% interest in reading the darn thing, but what choice did I have? I had to keep up my front.

I almost sprained my arm pulling home the nine regular-sized mystery books and the other giant one Miss Peshong gave me in my Radio Flyer wagon, but I knew that baby-smelling librarian meant well, so I didn't hold it against her. I also knew that she would ask me what I thought of *Modern Detection* the next time I stopped by the Finney, because she had to, *if* I wanted the book to count for the Billy the Bookworm contest, which I did. So to have at least a little something to make her believe that I'd read it, I reluctantly cracked it open that night, but in no time at all . . . I found myself flipping through those pages with fingertips that felt on fire! And at Mass the next morning, I went ahead and said a few Hail Marys for Miss Peshong, because it was thanks to her that I learned I could play both sides of the fence. I could steal a cake and eat it, too!

Due to extenuating circumstances—my mother—I hadn't found the time to finish the book that has turned out to be such an eye-opening life changer, but I *had* learned in Chapter Two of *Modern Detection* that when it came to crime, it was extremely important for me to arrive at the scene of it sooner rather than later. So I snatched the double-Dutch jump rope from the closet, knotted it to the bedpost, and got ready to climb out of my bedroom window. The second my feet hit the ground, I was going to run across our backyard to the black iron fence that surrounds Holy Cross Cemetery and monkey over it faster than King Kong scaling the Empire State Building to do some gumshoeing.

On the *other* hand—I've come to learn that there is *always* another hand to slap you around, usually about the time you're feeling like you got the world by the tail—no matter how much my detecting mind was telling me that heading over to the cemetery in the dead of night was a swell idea, my guts were reminding me about that other famous saying, "Haste makes waste," which means a person should never be too fast to act or they could end up holding the shit end of the stick.

Believe me, if I coulda, I woulda shaken awake my sleeping sister so we could snoop at the cemetery together, but since there wasn't a snowball's chance in h-e-double-hockey-sticks that I could get Birdie up and running at that hour of the night—she has never been much of a night owl—it was just me and my churning tummy that wrestled my trusty Roy Rogers flashlight out from under the mattress, slid Daddy's lucky Swiss Army Knife from under my pillow, and got down to business.

Watching my father die taught me the most important lesson I'll ever learn in life—BE PREPARED—so I was already wearing my regular snooping clothes—black shorts, a navy-blue T-shirt that matches my eyes, and filthy white sneakers—when I slid my always nicked-up legs out of our bedroom window, shot a quick look over at Holy Cross to plan the quickest route to where I thought the voice and the scream might've come from, and . . . and . . . lo and behold! In the glow of one of the flickering streetlights alongside the road that snakes through the cemetery, I caught sight of a guy slithering through the gravestones with what looked like a limp body in his arms seconds before he disappeared behind Mr. Gilgood's mausoleum!

FACT: That tall, thin man definitely *wasn't* Mr. Howard Howard.

PROOF: Due to my weekly surveillance of his Precious Gems and Jewelry store on North Ave. that I might have to heist someday if things go from bad to worse around here, I've watched the stumpy owner lock up his shop and waddle next door to Dinah's Diner dozens of times to stuff his mouth with jelly donuts and wash them down with a cup of joe with three sugars.

So there I was, all set to sleuth after that mystery man and the no-longer-screaming gal he was lugging around, when my wiggle over

5

the windowsill was stopped in its tracks by even *more* suspicious noises ripping out of the black, velvety night. Not more shouting or another screech coming out of the cemetery. These sounds hit even closer to home and were even more blood-curdling. Elvis Presley was warbling about a hound dog out of a car radio, and then the hot rod that belongs to our mother's new boyfriend laid squealing rubber down Keefe Ave.

12:21 a.m. I barely had enough time to scramble back into bed and yank the sheet up to my chin before our mother, Louise Mary Fitzgerald Finley, came through the front door of our two-story wooden house that looks about the same as most of the other two-story wooden houses that beam out in blocks from St. Catherine's Church and School like rays on a holy card.

After Louise turned on the bathroom light so she could swipe off her makeup with Noxzema cream and tinkle out the beer she wet her whistle with at Lonnigan's Bar, she kicked her red high heels off in front of the Finley sisters' bedroom door. All she probably wanted to do was hit the hay after her big fat date, but she *had* to make sure that Birdie and me weren't sneaking around the neighborhood the way we do any time we get the chance, because she's got something she wants really bad and she's worried our "shenanigans" might screw it up for her. (For a gal who blew out twenty-nine candles on her last birthday cake, our mother is such a sucker. She's fallen for the old stuff-pillows-under-your-sheet prison trick at least six times. In the last month.)

Of course, I kept my eyes shut when she came to the side of our bed, but I knew she was looking down at Birdie and me. I could smell the beer and peanuts wafting off her, the same way they did when Daddy would come home from working his late-night shift at Lonnigan's. Only *he* wouldn't stand next to our bed and sigh. "Good Time Eddie" Finley would belly flop onto the mattress between my sister and me, gather us in his strong arms, and belt out his favorite song. But instead of him sticking to the real words, "We belong to a mutual admiration society, my baby and me," Daddy would wail, "We belong to a mutual admiration society, my *babies* and me."

But there were other nights when the smartest and sweetest, handsomest and funniest man in the whole neighborhood wouldn't sing. He'd lean his ladder against the side of our house, crawl through his "babies'" bedroom window with a black nylon stocking pulled over his face and a five and dime gun in his hand. "This is a stickup! Give me all your hugs," he'd growl like a bank robber, only a lot slurrier. When Birdie and me would yank the covers over our heads and pretend to scream if we were waiting for him, or really scream if we weren't, Daddy would slap his knees and say, "Ha . . . ha . . . ha! *Gotcha!*" because he adored jokes of all kinds, but he got the biggest charge out of the ones that practically scared the poop out of a person.

But as soon as our mother got done pressing her salty lips against Birdie's and my foreheads a little bit ago and clicked the door shut behind her, I rolled over and wrapped my sweet-smelling sleeping sister in my arms and popped the top offa my biggest grin. Sure, the worst party pooper on the planet might've wrecked my investigating what went on in the cemetery as fast as I would've liked to, but when the sun came peeking through the cracks in our bedroom window shade, believe you me, the Finley sisters would have the last laugh. All the way to the bank.

I'm not so good at arithmetic, but one guy yelling + one gal screeching + the both of them disappearing behind the Gilgood mausoleum in the middle of the night? Any idiot could see that added up to one thing and one thing only.

The Mutual Admiration Society had a bloody murder case on our hands!

2

COME HELL OR HIGH WATER

"Good Time Eddie" Finley's last words to me were, "What a great day to be alive and out on the water with one of my favorite girls."

DADDY'S REMAINS

1. Birdie.
2. Jokes.
3. A hankie.
4. The Swiss Army Knife.
5. His Timex watch.
6. A brown belt.
7. Famous words of wisdom.

If only he hadn't borrowed *The High Life* boat from his friend Joey T so him and me could do a little fishing on Lake Michigan in Milwaukee, Wisconsin, on August 1st, 1959. And after he slipped on the bottles of beer rolling around the bottom of the boat, hit his head, and fell overboard, if only I hadn't sat there laughing my head off because I thought at any second he was going to swim to the surface and say, *Thought I was a goner, didn't ya, Tessie? Ha . . . ha . . . ha. Gotcha!*, Birdie and me wouldn't be able to see the curve of his gravestone out our bedroom window.

With every beat of my heart, every breath, every lightning bolt, and every joke, I miss him. There is not a minute that goes by day or night that I don't wonder how I'm going to live to the next minute without him. But I *had* to force myself to stop bawling every time I pressed Daddy's watch against my ear or when I smelled his Old Spice stuck in the seams of the white hankie or felt the weight of his Swiss Army Knife in my hand. And when I waited outside of Lonnigan's Bar, I had to stop pretending that the only reason the best bartender in the world didn't come laughing and stumbling out of the back door after his shift was because I got my nights mixed up. What choice did I have? A broken heart is so heavy to lug around that a kid can feel the life seep out of them with every step, and I needed every ounce of strength I had left to honor the promise I made to myself to step into Daddy's shoes. It was the only way I could figure out to pay penance for not even trying to save him.

6:30 a.m. I'm so excited to tell still-snoozing Birdie that I'm 95% sure a murder got committed in the cemetery last night, but from years of experience, I know that if I don't want her to go unruly on me, I have to settle myself down and follow *her* TO-DO list instead of mine. It'll take me four tries to wake her up. It does every day. That's her favorite number.

I wipe her too-long bangs off her forehead and say, "Morning!"

Neither one of us are even close to being as beautiful as our Irish mother. My sister and me got more of Daddy's English blood running through our veins, thank God. But with her blah-brown hair and nose that's turned up a little too much and slightly bulging eyes, my sister is the much better looking of the two of us, which is good by me, because the poor kid doesn't have much else going for her.

On try #2 to wake her, I slip my hand under the top of her pink baby-doll pajamas and play her ribs with my pointer finger like they're a xylophone. "Time to face the music!" (Joke!)

Since I turned eleven two weeks after Daddy died, that makes Birdie ten years old, because we have the same birthday—August 15th, which just so happens to also be the Catholic holy day of the Assumption of the Virgin Mary. (Probably why I have such a horrible tendency to *assume* things.)

We weren't supposed to be born on the same day, but even before she came into this world, Robin Jean Finley couldn't stay put. She popped out of our mother two months too soon at St. Joseph's Hospital on Burleigh St. weighing too little under five pounds. After the nurse cleaned her up and placed her in Daddy's boxing arms and he got a load of her fluffy hair, big eyes, and little bones, he smiled and declared my new baby sister a "featherweight." He tried out a couple of different nicknames but settled on Birdie, which was darling once upon a time but had a bad ending. (How was he supposed to know that "Birdbrain" would be just one of the names kids in the neighborhood would end up calling her if I'm not around to set them straight?)

And no matter how much I wish and pray it wasn't so, as the *Titanic* would say, when it comes to my sister, being dumb is just the tip of the iceberg. (Joke!)

Try #3. I whisper straight into her ear, "Time to get the show on the road, kiddo."

I still haven't found any information on this subject at the Finney Library, but it sure seems like being born before the time you're supposed to be can cause a lot of weirdness to set up shop in a kid's brain, because even *I*, who love her most of all, now that Daddy's gone, have to admit that Birdie is one odd duck. And sad to say, according to this movie her and me saw at the Tosa Theatre called *The Snake Pit* that we thought was gonna be another one of those animal-dying movies like *Bambi* or *Old Yeller* but turned out to be about this shapely brunette who ended up in an insane asylum, my sister also greatly resembles another one of her neighborhood nicknames—"Loonatic." (The harmless kind. Not the kind like Ed Gein, who got everyone so worked up around here after he murdered a bunch of people near our state capital of Madison and sewed lampshades and slipcovers outta their skin. Birdie would *never* do something like that. She can't even thread a needle.)

Sure, some days go so bad around here that it might seem like she has, but Birdie has not yet gone *completely* nuts.

She doesn't have #10 and #11 on the list yet, but if she starts doing those anytime soon, we're going to have to scram out of the neighborhood before the men in the white coats show up, which is one of the main reasons I started up The Mutual Admiration Society in the first place. To save up a lot of running-away money, because Daddy wouldn't like it if I let our mother toss my sister into the county nuthouse, which, believe you me, is getting less far-fetched by the day.

SURE SIGNS OF LOONY
1. Seeing, hearing, and smelling stuff that nobody else can.
2. Acting more high-strung than a Kentucky Derby winner.
3. Wearing clothes that don't go together.
4. Not understanding what's going on in movies or television shows or the neighborhood.
5. Wetting the bed ~~all the time~~ sometimes.
6. Wild-streaking.
7. Extreme stubbornness.
8. Having a leaky memory and a drifting brain.
9. Not getting jokes and the ones they tell are lamer than Tiny Tim.
10. Murdering.
11. Drooling, when not asleep.

On my fourth and final try to get my sister up and running, I tell her what Daddy told her every morning since she was born, "The early Bird gets the worm!" And after she pops open her run-of-the-mill blue eyes that I tell her are a gorgeous *Robin*'s-egg blue—she loves to be buttered up, and if you can throw her name into the mix, that's frosting on the cake—I hold up the little gift she left under my pillow last night. It's a nickel. 1958. "Thank you, honey. It's the shiniest one I've ever seen!"

After I bounce out of bed, I toss her the pile of clothes that I picked out before we turned in last night, because if I let my sister choose what to wear, she'll slip on a pink-striped T-shirt with a pair of yellow polka-dot shorts and running around the neighborhood like that is not only #3 on the LOONY list, it's the worst possible getup for snoops and blackmailers to parade around in. We gotta blend in. (Green is good to wear in the springtime and summer, brown or tan is best for the fall, white when the snow flies, and no matter what time of year, black or navy are our go-to outfits on night missions.)

"Hurry and get dressed. We got a big, big day ahead of us," I tell Birdie. "You're not gonna believe our great good luck! When I was in the middle of practicing my Miss America routine last night, I heard this shouting, and then . . ." Shoot. It's going to take forever to explain what I heard and saw while she was sawing logs and even longer for her to understand. It usually works out better if I play *show* instead of *tell* with her. "Pull your shorts up. We gotta get over to the cemetery ASAP. There's something I really, really, really, really want to show you!"

'Cause Birdie loves our home away from home as much as me, I'm so positive that she is going to love this idea that I can't believe my ears when she says, "I'm sorry, but we can't go over to the cemetery this morning to look at whatever you really, really, really, really want to show me, Tessie."

Oh, boy.

Most of the time she's real easy to boss around, but sometimes, for some unknown reason, the kid can go more stubborn than a bloodstain on me. This better not be one of those times. I got a good feeling that today could be the start of something big and I'm not the only one who thinks so. I have what *Modern Detection* calls in Chapter Four "corroborating evidence."

Daddy used to be the one to answer all my questions, but when I get stymied these days, I have to rely on the next best thing. My Magic 8 Ball. I keep it hidden in my closet so our mother doesn't find it, because she'd blow her top if she did. It's a sin to ask anything to foretell your future, only God's supposed to know that, but honestly, I already got so many sins, what's one more? Especially since after I asked the Magic 8 Ball this morning, "Will today change our whole lives?" the little white paper that floated up informed me, *It is decidedly so*!

"Did you forget that we go over to the cemetery *every* day to visit Daddy?" I ask as I wiggle Birdie's tan shorts up to just below her protruding tummy that's the only chubby part of her, so from the side she looks like a pelican.

"No, I didn't forget that we go over to the cemetery *every* day to visit Daddy, Tessie, but we can't go over there right now, 'cause . . ." She cocks her little head. "Listen."

There are so many sounds in our neighborhood this morning, the same ones there always are: WOKY AM blaring rock 'n' roll songs out of the car radios that belong to the fathers on their way to their shifts at the American Motors plant or the Feelin' Good Cookie factory, milkmen delivering their clanking bottles, the *Milwaukee Sentinel* landing on front porches, St. Catherine's "St. Kate's" church bells clanging, dogs barking, and moms and dads hollering at their kids from their front porches to get outta the street.

None of those everyday noises have ever kept the Finley sisters from running over to the cemetery before, so what is Birdie picking up on that I'm not—oh, dang it all!

FACT: The kid's got better hearing than Lassie when that pooch goes looking for Timmy Martin in an abandoned well.

PROOF: I didn't notice the way she did that Trouble with a capital T is up much, much earlier than usual, brushing her teeth and gargling in the bathroom down the hall, which is probably why Birdie is digging in her heels.

In a tiny portion of her tiny brain she might be remembering our mother's #1 Commandment that we're never, under *any* circumstances, supposed to go over to the cemetery. If she is, we could wait a half hour or so and my sister with the terrible memory would probably forget that rule, but I don't have that kind of time on my hands this morning. Louise will be breathing down our necks soon, and I'm almost positive a murder has been committed in a neighborhood that hardly nothing goes on in without somebody finding out about it in five seconds flat and spreading it around even faster. You spit a loogie around here and before it hits the sidewalk you'll read about it in St. Kate's *Weekly Bulletin*.

One of our nosy neighbors *had* to have heard the ruckus going on at Holy Cross last night the same way I did and they might've already called the cops. I didn't hear any sirens or see any flatfeet from the Washington St. police station stomping around the cemetery when I checked about a million times this morning out our window while I was waiting to wake up Birdie, but I'd bet dollars to donuts the cops are over there somewhere doing their jobs, the same way the snooping Finley sisters oughta be.

I don't want to ask Birdie if the reason she's refusing to go over to Holy Cross with me this morning is because she's remembering that our mother who she loves so much doesn't want us to, because if she *isn't* remembering that, I would've blown it. I just quickly tug the brown T-shirt over her head and say, "C'mon. Don't be a wet blanket. We got plenty of time to run over to the cemetery." The church bells are letting me know the time, but I double-check Daddy's watch that I keep on me at all times, and sure enough, it's 6:45 a.m. on the dot. It takes Louise at least a half hour to get dressed and fix her hair after she's done brushing her teeth. "No sweat."

A person wouldn't have to be a detective to see that my sister doesn't go for that idea.

She starts flapping her arms like crazy and if I don't soothe her ruffled feathers, she'll do the next weird thing she does when she gets really riled up or very hungry. She'll throw her head back and squawk. Louise will hear for sure. The whole neighborhood will hear for sure. This little kid has got such a big set of lungs on her that she could be an opera singer when she grows up. *If* she grows up. I'm not sure how long somebody with her condition lives.

"Okay, okay, simmer down, honey," I tell her *sotto voce*, which means *very softly* in the Italians' language. (You go to school with as many wops as I do, live four houses down from Nana Cavallo, who only listens to Sicilian funeral music on her record player, and watch as many gangster movies as me, ya pick things up.) "I really, really, really, really want ya to climb the cemetery fence this morning with me, but . . ." I have to tie on my thinking cap and come up with another idea to get Birdie to do what I need her to do. Believe me, it's for her own good. "How about if we . . . hmmm . . . hey, I know! Instead of going all the way over to Holy Cross, how 'bout we just head down to the back porch and see if we can see from there the great-good-luck something I wanna show you that you're really gonna love?" We might be able to catch the cops dusting gravestones for fingerprints or tripping over a fresh corpse with a dagger sticking out of its throat from the porch that overlooks the cemetery, which isn't nearly as good as being at the scene of the crime, but better than nothin'. "Whatta ya say?" I stick my hand in my pocket and furiously rub my fingers on Daddy's Swiss Army Knife for luck. "You in?"

Things can change minute to minute with my weird, loonatic sister, but I'm currently having very high hopes that I won't be heading down to the back porch alone to see what I can see in the cemetery. Even though Birdie has parked herself on our bedroom carpet with that you're-not-the-boss-of-me look on her face, I have one more trick up my sleeve that's been working like a charm lately to get her going full speed ahead.

Our parish is full of juvenile delinquents nicknamed "greasers," and busybody neighbors nicknamed "killjoys," so if you're the kinds of kids who are snoops and blackmailers who are on their own because their mother doesn't like them very much and they don't have a father anymore who would beat the living daylights out of anyone who dare lay a finger on his "babies," you better be fast on your feet around here, and unfortunately, only one of the Finley sisters can make that brag.

Even though I'd gotten a heckuva shiner from Butch Seeback, the meanest and greasiest of the greasers, due to Birdie's dawdling, I'd been having the worst time making her remember that if we suddenly found ourselves in a rough-and-tumble situation, which seems to happen to us all the time these days because of our dangerous lines of work, we had to haul our heinies away from whatever fix we were in ASAP! No ifs, ands, or buts.

I'd just about given up on getting through to her and felt doomed to spending half of my life with beefsteaks on my eyes, when the answer to my problem came out of nowhere the night Birdie and me were in the middle of playing the umpteenth game of cat's cradle on our front porch steps a couple of weeks back.

There we were, breathing in that ripe red apple smell that's been hanging over the neighborhood, passing the bakery string back and forth, when my sister's most favorite song in all the world—"Rockin' Robin"—came drifting down the block. The second she started to snap her fingers and got that irresistible smile on her face, I knew Birdie was going to take a powder, but my hands were tied. Before I could shake the string off my fingers to stop her, she hopped down the porch steps and took off like she was a rat following the Pied Piper toward where the tune was coming from, which turned out to be the Tates' house five doors down.

When I was chasing after Birdie, my keen detecting mind couldn't help but wonder just what in the hell stick-in-the-mud Mrs. Nancy Tate would be doing up at 10:47 p.m. listening to rock 'n' roll music when her husband was laid up at St. Joe's Hospital with the broken leg he got when he was playing football at the yearly St. Kate's Men's Club game.

At that time of night, you can usually find *somebody* in the neighborhood up to no good, but whatever that particular gal was doing, I was positive that it would *not* be blackmailable or mysterious and therefore a huge waste of my precious time. Mrs. Nancy Tate, the current treasurer of the Pagan Baby Society, who our mother is running against in the election in a few weeks, was probably up doing something boringly holy. Something like humming along to a stack of 45s while she was sewing patchwork quilts for heathen African children on her Singer machine.

So all I'd been thinking about doing when I finally caught up to Birdie was scolding her and dragging her back home, but after I caught a handful of her T-shirt in the Tates' backyard, the poor thing was looking so eager to peek into the window the music was coming out of that I caved in. Sure, I was 100% positive that nothing would come of it, but I figured as long as we were there, what the heck. I gave my sister the shhh sign and took outta my shorts pocket the two things that I *always* keep on me after the streetlights come on. And once I got done wiggling down over our faces the exact same black nylon stockings that Daddy used to wear when he snuck up on *us* in the middle of the night, the sweaty Finley sisters crept hand in hand toward the Tates' rumpus room window, ready, willing, and mostly able.

Because we weren't on one of our regularly scheduled missions, but on one of Birdie's regularly unscheduled missions, I didn't have the chance to grab our coaster wagon that's got the soda crate in it for my sister to stand on so she can see into our neighbors' windows,

18

so I ended up having to piggyback her. Once we got squared away, we peered through a crack in the curtains on the Tates' wide-open window the music was booming out of and . . . lo and behold! Holy Mrs. Nancy Tate *wasn't* humming along to Birdie's most favorite song in all the world while she was pumping the pedal on her Singer machine the way I thought she'd be. Holy Mrs. Nancy Tate was humming along with "Rockin' Robin" and pumping something else! She was shimmying around her wood-paneled rumpus room in a white pleated Washington High School cheerleader skirt for a traveling vacuum cleaner salesman. His back was to me, but I knew who it was. One of his uprights was standing next to the chair he was sprawled out in, and he was holding in his hand the same drink he always orders at Lonnigan's Bar whenever he comes into town. Vodka on the rocks + a Hoover machine = Mr. Horace Mertz.

Everything was going along peachy keen—Mrs. Tate was giving us real blackmailing eyefuls—*until* it got to the part in the song that my sister just goes absolutely crazy for. The part when the rockin' robins start flapping their wings and singin', "Go, bird, go." I was so impressed by that old cheerleader's splits that I forgot all about paying attention to you-know-who, and by the time that I did, Birdie was singing really loudly along with the song and I couldn't slap my hands over her mouth the way I normally would've because I was using my arms to hold her up.

When it hit Mrs. Tate that she wasn't performing a solo anymore, she dropped the red pom-poms she was using to cover up her long boobies, ripped open the curtains we were peeking through, hollered something at us that should get her kicked out of the Legion of Decency, and then you know what that half-naked rah-rah gal had the gall to do? She sicced her wiener dog on the Finley sisters! Slid Oscar straight through the rumpus room window!

Of course, animal lover Birdie, who was still wailing away at the top of her lungs, wanted to stay and pet the pooch instead of hightailing it out of there before we got our faces chewed off by that vicious little foot-long, so praise be to whoever is the patron saint of genius ideas for *finally* delivering the answer to the problem I'd been having of getting her to scram from life-threatening situations, because it worked like a charm that night and on many more snooping missions since.

Even if my partner in crime is being stubborn, scared, or overly friendly with a dangerous guard dog or greaser, all I have to do to get her moving toward a safe location is to remind my little candy worshipper that I, her one and only, the sister who loves her like no other, will reward her with a yummy Hershey's kiss if she beats me in a race to wherever I tell her to run to. (I'm ten times faster, of course, but I let her win. She wouldn't play along if she didn't get *something* out of the deal. She's weird and a loonatic, not some chump.)

So *this* morning, the start of the day that our Magic 8 Ball told me would change the Finley sisters' entire lives, the beautiful Indian summer morning that I'm hoping to start investigating our very first murder case from the back porch of our house, I pluck my sister's flapping hand out of the air, press it down on my shorts pocket that's bulging with chocolate kisses, and tell her the same thing I told her in the backyard of the Tates' house the night we needed to escape from the jaws of the wiener dog. "Race ya to the back porch! One for the money, two for the show, three to get ready, and—"

Sure enough, just like I was *almost* positive she would, the kid with a sweet tooth a mile long sings the words from her favorite song in all the world over her shoulder as she shoves past me and runs out of our bedroom door, "Go, Bird, go!"

3

LIKE A NECK TO COUNT DRACULA

After Birdie and me scramble down the stairs, skid across the green linoleum kitchen floor, and burst through the squeaky back screen door that Daddy kept meaning to oil, my sister throws her arms in the air and announces with a gloating smile, "I win!"

When I drop the first-place chocolate kiss candy into her hand that she's waving two inches from my face, I want to, but I resist the temptation to tell her for the millionth time that she's really gotta work on being a better winner, and I get busy doing what I came out here to do in the first place.

I lean the top part of me over our peeling porch railing, swivel my head as far as it will go to the left and the right, and what to my wandering eyes should appear but . . . a big fat zero. What the heck? Where's the fuzz searching the cemetery for clues under the red and orange leaves, carting off a stiff through the tombstones, or holding back a pack of slobbering bloodhounds near Phantom Woods?

Wait just a cotton-pickin' minute.

Is it even humanly possible that not one of our neighbors called the Washington St. station house to report what they heard and saw in the cemetery last night? Am *I* really the only one who knows about the crime that was perpetrated? Well, while I would just love to believe that, I learned my lesson. I can't screw up again, not the way I did when I assumed it was half-in-the-bag Mr. Howard Howard ranting over there in the wee hours. So I remind myself again how *Modern Detection* warns gumshoes to look at *all* the different answers to problems that pop up during the course of an investigation, not just the ones they go crazy for right off the bat. "An investigator must remain skeptical of easy solutions," Mr. Lynwood "My friends call me Woody and my enemies call me their worst nightmare" Bellflower, the writer of the detecting book whose words I take very much to heart, warns in Chapter Four.

So from here on out, I, Theresa Marie "Tessie" Finley, hereby do swear that when something mysterious happens during the course of this investigation, I will examine *all* possibilities before I draw any conclusions *and* I will not let my emotions get in the way of doing my job again, either. I will ask *myself* the tough questions in a very coldhearted way, the ones I'd ask Daddy if he was here, or the ones I ask my Magic 8 Ball because he isn't.

Q. Am I not seeing the police looking for footprints or searching for a body with a knife sticking out of its neck because there *wasn't* a murder in the cemetery last night after all?

A. *Reply hazy try again later.*

Q. Could it be possible that I want to solve a crime that'd give Birdie and me a big reward or a bushel of blackmailing bucks so much that I let my imagination run away with me?

A. *Cannot predict now.*

Q. Could I have accidentally drifted off last night and dreamt the murder up?

A. *Ask again later.*

I'm so wrapped up in giving myself the third degree that I jump about a foot when Birdie taps my shoulder and asks me with a chocolaty grin, "Whatcha doin', Tessie?"

A. *Better not tell you now.*

"I'm . . . I'm lookin' around for that great-good-luck something I wanted to show ya," I say, before I go back to bobble-heading over the porch railing, only this time in a much more desperate way.

But no matter how hard I stare at the cemetery in every direction, all I can see and hear is cemetery caretaker, grave digger, and Birdie's and my good friend, Mr. McGinty, shouting something about funeral flowers at the hard-of-hearing widow of Mr. Peterman, whose heart attacked him a few days ago in aisle four of Melman's Hardware when he was testing out a new toilet plunger. When the now *ex*-foreman over at the Feelin' Good Cookie factory tried to pull the stuck plunger off the store's floor, that's when his ticker punched its time card. (No joke.)

"What kind of great-good-luck thing are you lookin' around *for*?" my sister leans in close and asks me. "A four-leaf clover?"

"Nope."

"A rabbit's foot?"

"Uh-uh."

"A—?"

"Corpse! Now zip it. I gotta concentrate."

"A corpse? Oh, no." Birdie puts her arm around my waist with a real forlorn look on her face. "I'm so sorry to be the one to tell you this bad news," she says like she's Nurse Barton getting ready to explain to a patient that they got a deadly disease. "Your good timing is very off this morning, Tessie." She reaches into my pocket and slides Daddy's watch out so fast that I don't barely feel her, because she has real potential as a pickpocket on account of her hands not being much bigger than the ones on the watch she's holding up. "I think it's around seven o'clock and Mister McGinty told us yesterday when he was digging Mister Peterman's grave that he's not gonna get buried until twelve o'clock today." She taps the face of the Timex. "That's when the hands are both straight up and they're not."

See who I'm working with here?

She can remember our mother's #1 Commandment, how important good timing is, and she can recall when the heart-attacked foreman of the Feelin' Good factory is getting buried today, but she can't keep in her memory any of the really important stuff, which is just about everything I need her to.

"A course I didn't forget that Mister Peterman is getting buried at noon today," I say crossly, because honestly, as much as I love the skin she's in, she can get on my nerves. "I'm not looking for his old corpse. I'm looking for a really fresh one."

"A really fresh *what*?"

Showing and not telling her what I heard and saw last night in the cemetery isn't working out, so I point at Holy Cross and come clean. "I'm ninety-five percent positive a murder got committed over there last night!" When Birdie's slightly bulging eyes go even bulgier, I go ahead and tell her the whole story, wrapping up with, "I couldn't see him real good because it was so dark and those streetlights are always flickering in that part of the cemetery, but I *could* tell that our suspect was tall and skinny before he disappeared behind the Gilgood mausoleum with a limp body in his arms, which is why it definitely couldn't have been Mister Howard Howard. He's built like a fire hydrant and he really likes—"

"Dinah's jelly donuts and three sugars in his Jim," Birdie nods and says, very knowingly.

"You mean three sugars in his *joe*."

"Roger that."

"That's why I wanted you to climb the cemetery fence this morning with me." I am feeling as deflated as my bike tire went when I rode over that broken glass last week behind Lonnigan's. (I know I gave it up, but I just couldn't help myself from wanting to stare at the back door of the bar one more time and wish Daddy would walk out of it.) "I wanted to show you that murder," I tell my sister.

"A murder?" she says. "Huh." She scratches her head. "You wanna show it to me *now*?"

I sure would, but we've run out of time. Two streets over, the bells of St. Kate's are clanging quarter past seven, which means Louise will be expecting breakfast on the table soon, so that's that. But when I turn to look back at what I can see of Holy Cross one last time to make sure I didn't miss anything, it hits me that my remorseful sister *might* be able to lend a hand after all.

Along with her excellent hearing, because her eyes bulge slightly closer to objects, Birdie can also *see* better than me or anybody else I know. (The kid can scout things out better than an Apache searching for a wagon train during a total eclipse.)

"We can't go over there anymore," I tell my almost-always-starving sister, "because it's almost time for breakfast and I know you wouldn't wanna be late for that."

She licks her lips and says, "No, I certainly would not want to be late for breakfast," and then her tummy growls to second that motion.

"But before we go back into the house," I tell her, "you know what you could do for me real quick?"

"What could I do for you real quick, Tessie?" she says, looking a little less hungry and more like she'd knock herself over the head with a rock if I asked her to, because she might have a really cruddy memory and all other sorts of weird problems, but she really does love me.

Quickly, before her big tummy can get control of her tiny brain again, I point at Holy Cross and say, "I've looked and looked, but I don't see any evidence of a murder taking place over there, so could you take a quick peek?"

"Why, what an absolutely splendid idea, young lady!" she cheers up and says. "I'd be delighted to lend a helping hand!"

Oh, boy.

25

She just started doing this lately. Out of the blue, for some unknown reason, she starts to act and talk old-fashioned. It's not like she's perfectly imitating voices the way I discovered I could do in St. Kate's choir loft last year. I thought it was some kind of miracle, ya know? Like turning loaves into fishes. There I was making fun of Sister Raphael behind her back like I always did and still do, because she makes me sing with the boys, when . . . lo and behold . . . instead of my own husky voice coming out of my mouth, I sounded exactly like that crabby penguin! And it wasn't just Sister Raphael. With some practice, I found out I could do pretty good impressions of just about anybody. That's *not* what Birdie does. She just suddenly goes really old-timey on me every once in a while. She might've picked it up from the ton of movies and TV shows we watch that take place in cowboy and Indian times, gangster times, and monster times, I don't know. I'm also not sure if I should make this problem #12 on my SURE SIGNS OF LOONY list. It's kinda hard to pin down.

My temporarily old-fashioned sister holds out her tiny hand bent at the wrist ladylike and says with a smile, "If you'd be so kind as to offer assistance, I'd be much obliged, Pilgrim."

Because she's short, almost a midget really, she has as hard of a time seeing beyond the porch railing as she does peeking into our neighbors' windows, so I "oblige" her by giving her an alley-oop, wait until she balances herself and has a chance to look around before I ask, "Well?"

"Nope, no abandoned well."

"Dang it all, Bird!" She's remembering where Lassie found Timmy on last week's episode instead of doing what I asked her to. "You're not lookin' for an abandoned well. You're lookin' for a fresh corpse or some cops or . . . or anything else that might have to do with the murder I just got done tellin' ya about a few minutes ago."

"Roger that," she says in her regular old voice and goes back to eyeing the cemetery. After a few more minutes of intense Indian staring, she shakes her head and looks down at me. "I'm . . . I'm sorry, but I don't see anything murderous, Tessie. All I see is Mister McGinty and Missus Peterman

26

talking, Johnny Mahlberg riding his bike down the road, and"—she puffs out her chest—"a *robin* redbreast perched on top of Daddy's tombstone."

This is *not* cutting the mustard.

I don't care how bad her and our mother want their breakfasts on the table by 7:30 a.m., I *cannot* let this life-changing, great-good-luck murder slip through my fingers. Birdie is such a spaz, but there's probably enough time for very coordinated me to do a solo snooping mission over the cemetery fence. If I'm quick about it, I can also make my way over to Mr. Peterman's final resting place to ask Mr. McGinty, who lives in a nifty shack not far from the Gilgood mausoleum, if *he* heard or saw anything suspicious last night. He is the caretaker, after all, and one of Birdie's and my closest friends, so I'm sure he'd cough up any information he might have.

That's a very solid plan except for the fact that only a complete moron would leave her 98% unpredictable sister on the back porch all by herself to get into God only knows what. So after I tell Birdie, "Get down offa there before you break your neck," I'm seesawing on whether I should lash her to the railing or the screen door handle with the cat's cradle string she's got in her pocket before I run over to Holy Cross, when wouldn't ya know it, the biggest party pooper on the planet wrecks my investigating plan, the same way she did last night when she got home from her stupid date.

"Theresa Maria," our mother shouts from inside the house. When I don't answer, she very foxily moves on to the smallest chick in our henhouse. "Robin Jean? Where are you?"

Uh-oh.

I spin back around and reach to slap my hand over my sister's mouth, but she ducks and shouts back, "Me and Tessie are on the back porch, Mommy!"

Damnation!

Birdie shouldn't have told her where we were *or* called her that, but she can't help it, poor thing. She cannot resist our mother the way I can. Louise is to my sister what necks are to Count Dracula.

FACT: After the widow Finley quit her job at the hat shop that she got so we could eat after Daddy died, she came up with the idea of finding a new husband to pay the bills.

PROOF: She didn't think she'd be able to catch a guy if he thought he'd be stuck with two more mouths to feed besides her luscious one. So if she should happen to come across Mr. Tall, Dark, Handsome, and Not Married when we were out doing errands, she wanted him to think she was a kindly relative or a do-gooder taking two little girls who weren't her daughters for an outing and not who she really was, which was our very foxy mother weaving a wedding web. "Once I get a decent man to fall for me, girls, when the timing is right, I'll introduce him to you two," she told Birdie and me with eyes that looked full to the brim with what I'm sure were probably crocodile tears. "After I seal the deal, you two can start calling me Mom again, but until then, you need to call me Louise."

She must've not heard Birdie call her the forbidden "Mommy," or me, "Tessie," because she doesn't say anything when she pokes her red head through the squeaky back screen door other than, "What are you two doing out here?"

Because I'm the Finley sisters' mouthpiece, I step up and say, "We were just—"

"I didn't ask you, Theresa," our mother says when she steps onto the porch with a look on her face that could freeze the cemetery pond in the middle of August. "I asked Robin."

Of course, I'd be worried as hell if I thought Birdie was going to cough up that information the way she did our whereabouts, but I can tell by the way she's giving Louise the once-over that my sister's mind hopped its rickety rails the second she got a load of our mother in the gray pencil skirt, black nylons with seams that run in a perfectly straight line up her bathing-beauty legs, a blouse the color of blooming lilacs, black high heels, and gold earrings.

When Birdie doesn't answer her quick enough, Louise snaps her fingers and says, "Pay attention, Robin. I want to know what you and you sister—?"

"Holy cow!" her daughter with the half-baked brain shouts at our mother. "You look good enough to eat!"

Now, I'd love to disagree with her, but I can't. This morning and every morning, noon, and even when she's sleeping, our mother really *is* one very scrumptious-looking broad.

Birdie sniffs the air—she's *also* got an excellent sense of smell—and adds on to the compliment that she already flung Louise's way, "And you smell so yummy, too. Like . . . like pears in the night!"

I have to try very hard not to laugh, because I get a big kick out of it when she gets mixed up like that, so did Daddy, but our mother, who must've gone to the little girls' room to stare at herself in the mirror when God was handing out funny bones, does *not* find Birdie telling her that she smells like pears in the night hilarious. So before Louise can get her pert nose pushed outta joint even further, I jump in and explain, "What Robin meant to say is that you smell very nice, too. Like your Evening in Paris."

Louise sighs strong enough in my sister's direction to fluff her too-long bangs, then does a sudden about-face and asks me, "You two weren't thinking about paying a visit to the cemetery, were you?"

She always had a conniption fit when someone tattled to her after they spotted Birdie and me visiting Holy Cross, but now that she's running for treasurer of the Pagan Baby Society she almost froths at the mouth when she gets wind of any gossip about the Finley *ghouls*, which is what some people around here call us instead of the Finley *girls*, on account of our never-ending love for the dead.

"I don't have all day, Theresa." Louise rat-a-tats her pointy fingernails on the porch railing. "Were you or were you not thinking about going over to the cemetery?"

"*Mea culpa*," I shout. "I see your lips moving, but . . ." I stick my finger in my right ear and wiggle it back and forth. "Did I mention to you that the school nurse told me that Micks can get something called potato ears and the only way to cure it is if you buy me some hearing aids soon as you can so—"

"Knock it off and answer my question," our mother tells me even more fired up.

Because I am always BE PREPARED, I tell her, "A course, we weren't thinkin' about going to the cemetery," with the wide-eyed look I practice every morning in front of the bathroom mirror that is a combination of Karen from the Mickey Mouse Club with a dash of Thumper thrown in. "We only came out here because . . ." I steal a peek over the porch railing to make sure what I'm looking for hasn't completely keeled over yet. "Because we wanted to surprise you with some flowers." I tilt my head toward them so Birdie understands which flowers I'm talking about and doesn't try to go running off to Bloomers florist shop to pick out a bunch. "We wanted to thank you for working your fingers to the bone for us, isn't that right, Bir—Robin?"

My forgetful sister, who believes that's the truth and not the snow job that it is, says, "That's right, Theresa Finley," and then she sticks her spindly arms through the rails, plucks the half-dead white flowers growing next to the porch, and offers them with one of her smiles that's so irresistible that even our chilly mother thaws a little.

Louise pats Birdie on the head when she takes the droopy twosome from her, and even says to me in a slightly less mean way, "Breakfast should be on the table, Theresa. What's the holdup?"

"Not a holdup, Mommy!" Birdie claps her hands and yells with her big opera lungs. "In the middle of the night, Tessie heard yelling and a bloody scream and then she saw a tall, skinny person who wasn't Mister Howard Howard 'cause he's short and eats too many jelly donuts with his Jim carry a limp body behind the Gilgood mausoleum so she is ninety-five percent positive that somebody got great-good-luck murdered in the cemetery last night!"

4

THE BUTTINSKY

"God*damn*it all, Theresa!" our hot-blooded mother says in a voice that I'd bet even money would set my hair on fire if she was standing a foot closer. "How many times have I warned you about filling your sister's head up with your . . . your foolishness? Doesn't she have enough problems as it is?"

How *dare* she?!

I spend a lot more time with Birdie than she *ever* has and I know a lot more about her "problems" than Louise *ever* will. The Finley sisters share *everything*. Missing Daddy, the cemetery, snooping, blackmailing, detecting, the Schwinn bike and Radio Flyer, a bed, head lice, and both of us go nuts for my fiancé, Charlie.

Feeling steamed about Louise's crack about Birdie, I'm about to turn the tables and read *her* the riot act, when who, of all people, should save me from going toe-to-toe in another losing battle with the Queen of Sheba, but our next-door neighbor, buttinsky, and #1 person on another one of my important lists, when she appears on the other side of the three-foot hedge that separates our backyard from hers to call out, "Good morning, Louise, dear." She looks down her nose at us. "Girls."

SHIT LIST

1. Gert Klement.
2. Butch Seeback.
3. Sister Margaret Mary.
4. The grease monkey who fixes cars at the Clark station and tries to peek in the little girls' room window when you got to stop to tinkle because your sister can't make it home from the Tosa Theatre after she drinks a large root beer.
5. Brownnoser Jenny Radtke.
6. What's-his-name.

Everybody's got to have a hobby or two to make life worth living, and one of Mrs. Gertrude B. Klement's top ways to have fun—besides being the president of the Pagan Baby Society, the most important and powerful club at St. Kate's—is doing everything she can possibly do to further tarnish my already not-so-sterling reputation. (No joke.) She's trying day and night to get me banished from the neighborhood immediately, if not sooner. When she's not at church with the other Pagan Baby gals boxing up patchwork quilts, Breck shampoo, Ivory soap, Pepsodent toothpaste, Kleenex, and Ban deodorant to send to little kids who live on the Dark Continent of Africa, Gert spends her every waking hour trying to gather enough evidence against me to prove to my mother that all I need to put me on the straight and narrow path is a much firmer hand, which just so happens to be the specialty of the nuns at St. Anne's Home for Wayward Girls.

Now normally, I'm highly against being held prisoner, but lately I been wondering if gettin' sent up the river wouldn't be that bad of an idea. Not forever, ya know, just long enough to learn how to hot-wire cars like Kitten Jablonski did the last time she was up at St. Anne's for slashing tires. That way, if Birdie and me can't save enough money from blackmailing or solving crimes to buy bus or train tickets out of town, I could jimmy the wires in our woody car and we could drive off into the sunset. Only problem with that plan is that I'd really miss my very nice fiancé and a coupla the other people in the neighborhood that the Finley sisters got on our side.

What would be better than running away is going to live with nearby relatives, ones who love us more than our mother seems to, but even though we're Catholic—a religion that gives extra credit for baby breeding—Birdie and me don't have the pick of the litter the way most everyone else around here does. All *we* got left in this world, besides one another, are Gammy and Boppa, our daddy's folks. I really miss them, but we haven't talked to or seen either one of them since right after he died thanks to our mother, who is having one of her 100% Irish temper tantrums. I'm not really sure why she's so worked up. I think it has a little something to do with how hard Gammy and Boppa cry when they hug Birdie and me, but mostly I think she's teed-off because our grandparents won't give her any money. They would like to I'm sure, but they don't have two nickels to rub together, either. So Louise won't let them come visit, hangs up on them when they call, and has "ways of knowing" if I try to call them. And when it comes to someone from *her* side of the family taking Birdie and me in? Rotsa ruck. Supposedly, her parents are "eternally resting." (They're probably just lying on some beach and won't tell her where.) She admits to having an older brother who is still alive and kicking, but she hasn't heard from him in years. (More than likely, Virgil changed his name to Pierre and joined the French Foreign Legion to get as far away from his bratty little sister as he could.)

For a while there, I decided that if Gammy and Boppa couldn't come to us Birdie and me would go to them, so I hatched a plan and packed our plaid suitcase and everything. We were going to run away to their cute rock house in the country, but that journey dead-ended around 73rd St. when my sister got hungry and I wasn't exactly sure how to get to our grandparents' place. I guess that worked out in the long run for the best. Because on the walk back home, I realized that

Louise might not know the first thing about diagramming sentences or the capitals of the United States or mothering kids, but believe you me, the gal is smart enough to hunt my sister and me down at Gammy and Boppa's house for no other reason but to bring us back to do her bidding while she's out painting the town red with what's-his-name.

FACT: Birdie and me are stuck between a rock and a heart place. (No joke.)

PROOF: I already got plenty of examples of Gert Klement trying to convince Louise to give me the boot, but in Chapter Four, Modern Detection warns detectives about the importance of gathering "substantial evidence" and I don't want to fall down on the job.

That's why I pay a confidential informant name of Kitten Jablonski, the most in-the know kid in the whole neighborhood, to keep me up on all the latest dirt about the Finley ghouls that gets spread around by our evil next-door neighbor. And thank all that's holy that I do, because Kitten told me last week that Gert added something new on her TO-DO list that's even worse than getting me sent away to the Catholic juvie home.

When Kitten and me bumped into each other at Dalinsky's Drugstore, she was buying ointment for her skin, and I just got done boosting a few more rolls of Tums, because my guts have been taking Daddy's death very hard. Of course, as usual, I was happy to see my lighthouse-tall eighth-grade informant that I look up to in more ways than one. (Joke!) But the same way I always do after I run into her, I had to take a giant step back. Not everyone knows this, but pimples are a kind of leprosy and I can't risk one of the dozen she's got marching across her face deciding to make a break for it and parachuting down to mine. (I've watched the Miss America contest on the television set many times, so I know that having peaches-and-cream skin and all your body parts is very important to the judges.)

Kitten, who must really believe in that famous saying about not giving up the ship, told me outta the side of her mouth in the drugstore's

BEAUTIFICATION aisle, "Ya better start watchin' The Bird's back even more than ya already are, Finley."

"Why?" I gulped. "What'd ya hear?"

"Gimme a dollar." After I dug a crumpled buck out of my pocket and handed it over, my confidential informant told me really fast, because she always talks like she's a desperado who's got a posse closing in on her, "What I heard is that Gert Klement's been openin' her fat trap at Wednesday's knitting circle. Tellin' all the gals how they gotta say novenas for your ma 'cause it was bad enough that your old man fooled around with Suzie LaPelt, but then he had the nerve to kick the bucket without leaving her any dough, and even worse . . ." Kitten swiveled her head around the drugstore to make sure nobody was listening because she is in the information business and does not believe in handing out free samples. "I'm about to tell ya the really bad part now, Finley, so get a grip on yourself." That's when I ripped open the Tums and chewed three on the spot, because if Kitten Jablonski tells you something is really bad, God help me, it really is. "Ya already know that battle-ax is tryin' to get you shipped off to St. Anne's, but what Gert's been spreadin' around lately is that if your ma ever hopes to get hitched again that she should put The Bird in a home with her own kind, too, because no man wants to raise another man's kids."

Along with a very smart brain and a very coordinated body, I got born with the personality of a trampoline so most of the ratty stuff people say about me bounces right off. And I already knew that Gert didn't like Daddy—I saw the way she always stared daggers at him over her hedge and across the aisle at Mass on Sundays—so it didn't surprise me when Kitten told me how our neighbor was cutting him down at her knitting circle for "fooling around" with Suzie LaPelt. That was so dumb, because of course "Good Time Eddie" Finley fooled around with his barmaid when they were working a shift together at Lonnigan's Bar. He was the most fun-loving bartender in the whole neighborhood.

But that other information Kitten told me about what Gert and her knit-one, pearl-two cronies were saying about my Birdie, *that* hit me hard in the breadbasket. I doubled over and went so wobbly and woozy that I had to sit down on Dalinsky's cold tile floor with my head between my knees, because my sister getting sent to a "home" to be with her own kind isn't far-fetched. Kids can disappear around here when they get to be too much to handle or if they're too different. Mrs. Fontaine sent *her* sweet daughter, Gail Ann, who had straight black hair, ate gum offa the sidewalk, and every once in a while pranced around the neighborhood in her birthday suit when it wasn't her birthday, to her new "home" in Mongolia. And the Jabos kid? The one whose real name was Doris but all the kids called Ducky because of those webbed fingers of hers? *Her* mother told everyone that she sent her daughter to "camp for the summer up north," but when school started, Ducky still hadn't flown south to start sixth grade with the rest of us. (No joke.)

But according to Kitten, the "home" that Gert Klement has been yakking about sending Birdie off to with those needle wielders in the church basement is *not* on the other side of the world or near Green Bay, Wisconsin. I looked it up in the telephone book, then I took the #7 bus to 10073 W. Plankinton Rd. and you know what I saw when I stepped off? They can call it County Hospital all they want, but I know a loony bin when I see one, and it'd be over my dead body that I let anybody keep me from doing #1 on my *most* important list.

TO-DO

1. Take tender loving care of Birdie.
2. Make Gert Klement think her arteries are going as hard as her heart.
3. Catch whoever stole over $200 out of the Pagan Baby collection box.
4. Practice your Miss America routine.
5. Learn how to swim.

6. Be a good dry-martini-making fiancée to Charlie.
7. Do not get caught blackmailing or spying.
8. Just *think* about making a real confession to Father Ted, before it's too late.

"Top o' the morning!" Louise calls back over the hedge to Gert in the pretty soprano that she leads St. Kate's choir with. "Thanks a bushel for keeping an eye on the girls last night." Whenever our mother leaves the house for any reason, she asks the worst next-door neighbor in the world if she'll keep tabs on Birdie and me, which, of course, our meddling mortal enemy is only more than happy to do. "Say good morning to Missus Klement, children."

Birdie follows directions, a *lot* nicer than me, because along with all of my sister's other "problems," she is an overly friendly and overly affectionate kid, a real tail-wagger.

"I was going to check in with you when I got home, but all your lights were out," Louise tells Gert. "Everything go hunky-dory last night?"

Our neighbor raises one of her penciled, black-as-a-funeral eyebrows up to her bone-colored hair and slowly repeats the way she does when she wants to make a point, which is almost always, "Did . . . everything . . . go . . . hunky . . . dory . . . last . . . night?" She looks right at me and sneer-laughs. "Far from it."

Damnation!

Did she see us?

I was so keen on working on #3 on my TO-DO list that I forgot all about doing what *Modern Detection* calls "reconnaissance" before we took off last night to do our snooping.

I desperately need to beat to the punch everybody else in the parish who's been trying to catch whoever nicked the money out of the Pagan Baby collection box up at church a few weeks ago. When I get my hands on whoever perpetrated that crime, I'm not going to rat them out. I'm going to tell them that I won't reveal their identity if they give me the money. I'm not gonna keep it. I'm gonna shove it under the bushes that grow against the side of the church, and then after Sunday Mass with so many witnesses gossiping about each other on St. Kate's steps, I'll wander over to where I hid it, pretend to be tying my sneaker, and pull out that stash of cash and yell, *Oh, my goodness! Look what I found in these bushes!* Because the way I see it, them Pagan Baby gals getting their moo-la-la back might go a long way in getting President Gert Klement off the Finley sisters' backs, and what the heck, who knows? Returning the money to its rightful owners could even win me some brownie points from our mother and the Almighty might cut me some much-needed slack, too.

The Mutual Admiration Society hasn't found any clues yet, but word around the neighborhood is that Skip Abernathy *might* be the no-goodnik thief that everyone's been looking for. That's why hours before the murder happened over at the cemetery, as soon as I saw the lights go out in Gert Klement's house, Birdie and me snuck out to our garage, loaded up our Radio Flyer wagon—besides bringing library books home in it, we take the coaster on all our snooping missions, except for the cemetery ones, because it's too hard to shove it over the black iron fence without all the tools and Birdie's snacks falling out—and under the cover of darkness we made our way over to the Abernathys'.

10:35 p.m. The Finley sisters were preparing to spy on our suspect at 7119 N. Keefe Ave.

I was, anyway. After all the brouhaha Birdie caused on the night pom-pom-waving Mrs. Tate was in her rumpus room pumping away for Mr. Horace Mertz, I didn't trust my sister to remember to keep her mouth shut, so I made her be the lookout.

FACT: If it turns out that Skip Abernathy really *is* the one stealing from little kids whose lives are already so cruddy because they are forced to listen to missionaries hour after hour, day after day, trying to convert them to Catholicism under the scorching sun in the Congo just so they can get shinier hair, blow their noses, and have no b.o., he should be very ashamed of himself. *Not* for thieving, of course. It would be two-faced of me to condemn him on that count, because hardly a week goes by that I don't ignore the *Thou Shalt Not Steal* Commandment.

PROOF: I'm a light-fingered Louie during the day and an even better cat burglar at night. (Secret God's work, that's what I'm doing. I don't remember the exact words, but He told somebody in olden times something like, "It's easier for a camel to get into Heaven than it is for a rich person." So even though our neighbors and the store owners don't deserve it, me sneakily lightening their load of worldly goods is greasing the hinges on the Pearly Gates for them.)

I most often make things disappear from Gert Klement's house because I want her to think that she's got that old-person sickness of going hard in her arteries, but sometimes I just swipe her stuff because I am a big believer in an eye for an eye. She's trying to steal so much from my sister and me, so tit for tat, right? And, okay, sometimes my fingers get sticky at Kenfield's Five and Dime, Dalinsky's Drugstore, and Melman's Hardware, too, but *only* if I run out of important supplies like Tums or Hershey's kisses or Three Musketeers bars, or if Birdie or Charlie need something important ASAP. Like the night-light I stuck under my T-shirt at the five and dime that's so powerful it lit up the insides of my sister's brain and made her nightmares stop and makes *me* feel like I'm already on the Miss America stage when I'm practicing my routine in the middle of the night. And the Bowie knife I stole from the hardware store? That was for Charlie, because whittling is one of his most important hobbies. And fine, there *was* this one time that I slipped two pairs of hose out of Janet's Dress Shop on Lisbon St. and stuck them in the bottom of Louise's unmentionables drawer when her last pair got a runner in them. (That was kind of a kooky thing for me to do, I know, but what the heck. All the gal's got going for her is her looks.)

So anyhoo, there Birdie and me were last night over at the Abernathys'. I was about to spy into Skip's bedroom window, hoping to catch him counting out the money he stole from the pagan babies, when his dad came banging out of the back door of the house to light up. Cigar smoke gives my sister a sneezing attack, which is why we had to hotfoot it out of there before we had the chance to get the goods on our suspect.

"As a matter of fact," our neighbor who's got her nose stuck into everybody's business, but the farthest into the Finley sisters' business, tells Louise so high and mighty from the other side of the hedge, "a very troubling incident took place in the neighborhood last night that I'm quite certain will turn out to be a matter for the police."

Uh-oh.

Just like I was afraid of, it looks like the wretched geezer got the better of me. She must've watched Birdie and me sneaking toward the Abernathys' out of her front window after she turned her lights off and she's about to rat us out *again*. Not only to our mother, but the men in blue, too.

Louise must also be worried about that, because her good-smelling Jergen's lotion hands are clamping down around Birdie's and my necks. She knows the cops showing up at our front door would wreck her chances to be the new treasurer of the Pagan Baby Society. Under no circumstances do those gals want one of their muckety-mucks to have jailbirds for kids, and that's exactly what's going to happen if Gert squeals on Birdie and me. Officer Mick Dunn, Davey Dunn's dad, came by the house to lecture us in the living room the last time we got caught spying into our neighbors' windows. He made Birdie and me sit on the sofa, but he stood and gave us a good talking-to. "I'll let you off with another warning," he threatened, "but if I have to come back one more time . . ." He looked over at our mother fuming in Daddy's favorite chair, and then he narrowed his already somewhat beady eyes at us and pointed to the handcuffs that were hanging off his creaky black leather belt. "You get my drift, girls?"

Birdie didn't, of course, because she was smiling her head off when she asked him if she could play with his billy club, but I certainly did.

And so did the gal standing next to me who's turned whiter than my Holy Communion dress. "A troubling incident?" Louise asks as she clamps her fingers tighter around her daughters' necks. "What kind of troubling incident?"

The #1 person on my SHIT LIST is not looking at our mother anymore, she's glaring even harder at *me* with eyes the color of an enemy submarine lying in wait at the bottom of the ocean when she says across the hedge, "Sister . . . Margaret . . . Mary . . . has . . . gone . . . missing!" My mother gasps, so Birdie does, too, but I gotta keep my wits about me. Getting questioned by Gert about *any* crime committed in the neighborhood from stolen merchandise to fires to broken windows is nothing new. She raked me over the coals about the missing Pagan Baby money, too. That's how come I'm 100% positive that I know what's gonna come out of her mouth next. "You wouldn't happen to know anything about Sister's disappearance, would you, Theresa?"

"Me?" I answer with my second-best most innocent look because I already used my first-best most innocent look up on Louise. "I certainly do *not* know anything about Sister Margaret Mary going missing, Missus Klement. Goodness gracious, that's . . . that's . . ."

The best news ever!

But, obviously, it'd be stupid to give my sworn enemy that kind of ammunition to use against me, so I put on my this-is-the-worst-news-ever look, the kind all the movie gals get—Loretta Young, she does the best horrified looks so beautifully—and say to Gert, "That's . . . terrible news!" even though it's anything but. In fact, I'm pretty sure what I might be beholding here is the living, breathing Holy Trinity of famous sayings!:

1. The Lord's one about giveth-ing and taketh-ing away.
2. Mr. Walt Disney's one about dreams coming true.
3. Daddy's one about never, ever throwing in the towel.

Here I was feeling so down in the mouth because I thought Gert was going to tattle on the Finley sisters to Louise and the coppers, and on top of that, it was starting to look like I'd imagined it all and bloody nothing took place in the cemetery last night, but now . . . my cup run-eth over-eth! Birdie and me are not going to get spanked and we're not going to the hoosegow, and sure, the Mutual Admiration Society might've lost the chance to solve a murder, but we just got our first-ever missing person case dropped in our lap instead!

Wait just a cotton-pickin' minute.

Now that I think about this, maybe THE CASE OF THE MISSING NUN is *not* one we should tackle after all. I mean, what if we actually *found* the despised principal of St. Kate's? I wouldn't put it past the pissed-off kids in the parish to drag us over to the Washington Park Zoo to do something biblically bad to get back at us. Something like throwing us to the lions.

On the other hand . . . searching for the school's top penguin might be worth taking the risk of getting eaten alive. Yes, I think Daddy would agree with me if he was here, because whenever he threw his paycheck into the pot when he was playing poker in Lonnigan's back room with the factory men, he'd lean down and whisper in my ear, "*Always* go for broke, kiddo."

Wait just another cotton-pickin' minute.

What if . . . what if there is more here than meets the eye of this private eye? The last thing I want to do is assume again, but I thought the screech I heard last night coming from the cemetery sounded familiar, so maybe our school principal isn't just missing, maybe she . . . dear, holy Mother of God. Did you just drop a fantastic twofer crime into The Mutual Admiration Society's laps?

Q. Did the limp body I saw getting carried behind the Gilgood mausoleum last night beneath the flickering streetlights belong to not just a *missing* principal, but a *kidnapped* and *murdered* principal?

A. *Outlook good.*

Well . . . amen to that, Sister.

Amen, amen!

5

JUST LIKE IDA LUPINO

The scrumptious-smelling red apple breeze is pushing around the yellow-and-white-checked curtains next to the avocado stove in our kitchen, where I'm putting the finishing touches on our breakfast while Louise puts the finishing touches on herself at the vanity table in her bedroom.

FACT: Daddy was our chief cook and bottle washer, but since I stepped into his shoes, I have to be the one to scramble the eggs and Spam in the black fry pan every morning. *If* Birdie and me want to live to see another day, that is.

PROOF: Louise Mary Fitzgerald Finley was the prime suspect on a recent detecting job that The Mutual Admiration Society didn't have to break a sweat to solve—THE CASE OF THE TROTS.

At St. Kate's potluck dinner last month that always takes place in our school cafeteria, parishioners who helped themselves to a scoop of the beef and whatever else it was that our mother stirred into the "gourmet" casserole that made it smell like toe jam got awful trots, and boy, oh, boy, were they ever sore. When the finger-pointing suspicion fell on Louise's mystery casserole almost immediately—unbeknownst to her, she has a reputation around here for being the antonym of Chef Boyardee—she didn't put the blame on the butcher for selling her bad hamburger, but she didn't deny the rumor after I started it, either. I really like Mr. Wisnewski, he tells the best Polack jokes in the neighborhood, so I felt like a louse after I thumbtacked one of my poison-pen letters on the church bulletin board:

ATTENTION PARISHIONERS!
BEWARE!
The meat at Wisnewski's Butcher Shop is no good!
Yours in Christ,
The Watcher

Like they say, "Charity begins at home," so what choice did I have?

I guarantee you, nobody would write down the name of a gal who almost diarrhea-ed them to death on the Pagan Baby election ballot and mark my words, if our mother loses out on being treasurer when that vote takes place, chances are that she'll blame Birdie and me and our "shenanigans" for messing up her chances.

This is far-fetched, but it *has* crossed my mind that Louise wants to be treasurer so bad because she's going to stealthily "borrow" some money out of the club's coffers to save our house from the First Wisconsin Bank. When Daddy was still here, her and him fought all the time about how much more hard-up we were than the other families in the neighborhood. Mr. Fleming, the father of Mary Jane Fleming, used to call the house once a week to ask where the mortgage money was, but now that we don't have some of Daddy's paycheck anymore, Mr. Fleming calls every day. (I think he wants to send us to the poorhouse.)

Of course, I ripped my poison-pen letter off the church bulletin board after the hullabaloo died down and posted another much nicer one that was also written with my left hand. (As a gumshoe, I knew that I shouldn't leave any evidence and I'm pretty sure my Palmer penmanship would be recognized by Sister Jane, who finds it "Quite good for a child of your background.")

ATTENTION PARISHIONERS!
FALSE ALARM!
Mr. Wisnewski's meat is as great as ever! Eat as much as you want! You won't get the trots!
Yours in Christ,
The Watcher

After I'm done slapping our breakfasts onto the white S&H Green Stamp plates Louise collects from the Red Owl every Wednesday, I know I shouldn't be doing that famous saying "Counting your chickens before they hatch," but I just can't help myself. Besides getting the chance to solve a kidnapping murder that could really pay off, if I can stay two steps ahead of Gert Klement's plan to get rid of Birdie and me, we won't have to run away. But because it's always good to BE PREPARED, just in case I come up a day late and a dollar short and we have to hit the road, instead of wandering around the countryside like two Gypsies who are sure to get their throats ripped out on a full-moon night—in the movies, where there are Gypsies, a werewolf is never far behind—the orange juice I'm pouring into the little glasses is reminding me that it's one of the chief exports of the final destination I finally came up with that Birdie and me will run away *to*, if come what may.

After studying TV shows and movies, combing through my geography book, visiting the Finney Library's travel section, and paying half attention during catechism class, I came up with a list of all the places that I thought might make a nice future home for the Finley sisters. Some of the locations sounded okay with pretty nice weather, which is something Birdie and me would have to take into consideration, because we won't have a place to live until we can get jobs or get to know everyone in our new neighborhood good enough to start blackmailing the snot out of them for enough money to stay at a hotel:

RUNNING-TO PLACES

1. France: *chief exports*: the perfume that my mother and most of the gals in the neighborhood wear, the movie *Gigi*, and sluts.
2. Mongolia: *chief exports*: Attila the Hun, pillaging, and homes for different kids.
3. The Congo: *chief exports*: head-shrinking Pygmies, cannibals, and pagan babies.
4. Lourdes: *chief exports*: crutches, rosaries, and Holy Water.
5. Fatima: *chief exports*: miracles, sheepherders, and appearances by the Virgin Mary.
6. New York City: *chief exports*: book writers, the Empire State Building, and crime.
7. Hawaii: *chief exports*: pineapples, the hula dance, and leprosy.

Unfortunately, hard work *doesn't* always pay off. I ended up having to pull the plug on all those spots, especially France, because everybody over there smelling like Louise all the time would make Birdie too sad and give me a headache. And even though I would love to shake the hand of the man who wrote *Modern Detection*, I don't want to live in New York City, either. It's known on a TV show as *The Naked City* and that sounds like a good way to pick up a disease. I also gave the boot to the new state of Hawaii—I don't want to bump into Father Damien and his lepers for Miss America reasons—and Fatima didn't sound like a whole hell of a lot of fun, ditto for the Congo, and the home of Attila the Hun.

It was just this past Sunday night, when Birdie and me were on the sofa watching the *Walt Disney Presents* show, that the end-all and be-all of where we should run away *to* came to me. I couldn't believe

I hadn't thought of it sooner. *Eureka!* I said to myself. *California, here we come!* I didn't mention anything to my sister, because sure, she loves Snow White because that black-haired beauty is also an animal lover, particularly of birds, and her best friends, the dwarves, are all about the same height as my sister, so they'd have that in common, but I'm still not positive that the eight of them are enough to tempt Birdie away from our mother, which is something I should probably add to my SURE SIGNS OF LOONY list. (If we *do* have to run away, I'm counting on my sister getting over Louise once we're in California and she feasts her slightly bulging eyes on the Magic Kingdom in living color.)

I hate for any opponent of mine to know what I'm feeling, so I'm very good at playing my cards close to my chest—Daddy taught me. But I must be accidentally smiling at the pictures I got in my head of Birdie spinning around in the flying teacups at Disneyland with Dopey, and Kookie Kookson the Third from *77 Sunset Strip* lending me his comb, because when Louise lowers herself down on the chair where our father used to sit at the head of the yellow Formica kitchen table, she doesn't guess that I'm thinking about the place where you can wish upon a star and make your dreams come true, but she *does* guess what's going on in the other part of my mind, which is how we're going to earn enough money to get us there.

"Wipe that smirk off your face, Theresa. Sister Margaret Mary's disappearance is none of your business," she says. "You hear me?"

I snap to and tell her, "Loud and clear," but when I pull my chair in next to Birdie and shovel a helping of eggs and Spam into my mouth, what I'm thinking is, *Oh, Louise, little do you know. Sister M and M's disappearance is exactly my business!*

My sister smiles, points next to our mother's plate, and says, so excited, "I got you a present. I got you a present. I got you a present. I got you a present."

Louise looks down, picks up the trinket with her napkin, and says, "How . . . how . . . mmmm."

The gal might be mean most of the time, but thanks to Miss Emily Post, she has excellent manners, so she's trying to think up something nice-ish to say about the doodad my sister left for her this morning. Birdie does this from time to time. Because she's not a thief like me, she doesn't steal the presents. She's more like a crow, ya know? Finders keepers, losers weepers and all that. When my sister comes across something shiny or fluffy, she puts it in her pocket and finds a time to sweetly surprise Louise or me with it. Like the 1958 nickel she left under my pillow this morning. Birdie used to leave feathers in Daddy's pants pockets, but now she lays them around his tombstone, and to Louise, she almost always gives a piece of fake jewelry that she might find in a sidewalk crack or under a kneeler at church or in a Cracker Jack box. But I'm not sure where she found the pink plastic heart-shaped ring with a red stone that's doing a terrible job of looking like a real ruby that our mother is holding in her fingers. (It will eventually end up in the garbage, which is fine, I guess. Birdie's memory is so bad that she won't remember giving it to her in the first place.)

Louise slips the crummy ring on her finger that used to hold her beautiful golden wedding ring that Daddy won in a poker pot, looks across the table at my sister, and says, "Thank you for the token of your affection, Robin. Now please stop kicking your leg against the table. I'm already on pins and needles about starting this new job at the Clark station and you're making it worse."

"She's not doing it on purpose," I swallow and tell our mother. "I told you her toes are going numb."

Louise was supposed to pick up a new pair of sneakers and saddle shoes for Birdie the day summer vacation ended, but she either forgot 'cause she's thinking all the time about what's-his-name or how short she is on money. Either way, I'm not going to make a federal case out of it this morning, because for now, my sister doesn't really need new school shoes from Shuster's anymore.

I know that most of the fathers around here work at foundries like Northland or factories like Feelin' Good Cookie, Pabst Brewery, and American Motors—you can smell where they do their shifts if you sit next to them at church—but one dad is a carpenter and my fiancé Charlie "Cue Ball" Garfield's old man dyes tools for a living and after Daddy died, Becky Winner's father was charitable enough to give Birdie and me lifetime passes to the Tosa Theatre that he owns. But I never heard of Molly Hopkins's father's job before last week. *He* gets a paycheck for sniffing around for trouble in old buildings. (With her excellent sense of smell, Birdie would be good at this job *if* she grows up, so further research at the Finney is required.)

Mr. Hopkins got called to our school on the afternoon Sister Prudence sent Tommy "Two-Ton" Thomkins to the basement to tell our janitor, Wayne "Creeper" Carlson, to wheel his bucket and mop up to the gymnasium so he could clean up the cookies that Davey O'Meara tossed on the floor during dodgeball. Fortunately, Two-Ton never made it down to that spooky room with the incinerator, the furnace, a calendar of Betty Grable loving a tractor too much hanging on the wall, a floor polisher, sawdust, and whatnot, where the janitor spends most of his time. Two-Ton fell straight through the basement steps and Creeper had to jerry-rig a hoist to pull him out!

After Mr. Hopkins got done inspecting the damage, he hung a **CONDEMNED** sign on the basement stairs railing and then, according to my confidential informant Kitten Jablonski, he also reported that he smelled an "unusual" odor drifting around the basement, which was such great news. "The school needs to be closed down immediately as a safety precaution. It could be gas," he told Sister Margaret Mary, who at that time was still present and accounted for. (I could've stepped in and told Mr. Hopkins that it definitely *was* gas he was smelling because he showed up on Beans and Wienies Wednesday to do his inspection, but no one except #5 on my SHIT LIST, brownnoser Jenny Radtke, would do something *that* repulsive.)

Louise, who's admiring herself in the oleo knife, says, "Since you're out of school until the repairs can be made, I expect the two of you to make yourselves useful. Dust and vacuum before I get home tonight, take out the garbage, and Theresa"—she gives me her evil eye—"go to confession today." The reason she didn't tell Birdie that she had to do the same is because she doesn't have to go into the wooden box to tell her sins once a week to Father Ted like me and all the other kids in the parish do. My sister got declared an "innocent" by the church two years ago on account of the fact that she would kneel down in front of the black confessional curtain every Thursday and start clapping her hands and laughing her heinie off because she thought she was about to see a puppet show.

7:49 a.m. The Finley sisters have big-deal detecting to do today and the sooner our mother is out of our hair the better, which is why I'm trying to come up with a compliment that could get her moving faster toward the front door. She usually falls for anything having to do with how good looking she is, that's how sweet she is on herself. But I don't know, sometimes I think I'm being too hard on the gal, ya know? If my long red hair fell down my back in perfect waves instead of looking like it got caught up in the spokes of my Schwinn if I don't stick it into a ponytail every morning, and if both of my ears laid close to my head and my right one didn't stick out like a handle, and if my cheeks were the color of baby pink roses instead of being covered with so many freckles that I can't fall asleep at my school desk without that nincompoop Chuckie Jaeger connecting them with a ballpoint pen, and maybe if my eyes were the color of shallow water instead of looking like the bottom of the deep-blue sea, one of my hobbies might be staring at myself as often as I could, too.

I lean back in my chair and tell Louise, "If you think you need to do more primping, don't bother. I'm not kidding, you look even better than one of Mister Skank's customers."

I listen to the Braves baseball games on the radio with my friend and business advisor, Mr. Art Skank, every other Saturday at his funeral home on Burleigh St., so that was not "hearsay" evidence. The undertaker is so good at fiddling with his customers that they end up looking like masterpieces, which is how he got his neighborhood nickname, "The Leonardo da Vinci of Undertaking."

FACT: Everyone around here tries to stay on Mr. Skank's good side, because he is known to hold a grudge.

PROOF: You should've seen what he did to one of his high school sweethearts who dropped him for another fella. Believe me, Mrs. Mitzi Kircher did *not* look anything like a framed picture of *The Last Supper* at her funeral. Mrs. Mitzi Kircher looked more like a box full of cafeteria leftovers at her funeral. (Joke!)

When Louise doesn't budge from the table, even though I just gave her that great Skank compliment, I move to my backup plan. I point to the clock above the sink and say, "Just like you're always tellin' Birdie and me how important it is to be on time, ya better hurry up if you don't want to be late for your first day on the job. What's-his-name is gonna pick you up at eight to take you to the station, right?"

Our mother slowly grinds out her L&M cigarette in her eggs and Spam scramble that she hasn't barely touched because she is always watching her figure, waiting for it to do what, I don't know exactly. "How many times do I have to tell you the name of the man I'm seeing, Theresa?"

What the heck comes over me?

I know that hope is something that should not be allowed to spring eternally when I'm in the vicinity of our mother, but for some unknown reason, I let myself believe sometimes that she misses Daddy as much as Birdie and me do. That's why I think she's about to make a joke to remember him by, the same way I do every chance I get. Like the kind ya hear up at Wisnewski's butcher shop and Lonnigan's Bar all the time. Daddy loved those "How many Polacks does it take to screw in a lightbulb?" jokes. (Three. One to hold the bulb, two to turn the ladder.)

"I don't know, Louise," I forget myself and say. "How many times *do* you have to tell me the name of the man you're seeing?"

But, of course, the second I see how tight her teeth are clenched, I knew what a hoping dope I'd been. And when she *does* open her mouth, I am shocked by how much she sounds like her idol, nasty Gert Klement, when she says, "For the last time, the name of the man I'm dating is Mister . . . Leon . . . Gallagher."

So *she* says as she shoves back her chair and sashays out of the kitchen in a cloud of smoke. Because he hasn't fallen into our mother's wedding web yet, Birdie and me haven't met "Mister . . . Leon . . . Gallagher," so there's no way to be 100% sure *who* he is. Chapter One of *Modern Detection* says: "A subject's identity must *always* be verified by loved ones," which would be the Finley sisters. Louise told us the ignorant slob she's trying to replace Daddy with works on the assembly line at the American Motors plant, but I'll believe that when I see it. I still think he might be #4 on my SHIT LIST. The grease monkey all the girls in the neighborhood call "The Peeker." (Judging from how many times I've caught him licking his lips and grinning at me when I'm keeping guard over Birdie outside the Clark station's restroom when she's tinkling out the root beer on our way home from the Tosa Theatre, The Peeker seems to have a taste for redheads, so *he* probably was the one who recommended Louise for the cashier job.)

While I might be feeling a little slowed down by my mother's chilly warning to mind my own beeswax when it comes to missing Sister Margaret Mary, believe me, I'm not about to throw in the towel. I immediately start working out in my head what the detecting Finley sisters have to get done today while I'm following Louise's orders and filling the kitchen sink up with warm water and a squirt of Joy.

Of course, the most important things I have to take care of ASAP are examining the scene of the crime over at the cemetery and calling a meeting of The Mutual Admiration Society to order. And if I want those things to happen ASAP, I got to remind forgetful Birdie she needs to step on it.

"Honey?" When I turn around to make sure she's quickly clearing the breakfast dishes like she's supposed to instead of lazily licking off the leftovers . . . lo and behold! I'm the Lone Ranger without my Tonto! Damnation!

I switch off the water faucet and call out, "Bir—Robin Jean?"

When she doesn't answer, *Here I am, Tessie!* the way she's supposed to if I lose sight of her, I wipe my soapy hands off on my shorts and run through the dining room to check for her in the living room. She's not on the green shag carpet in front of the Motorola television set, and she wouldn't go into the basement by herself, so I dash back through the kitchen and head up the stairs two at a time. "Honey?"

After I poke my head into the bathroom and our bedroom and come up empty, that only leaves the last place that I was dreading looking for Birdie in the first place. I really don't want to find my sister in what was once the most special spot in the house. It used to smell like Daddy's Old Spice, and there were always matchbooks and a pack of his Lucky Strike cigarettes on his bed stand, and a deck of cards sitting on top of the bureau, and just being in there filled me to the brim with love. But ever since we lost him, when I even think of going in there, a missing sadness comes crashing down on me, the same way it's doing right this minute. I have to plaster myself against the hallway wall to keep myself from getting knocked to my knees. But what choice do I have? I made a solemn vow to step into Daddy's shoes and I'm not going to let him down. Not again. I promised to take tender loving care of Birdie and that's what I'm going to do. Come Hell or high water.

So I take a deep breath and try to push away the missing sadness the best I can, take shaky baby steps down the hall, and through the bedroom door. Because I'm feeling roughed-up when I plop down next to my sister on the edge of the bed Daddy used to snore in, I take an extra tight hold of her little hand. To steady myself, of course, but also to keep her glued to me. If Birdie starts to act up and do something really weird and loony, Louise, who is sprucing herself up at her vanity table, could change her mind and decide that "somebody more qualified" needs to keep watch over my sister today instead of me. I can't risk that. The Finley sisters got what I'm almost positive is a kidnapping murder to investigate that could earn us great running-away bucks. That means getting stuck on Gert Klement's front porch all day so she can keep her evil eye on Birdie and me while Louise is at her new job is completely out of the question.

I know that our mother has got to report to work by 8:15 a.m., but what I don't know is how *long* she'll be taking money for gas or tire-changing or whatever else a cashier at a filling station does, besides hopefully steal some of the big bills out of the till so we don't lose our house. Will she be up at the Clark for the same eight hours that she spent at the hat shop called Turner's Toppers that she quit after two weeks? It's not like I'm going to miss her or nothin', I just need to know when she'll be back, so Birdie and me don't get caught with our hands in the cookie jar.

I fake-yawn and ask Louise very ho-hum, "When will you be home for supper?"

"I won't be," she says as she brushes one more coat of polish on the last of her nails. Usually she chooses something eye-catching, but I guess clear polish must be better for cashiers than Revlon's Matador Cape. "Mister Gallagher and I are going out to Mama Mia's to celebrate my first day on the job."

Hmmm. It's good news that she's going to be gone all day and into the night, because it gives my sister and me lots of time to do our snooping. And usually I'd also be 100% glad that we wouldn't be saying Grace tonight over one of her revolting "gourmet" meals, but I am *not* happy one iota about her going out to eat with what's-his-name at Mama Mia's *Ristorante*. The last time the Finley family ate there together, we had such a swell time. We were celebrating ten years of Louise and Daddy's being married. She was still called Mom then, and her and him slurped spaghetti like Lady and the Tramp, and on the drive home, I laughed so hard at Daddy's jokes that I got the hiccups and Birdie stuck her head out of the woody car window and lapped the fast air the way she loves to, and Louise sang "That's Amore" and didn't even mind that her hair got mussed when her husband pulled her closer.

I haven't figured out yet how to stop memories of the good old days from squeezing my heart so hard, so the missing sadness jumps out of the shadows and bushwhacks my heart again. It travels up my throat and wants to come out of my eyes, but I'm trying with every ounce of strength I got not to break our mother's #2 Commandment—"Stop crying or I'll give you something to cry about"—because blubbering could tick her off enough to sentence us to Gert's porch for the whole day, too.

So I swallow, snort back the sad, and ask her, "If you're goin' out, what are Robin and me supposed to eat for supper?"

"TV dinners."

At that news, Daddy's "little dreamboat"—another nickname he called my sister, whose brain doesn't have an anchor, so she tends to drift off to parts unknown—shouts, "Ship . . . ship . . . hurray!" because she *really* adores the gummy brownie that comes in Swanson's fried chicken dinner and she is not at all good at remembering famous sayings.

"Theresa." Louise snaps her gold compact shut and drops it into her red pocketbook. "Missus Klement has agreed to check in on you two until I get home tonight, and if she has to call me at work to report that you and your sister left the house for *any* reason other than to take the garbage out or go to confession—" The ah-OO-ga horn that belongs to her new boyfriend's Chevy blares below the bedroom window. "Do *not* climb over the cemetery fence or peek in people's windows or . . . or get yourselves into any other fixes, or I'll . . ." It must be a wave in the mirror or my eyes playing tricks on me or something, because her reflection looks sad when she says, "I'll have to take away your Three Musketeers bars for an entire month, Robin."

Uh-oh.

Birdie's "all for one and one for all" bars are almost as important to her as Daddy's Swiss Army Knife is to me, because besides being delicious "The Three Musketeers" is a nickname he used to describe him and his girls when we'd snuggle in bed or be up at Lonnigan's Bar together or gazing at the constellation called Orion on our back porch or anyplace else Louise wasn't.

But instead of Birdie doing her impression of a chicken about to have its head cut off after Louise threatened to take away her most important candy the way I was almost sure she would, the unpredictable kid whips her hand out of mine, jumps to her feet, and shouts at our mother at the top of her opera lungs, "You are so, so, so, so beautiful! You remind me of Ida Lupino!"

Oh, for the love of God.

Just once, *once*, couldn't she remember that Louise despises Ida Lupino?!

"She meant to say that you remind her of Maureen O'Hara," I quickly tell our mother as I wrap my hand around my sister's bony leg, pull her down, and slap a pillow over her mouth before she can stick her other foot in it.

I guess Louise is too busy giving herself two thumbs up to care about the Ida Lupino crack, because after she checks herself out one more time in the mirror and likes what she sees, she doesn't roll her eyes at Birdie or me. She just stops to remind us on her scoot out of the bedroom door, "Do your chores, no shenanigans, and Theresa"—her lush mouth foxily curls up on one side—"don't think for a second that I won't check with the Radtke girl to make sure you went to confession," and off she goes. The only evidence she leaves behind is the smell of her Paris perfume, the heart-shaped ring she found next to her plate this morning sitting on the vanity next to her red lip prints on a piece of Kleenex, and a little kid who loves her like nobody's business.

Because I can't trust Birdie not to chase down the stairs after her yelling, *Hey, Ida Lupino, how about a little hug?*, I sit on her round tummy, pin her down to the bumpy white bedspread, and wait until I hear the Chevy squeal away from the curb to tell her, "She's gone and we got important detecting to do. I'm gonna finish the dishes and I want you to go up and dig around in our closet for my old sneakers, then get the white towel out from under the bed and hang it outta the window to let Charlie know to meet us under the weeping willow soon as he can. Do *not* hang the yellow towel. That's the signal to meet us in his bomb shelter." Birdie is looking up at me from the bedspread blanker than a gravestone before it's engraved. "Can you remember all that, honey?"

"Can I remember all *what*, Tessie?"

"While I finish doing the dishes . . ."

But before I can finish repeating what I just got done telling her about the shoes and the towels, my wiry sister bucks me off her pelican tummy, rolls off the bed, and skips out of the room chuckling to herself like she pulled a fast one on me. Poor thing.

6

THERE'S NO FART LIKE AN OLD FART

Birdie can go even more high-strung and ornery if her next meal isn't within grabbing distance. So after I dried off the dishes, I slapped together her favorite sandwich—peanut butter and marshmallow, nicknamed P B and M—and toss it into her favorite brown bag that's got the picture of a Red Owl on the front before I move on to the last *very* important thing I need to do before the Finley sisters can get over to Holy Cross and get down to work. I tug the folded-up piece of paper and stubby yellow pencil out of my shorts pocket, smooth the paper out on the kitchen counter, add on a new #2, and move everything else down.

TO-DO
1. Take tender loving care of Birdie.
2. Solve whatever happened to Sister Margaret Mary for big blackmail or reward bucks.
3. Make Gert Klement think her arteries are going as hard as her heart.

4. Catch whoever stole over $200 out of the Pagan Baby collection box.
5. Practice your Miss America routine.
6. Learn how to swim.
7. Be a good dry-martini-making fiancée to Charlie.
8. Do not get caught blackmailing or spying.
9. Just *think* about making a real confession to Father Ted, before it's too late.

Once I'm happy with the order of things, I slide outta my back pocket my detecting and blackmail notebook that matches my navy-blue eyes. Next to Birdie and Daddy's Swiss Army Knife and his Timex watch, this notebook that's full of facts, proofs, blackmails, dollar amounts, snooping times, and loads of other top-secret information is my most prized possession that I printed **KEEP OUT! THIS MEANS YOU!** on the front of, because I shudder to think what my fate would be if Louise ever got a hold of it. After I flip it open to a clean page, I write:

THE CASE OF THE MISSING NUN WHO MIGHT BE KIDNAPPED AND MURDERED

I am going by the book, and I cannot be sure my suspicions about Sister Margaret Mary are 100% correct until I can check off all the steps that *Modern Detection* taught me I needed to do after a crime has been perpetrated:

1. Find a dead body.
2. Search for a suspect with the means, motive, and opportunity to commit the crime(s).
3. Gather evidence against said suspect through observation and interrogation.

Because I'm pretty sure that Birdie and me are going to find kidnapped and murdered Sister M & M behind the Gilgood mausoleum, I tick that one off and go straight to the next step.

The first time I came across #2, I thought that Mr. Lynwood "My friends call me Woody and my enemies call me their worst nightmare" Bellflower had written "*mean*, motive and opportunity," so I almost closed up my detecting business before it even had a chance to take off.

There are so many *mean* people in the neighborhood that my suspect list for a crime would be too heavy to carry around in my pocket without my shorts falling down around my ankles. It wasn't until I went back and reread #2 that I saw it was *mean* with an *s*, but that threw me into a tailspin, too, because other than meaning more than one mean person, I had no idea what *means* meant. So, of course, as a kid who takes reading and spelling *very* seriously, I did what I always did when I got confused over a word. I rode on my Schwinn bike to North Ave. and looked it up at the Finney Library that I really love. (I would steal the big dictionary they got up there if I could, but I think Mrs. Kambowski, the crabby librarian who works with nice Miss Peshong and acts like she owns the joint, might have my number, because I think she nailed it to its pedestal.)

When it comes to detecting, *means* was defined by Merriam-Webster as having the *ability* to commit a crime. For example, you couldn't be guilty of running somebody over if you didn't know how to drive a car, or you couldn't stab someone seventeen times if you didn't have any hands to hold a butcher knife in, or if you wanted to sew slipcovers out of a person's skin—you couldn't do that, either, if you didn't own an upholstery knife. So if Sister M & M *is* dead, like I think she is, The Mutual Admiration Society is going to have to look for a suspect who is strong. I can't really tell just by looking if our principal has any muscles underneath her black habit, but I *have* seen her break a chalkboard pointer in her bare hands, so she would put up a good fight. And if nuns were allowed to play basketball, she would be a starting forward, so she could not be kidnapped and murdered by a guy who only came up to her rosary beads on a good day.

Figuring out the *motive*, which is *why* somebody would want to kidnap and murder Sister Margaret Mary, well, that's going to be a lot tougher, because nobody likes her, except for my bighearted sister, who likes everybody. But take it from me, a person of much sounder mind, the Creature from the Black Lagoon has a better personality than the principal of St. Kate's.

But tracking down someone who had the *opportunity* to commit the crimes? That should be a breeze. All The Mutual Admiration Society has got to do is search for someone who could've been in the cemetery last night at 12:07 a.m. yelling, "I'm warning you! Watch yourself! You're treading on dangerous ground!," not someone who had laryngitis or was working the night shift at one of the factories.

Because I'm their leader, I can't turn up at our Mutual Admiration meeting under the weeping willow tree without a couple of smart detecting ideas. My partners in crime are counting on me as much as all of us are counting on President Dwight "Ike" Eisenhower. So while I'm waiting for Birdie to come back downstairs wearing my old sneakers after she hung out the white towel from our bedroom window that'll let Charlie, our Sergeant of Arms, know where to find us, I flip another page of my navy-blue detecting notebook over and jot down a new list:

QUESTION OR SURVEIL

1. Mr. McGinty.
2. Kitten Jablonski.
3. Butch Seeback.
4. Mr. Johnson.
5. Suzie LaPelt.

Of course, after I tell my fiancé about our new case, I'll listen to what he has to say, but since we'll already be at the scene of the crime soon, my vote would be to talk to our good friend Mr. McGinty first. The way I wanted to earlier when I saw him from the back porch talking to Mrs. Peterman about her husband's burial. Hardly nothing happens in the cemetery that the caretaker doesn't know about.

8:14 a.m. Birdie *still* hasn't shown up in the kitchen, which means she probably forgot why she went upstairs in the first place. I bet she's in our mother's bedroom. Sitting at the vanity table and trying on her shiny jewelry and smelling her lotions and playing with her makeup, because unlike me who really doesn't go for that sort of thing, Birdie is a lot like Louise in some ways. She can't help it, poor thing, that's just the bad luck of the draw of blood.

I take a giant step to the bottom of the stairs, and yell up, "Get down here ASAP!"

Due to her dawdling, I'm sure that's gonna take her a while, so just as I'm about to take the garbage out the way Louise told me to, I'm surprised to hear the running of little feet over my head and my sister hollering back, "I'm ready, Frank!"

When Louise is gone for the night, I like to pop some corn and curl up on the sofa and watch TV shows like *77 Sunset Strip* and *Hawaiian Eye* so I can get some free detecting pointers, but those whodunnits? They're *way* too hard for Birdie to keep straight in her brain. Besides *Walt Disney Presents*, what tickles *her* fancy are game shows. She's not smart enough to shout out any of the answers to the questions the way I do, she just loves the shiny prizes, and when the duck comes down on one of her favorite shows of all, that's *always* good for one of her great belly laughs that can give even the saddest person a little hope.

Because she loves all my impressions, to reward her for doing what I told her to, after she hops off the last stair and makes the turn into the kitchen, I reach around and grab my ponytail, hold it over my lip, and tell her like Groucho Marx, "Close, but no cigar, little lady." She laughs so hard that her pelican tummy jiggles out of the top of her shorts and I have to stop walking around with my knees bent and stick it back in.

"By the way, honey, the famous saying is, I'm ready, Freddy, not I'm ready, Frank, and . . ." I point down. "You got the right sneakers, but they're on the wrong feet." I bend over to switch them up. "This is a big, big day that could change our whole lives, so ya gotta keep trying your hardest to listen to me and do whatever I tell ya to, okay? Try to keep your drifting to a minimum, and especially"—I make bunny ears in the sneaker laces and change my voice to my most serious one, the one Perry White of the *Daily Planet* uses when he's talking to Jimmy Olsen, who can get flighty, too—"you can't do any wild-streaking, okay?"

Wild-streaking is the bottom of Birdie's barrel. Out of nowhere, she'll take off to parts unknown without me, and it can be hours before I finally find her at Daddy's pretend grave or the Finney Library or the candy aisle at Dalinsky's Drugstore or the flower shop with her nose in a bouquet of pink roses or etc. You name a place in the neighborhood and I've found my wild-streaking sister there. Even the last place *nobody* wants to find themselves in. Up a tree in the cemetery's Phantom Woods. And maybe the worst part of all is that I can't even BE PREPARED for one of her streaks. They're like the weather in the month of March. They blow in like a lion and go out like a lamb, and as far as I can tell, I don't think she's in charge of them, any more than she's the boss of when she drifts off to parts unknown or any of the other weird stuff she does. But over the years, I *have* noticed that if Birdie gets too starved or too bored, a wild streak is *much* more likely to rain on our parade.

I've lectured her about listening to me, and I've already taken care of keeping her tummy happy when I made her the P B and M, so after I get the sneakers laces double knotted, I slip off the rubber bands I got around my wrist, and tell her, "Time for your beautification routine." This is one of her favorite parts of the morning, so I don't even have to tell her to turn around. I finger comb her hair into two blah-brown pigtails, then I come back to the front of her, lick my pointer finger, and wet her eyebrows down so they all go in the same direction, pinch off a booger that's hanging from the bottom of her upturned nose, and rub off most of Louise's red lipstick she smeared way outside the lines of her lips when she was upstairs messing around with our mother's things. But there's nothing I can do about the Evening in Paris perfume she dabbed behind her ears except hook her too-long bangs behind them to hide the smell. That's the best I can do until we catch up with Charlie and he raises Birdie's bangs with his sharp whittling knife. I could it do with a scissors, but she thinks I make her look like Moe from the Three Stooges and she's right.

When I'm done straightening her out, she bats her eyes and asks me the same thing she asks me every morning. "How do I look, Tessie?"

So I say back to her the same thing I say to her every morning. "You are so, so, so, so beautiful. You remind me of Ida Lupino." Then I wink at her and then she winks back at me in her adorable slightly bulgy-eyed way and that can go on forever, so I put a halt to it by pointing down to her right shorts pocket to make sure she has what she needs to keep her tiny mind occupied when we're over at the cemetery. Birdie cannot, I repeat, *not* do any bored wild-streaking on this life-changing day. We're on a deadline. "You got your hobbies?"

"Yes, Tessie, I got my hobbies." She slides her playing cards and a cat's cradle string out of her pocket with a very proud smile and I don't blame her. Dick and Jane might be too hard for her to read, and keeping track of what goes on in movies or television shows is too confusing, and our Mutual Admiration meetings might be above her head, but you hand this kid a deck of cards—I think she got her love of the "52" from Daddy—or give her a white string off a Meuer's Bakery box that still smells like sugar? She turns into a regular Albert Einstein.

All set to hit the investigating trail now, I grab the Red Owl bag off the counter, point to the back door, and tell her the last thing I gotta tell her to get her going in the right direction in my voice that's sure to fire her up. "Race ya to the cemetery fence! One for the money . . . two for the show . . . three to get ready, and . . ."

I wait for her to fill in the blank, but she doesn't shout, *Go, Bird, go!* like she's been doing.

She could be going stubborn on me again or . . . or maybe she just has to tinkle. Yes. She can forget if I don't remind her. "You gotta go before we go, Bird, go?"

"No, I don't gotta go before we go, Tessie."

Hmmm.

"Did you just remember ya hung the wrong-colored towel out of the window?"

"No, I hung the white towel out the window just like you told me to, Tessie," she says, sure-enough-sounding that I believe her.

Because I'm all gassed up and ready to go and she is doing an excellent impression of a roadblock, I lose my patience that I don't got a lot of in the first place, because in this way, unfortunately, I resemble my mother by a bad-luck draw of the blood.

So it's not really my fault that I ask Birdie snippier than I should, "Then what's the damn problem?"

She looks down at the green kitchen floor that could use a good scrubbing and tells me in her tiniest voice, which is already quite tiny, "You're gonna get mad-der if I tell you."

"No, I won't. I promise, no, I *sister*-promise." For some other unknown reason, the kid who forgets 99% of what I tell her *always* remembers that's the most serious kind of promise there is. A *sister*-promise can *never* be broken, no matter what. Even if some dumb greaser forces me to eat maggots on a saltine cracker before he'll give Birdie back to me, she knows that I would rather do that than break a *sister*-promise. "C'mon." I make my voice less ticked-off sounding and more sugary-sounding. "Tell me, honey." As much as I want to, I can't go over to the cemetery without her, because I cannot leave her alone. "Why aren't you raring to go with me to Holy Cross?"

"'Cause . . . 'cause . . ." Birdie says, barely above a whisper, "I don't want Mommy to take away my all for ones and ones for all."

"You mean you don't want *Louise* to take away your all for ones and ones for all."

"Roger that."

My sister was so wound up at the time that I didn't think she heard our mother warn us not to visit the cemetery or do any peeking into our neighbors' windows or she'd take away the Three Musketeers bars before she left for work, but I'm not all *that* surprised that threat got through her adorable, thick skull. Candy of any kind is a *very* important topic of conversation to Miss Birdie Finley.

If she was walking down Keefe Ave. and Mr. Ed Gein pulled up next to her and offered her a piece of disgusting black licorice to get in his car with him after he escaped from the Big House for murdering all those people, my sister would fall for that. She'd tug open the car door and tell that crazy murderer with one of her irresistible smiles—*Thanks for the candy, mister. Sure, I'd love to go for a spin! I'm just crazy about your upholstery, by the way.*

Birdie can see that she's disappointing me, so she starts flapping her arms. She'll throw her head back and start squawking next and it can take forever to work her out of *that* state, so I tell her, "Don't get yourself all lathered up, okay?" and then I pet her little back in long strokes, the way she likes. "Remember? Louise is only gonna take away your candy bars if we get *caught* over at the cemetery and that's not gonna happen." Birdie still doesn't look ready to rumble, so I need to up my ante. I pick up her hand and place it on the front of my shorts. "That's a whole pocketful of Hershey's kisses, and look!" I wave the Red Owl bag in front of her face so she can get a whiff of what's inside with her special smelling power. "I made you a P B and M." It can't hurt to throw one more chip into the pot to convince her how much is at stake here. "And if you mind your p's and q's, I'll nab the box of chocolate-covered cherries offa Mister Lindley's grave and you don't even have to give me any." Next to Three Musketeers bars, Birdie loves those creamy, gooey cherries best of all, so she must be very scared about heading over to the cemetery, because she's perked up some, but she still doesn't look like she's burning with desire.

I'd mention to her our new case and how life-changing important it is to us, but that won't be enough. I don't think she understands or cares all that much about solving the kidnapping murder. She might not even remember it anymore. No. I'm going to have pull out my big guns to get her moving toward the black iron fence.

Visiting Daddy's pretend grave *always* makes his little dreamboat feel like her ship has come in (Joke!), and she also goes very gaga for my nice fiancé, Charlie "Cue Ball" Garfield, almost as much as I do, which is gonna work out so great after him and me become Mr. and Mrs. When we get back from our honeymoon in Wisconsin Dells that my sister will go on, too, of course, because it's our version of Disneyland—my little animal lover will just adore petting the deer and seeing the statue of Paul Bunyan's ox, Babe—The Mutual Admiration Society will live happily ever after in the house on Hadley St. that I like so much. The solid-looking redbrick one with the white shutters and pretty maple tree out back that shades the bedroom off the kitchen that will belong to Birdie. Charlie and me will take care of her for as long as she lives. The same way Mrs. Obermeyer across the street watches over her sister Audrey, who got polio. Even after being in an iron lung at Sacred Heart Sanitarium for a year, the gal still has to wear those steel braces.

I give Birdie's back a few more kitty-cat strokes and say into her ear, "I know you're worried about us getting caught and Louise takin' away your ones for all and all for ones, but . . ." I rub Daddy's Swiss Army Knife, because I'm about to fire off my end-all-and-be-all trick. "You really, really, really, really wanna go to the cemetery to visit with Daddy and Charlie, don't you?"

Ha!

You Bet Your Life she does! (Joke!)

My future bridesmaid yells, "Go, Bird, go," and pushes me out of the way, pops through the squeaky back door of the house, and thank goodness I caught a hold of her arm before she jumped down the steps and ran across the backyard toward the cemetery fence.

I yank her toward me and tell her, "I like your enthusiasm, kiddo, but before we can go say hi to Daddy and Charlie, we got a *very* important caper we gotta pull off first."

Along with all the other putridness Gert Klement does to Birdie and me, she put a real crimp in our cemetery visits after she paid to get a gigantic picture window put in above her kitchen sink. So now, whenever she's doing the dishes or cooking or baking or pondering evil plans, she can keep tabs on Birdie and me better than she ever has. And believe me, nothing, and I mean *not . . . one . . . thing* on God's green earth, even pagan babies, fills the black heart of that old biddy with as much joy as catching the Finley sisters in the act.

Birdie looks up at me, cocks her head, and asks, "What *very* important caper do we gotta pull off first, Tessie?"

This is not the time or place for this kind of sentimental sloppiness, but I can't help myself. She is just so darn cute that I give her an Eskimo kiss before I narrow my eyes at the house next door and tell her, "We gotta sneak past the old fart first."

7

LOOSE LIPS SINK SHIPS

After sitting Birdie down on our back porch steps and giving her strict instructions to stay put until she hears my coast-is-clear signal, I got busy doing reconnaissance from behind a tree in front of Gert Klement's house.

I'm peeking around the trunk to make sure that everybody who is out and about on the block is so busy paying attention to something else that they won't notice me and report back to Gert that they saw me on the morning in question. So far . . . so good. A group of around twenty kids are playing a rough game of Red Rover in the middle of Keefe Ave. Looking like death warmed over, Mrs. Stewart is barely pushing her tenth colicky baby in a ratty-looking carriage on the opposite end of the block. And four houses down, Louise's opponent in the Pagan Baby Society election is working up a storm.

I've heard our mother refer to Mrs. Nancy Tate as "a lame duck," but in my opinion, instead of wasting energy calling the gal she's running against names—I'm rubber, you're glue and all that—Louise should get busy doing *exactly* what Mrs. Tate's been doing. And I don't mean she should dance half-naked for traveling vacuum cleaner salesman Horace Mertz while listening to "Rockin' Robin" when the mood comes over her. What our mother should be doing is some *advertising* if she doesn't want her clamdiggers beat off her two weeks from now.

The reason I know how important getting the word out is in the scheme of things is because every other Saturday afternoon this summer, besides teaching me a lot about the Braves baseball team—boy, that Eddie Mathews is really something and so is Hammerin' Hank Aaron—the owner of Skank's Funeral Home has "undertaken" the job (Joke!) of teaching me free of charge about embalming fluid, how to apply makeup to a corpse for the most lifelike appearance, high-quality casket linings versus tacky ones, and most importantly, how to run a successful business. "There are only so many dead bodies to go around, and more parlors are popping up every day," Mr. Art Skank told me when he was putting the finishing touches on Mr. Otto Cooper, who died of old age week before last. "It's crucial to draw attention to your business, so besides my usual advertisement in the Yellow Pages, I recently purchased a billboard." He dabbed a little more pink lipstick on Mr. Cooper's lips. "Have you seen it, Tessie?"

I *had* seen the **WORKS OF ART** sign on top of the abandoned Goodyear tire store on North Ave. I thought that was a really good slogan, but in my opinion, Mr. Skank should've stopped while he was ahead. He shouldn't have put the sign on top of that particular store, and he should also *not* have included a picture of himself standing next to a casket in a Leonardo da Vinci costume. Firstly, you croak, you're never gonna make somebody believe it's a good year. Second off, from hanging around so many dead people, hate to say it, but they have kinda rubbed off on the short-necked, unusually hairy-armed, and generally not-very-good-looking-in-the-first-place mortician.

But, in answer to his question, of course, I did what any good friend would do. I fudged a little and told him, "I *did* see your billboard, sir, and it's . . . it's a *huge* masterpiece!" That seemed to make him happy, because he perfectly rouged Mr. Otto Cooper's cheeks. (Mr. Skank was doing a little showing off, ya know? The way people do to make the compliment you just gave 'em seem true.)

If The Mutual Admiration Society ever needs to get more detecting customers, but not blackmail customers, we have plenty of those because there is never any shortage of people doing bad things around here, I'll BE PREPARED to do some advertising. We'll need a snappy slogan, like the ones Mr. Art Skank and his sister, pom-pom-shaking Mrs. Nancy Tate, came up with. He must've lectured *her* about the importance of "getting the word out," too, because from behind this tree in Gert's front yard, I'm watching our mother's opponent in the Pagan Baby election pound *another* sign into her lawn and she's really putting her back into it.

TWO-FOUR-SIX-EIGHT!

SCORE A TREASURER THAT'S REALLY GREAT!

CAST YOUR VOTE FOR NANCY TATE!

After I take one more good look up and down the block and I'm positive that the kids playing in the street are too wrapped up in sending "Timmy" over, Mrs. Stewart is sticking a bottle into the ratty carriage, and Mrs. Tate is busy with another one of her u-rah-rah signs, I stick my two pointer fingers in my mouth and whistle *wooo ooo whoot*, which is the signal to let Birdie know that it's time for her to jump off our back porch steps and run like crazy to the bushes in front of the cemetery fence and wait for me in the usual place.

On account of the great Indian weather we're having, like everybody else's on the block, all the windows are open in Old Lady Klement's house, so I can hear Bishop Sheen sermonizing when I'm standing at her front door. She's listening to his show on the radio in her kitchen, and something smells really good and I'm 100% sure it's not her. I think she must be baking a devil's food cake, because, of course, that would be her favorite on account of that famous saying "Like attracts like." (No joke.)

FACT: I know the layout of her house.

PROOF: It's easy for me to jimmy the lock and wiggle through her basement window.

Daddy always said, "Throw the first punch," so by pocketing our next door neighbor's change and moving around stuff in her house when she's asleep or up at church, I'm working on #3 on my TO-DO list: Make Gert Klement think that her arteries have gone as hard as her heart. That way, when her granddaughter, Lily Klement, who is so sweet and nice that she *had* to have been adopted out of St. Rose's Orphanage, enrolls Gert in the kind of "home" she'd like to send Birdie and me off to she will not put up a fight. The day the moving truck pulls up in front of her house to lug her and her belongings up to the Catholic Home for the Aged on Burleigh St. will be a big red-letter day for Birdie and me, because I am 50% sure that Louise wouldn't get rid of us once that buttinsky can no longer whisper not-so-sweet nothings about us into her ear.

On the other hand . . . timing really *is* everything, so I have to BE PREPARED that the artery-hardening plan won't work before the men with the nets show up to take Birdie away or before I get sent to live at the juvie home, so I'm feeling a *big* desire to solve this kidnapping murder case for lots of running-away bucks when I lean on Gert's doorbell.

When the old witch hears the doorbell ding-dong, she slams a kitchen cabinet shut, turns the radio down, and hollers, "You better not be another Fuller Brush man or vacuum cleaner salesman interrupting the bishop and my baking!"

Ha . . . ha . . . ha . . . *Gotcha!*

She thinks she's so smart, but she's doing one of the worst things she could possibly do, according to my expert boxer Daddy. Just like Louise is underestimating her opponent in the election, Gert is underestimating me. I *know* she can give door-to-door salesmen the boot, but it's a huge sin not to help St. Kate's raise money, which is why I lower my voice that is already so deep and yell back at her "Church paper drive!" before I jump the porch railing and take off around the side of her house.

8:33 a.m. *I* can make the round trip from Gert's kitchen to her front door in under ten seconds, but once she sees that nobody's come from St. Kate's to collect her old newspapers, it'll take her around three minutes to shuffle back to Bishop Sheen and her picture window, depending on how much her bunions that I gave her by praying every night for a month to Mary Magdalene, the patron saint of feet, are bothering her this morning.

Keeping track of the time on Daddy's Timex with one eye after I make it across our neighbor's backyard and into ours, I use my other eye to get busy looking for Birdie in the bushes in front of the cemetery fence where she's supposed to be hiding. I need to guide her over the pointy spears on top, because I get too petrified that one of these days her little hands are going to lose their grip and she'll end up looking like a lollipop.

When I can't get a bead on her right away, I go nervous, but not straight into shock. This is just another example of that famous saying about a Bird in the hand being better than a Bird in a bush. (No joke.) It's also not the first time she's pulled something like this and I'm 100% positive it won't be the last. Considering how often she gets away from me, I can only think of one good reason why the Finley sisters shouldn't have been born connected at the hip like the two Siamese sisters we saw at the freak show at the Wisconsin State Fair.

Q. How do Ling and Ming go to the bathroom?

A. *Outlook not so good.*

I whisper-holler into the bushes, "Bird?"

Not a peep.

"Tweetheart?"

That's my forgetful sister for ya in a nutshell. Instead of running over to these bushes when I gave her the whistle signal, she musta ran somewhere else. I'd go it alone, but I can't. It's never a good idea to let Birdie out of my sight for too long. If she doesn't answer me this time, I need to go find her and work out another plan. "Honey?"

She pops up in the bushes on the *other* side of the black iron fence that I never want her to climb over without me and says with a funny little smile, "You rang?" like beatnik Maynard G. Krebs of *The Many Loves of Dobie Gillis* show, which is kinda strange. She doesn't get jokes and is not supposed to know how to crack a funny "You rang?" one about me ding-dong ditching Gert Klement.

8:45 a.m. According to the second hand on Daddy's watch, our neighbor is going to be standing at her kitchen window that'd give her a great view of Birdie and me in 5 . . . 4 . . . 3 . . . , so I hurry over the fence and pull my giggling sister deeper and lower into the bushes and not a second too soon.

Through the parted leaves, Birdie and me watch as The Wretched One flattens her nose against her giant picture window. She's locked on to the spot where we've hidden from her a gazillion times before, so I know she can't see us, but we gotta be careful that she doesn't hear us, because just like The Mutual Admiration Society, our enemy has got what Chapter Five in *Modern Detection* calls TOOLS OF THE TRADE of her own. "A *fedora* may be worn low over one's eyes to conceal one's identity," the book says, which makes sense. Eyes can tell somebody everything about you because they are the windows to our soul. I couldn't find a fedora hat to fit me at Toppers, so I boosted a pair of sunglasses from the five and dime last week to keep my peepers hidden. A *trench coat*—a tan coat that has nothing to do with sickness of the mouth—also comes highly recommended, but I figure a beige top and shorts would work just as good. And an *ordinary drinking glass* is also nice to have on you if you want to listen to people talking on the other side of walls, and I keep one of those in our Radio Flyer.

But as good and helpful as hats, shades, and drinking glasses are, I got my sights set on something much, much better. I want the same TOOLS OF THE TRADE that Gert's got. Hearing aids. They're not much to look at, but I'm not kidding, those little plastic shrimp that hook around her long ears are so powerful that she can hear you burping the alphabet or making farting noises under your armpit in the front pew of the church when she's all the way in the back. Oh, having hearing aids of my own would be so helpful for blackmail and detecting eavesdropping! Betcha I could be five cars away and still hear a greaser bragging to one of the gang at the Milky Way Drive-In, *I scored third base offa Mary Catherine O'Donnell at the necking tree last night* or *It's me who stole over two hundred clams outta the Pagan Baby collection box*, or the best confession ever, *Yeah, I was the one who snatched and murdered Sister Margaret Mary, ya wanna make something of it, Clyde?*

From where Birdie and me are hiding, I watch with held breath as our rancid neighbor with the A+ hearing moves from her picture window over to her smaller shouting-at-us window. "Church paper drive, my foot!" she screams. "I see you and your sister crouched in those bushes, Theresa Finley, you little banshee!"

"No, she doesn't. She's trying to trick us," I whisper to Birdie.

"If you don't come out, I'm calling your mother and telling her what you've been up to!" Gert bellows.

When I feel Birdie tighten, I tap my finger against her cute mouth and say, "Zip it, lock it, and stick it in your pocket," because I wouldn't put it past her to jump up and shout back to Gert, *Tell Mommy I'm sorry . . . I'm sorry . . . I'm sorry . . . I'm sorry!* So just to make sure she doesn't, I wrap my arms around her little body and start singing softly the same thing I always do when we're hiding. "One Mississippi, two Mississippi, three Mississippi." When I reach, "twenty-one Mississippi," which is *my* lucky number, because it was Daddy's, I remind my partner in crime one more time to keep her trap shut before I separate the bush branches to check and see why Gert has suddenly gone quiet as a tomb.

Damnation!

Her bunions must not be bothering her this morning as much as I wanted them to, because our bulky neighbor has made it out her door, down her porch steps, around the prickly hedge, and to the back of our house in record-breaking time. She must've decided that we weren't crouched down in the cemetery bushes after all, which is good, but now she's coming over to check on us the way Louise asked her to before she left for the Clark station, which is not good.

"Open up!" Gert bellows as she pounds on the back door of our house.

When Birdie and me don't do her bidding, she takes something out of her flowery housecoat pocket in a frenzy and starts talking in the secret language they teach at St. Nazianz Seminary, which is where boys go to become priests after high school if they can't get any girls to put out for them.

"*Dominos vobiscum*," Gert shouts in Latin.

What *is* that she's choking in her meaty hand? Is that . . . no. That can't be her precious bottle of Holy Water she brought back from her pilgrimage to Lourdes, could it?!

"Theresa Marie Finley, in the name of His Holiness Pope John the Twenty-Third and our savior, the Lord Jesus Christ, and His mother Mary," Gert yells as she dips her fingers into the purple bottle and makes the sign of the cross on our back door. "I demand you show yourself immediately!"

What . . . in . . . the . . . hell . . . is . . . she . . . doing?

It sorta looks like something that Kitten Jablonski told me the church had to do to her older sister, Dawn, who got in Dutch for getting caught too many times with her blouse off in the back of some boy's hot rod. When my confidential informant was describing it to me, her exact words were, "It's called an *exercism*. The bishop sent a special priest to our house to shout a bunch of Latin, throw Holy Water on Dawnie, and force her to do Royal Canadian push-ups so the devil would hop outta her."

Even though Kitten's information is usually so reliable, I didn't believe her at first because that *exercism* business sounded sorta off the wall to me, but whatta ya know? Here's Gert Klement proving once again that famous saying "Seeing is believing."

Gert says as she holy sprinkles our house again, "This is your last chance, Theresa, before I . . . I . . ."

Before you what, you holier-than-thou hag? Call your friend the bishop and tell him to send a special priest over to our house tonight who'll force me to drop and do fifty in our living room?

That'll be the day.

But my fragile sister, she doesn't feel the same way. Birdie doesn't do so good with yelling, orders, or threats of any kind, no matter how much Hershey's chocolate I jam into her mouth. If she gets too worked up, she's going to start squawking so loud that our neighbor wouldn't even need her hearing aids to find us.

Gert threatens again, "I'm calling your mother!"

"Keep your cool," I whisper to the kid whose slightly bulging eyes have got more white in them than they should. "Even if she *does* get a hold of Louise at the station, I'll explain to her that the reason that we didn't answer the door when Gert knocked was because . . . ummm . . . you and me went up to church so I could confess with the other kids." Birdie won't figure out that I'm lying to her to keep her from going berserk, because she won't remember that I can't say my sins for a few more hours and she can't tell time. "Exactly the way she ordered me to do before she left for her job."

That famous saying about pride goeth-ing before a fall is very correct, because I'm so busy giving myself a pat on the back for thinking up that whopper that when my sister starts looking even more agitated and begins shaking her head low and slow, it takes me a second to figure out why the confession lie didn't calm her down the way it shoulda.

I could just kick myself! It's too late now, but I should've come up with a different fib about a subject that Birdie is not so dang touchy about.

Sure enough, sadder sounding than the seagulls who circled over my head on the day Daddy drowned, my sister reminds me about #9 on my TO-DO list. "Please just *think* about making a real confession to Father Ted before it's too late, Tessie."

Her and me agree on most topics of conversation, but on this particular one, the Finley sisters are more parted than the Red Sea.

Every night lately after we kneel next to our bed to say, "Now I lay me down to sleep, I pray the Lord my soul to keep. If I should die before I wake, I pray the Lord my soul to take," Birdie throws her arms around my neck and cries on my shoulder.

Dying in the middle of the night must happen all the time to Catholic kids or there wouldn't be a prayer to ward it off, so I understand why she gets herself all hot and bothered. We already lost Daddy, and my sister is petrified that she's going to lose me, too, not just in this lifetime, but for all eternity if I should croak in the middle of night when I'm slipping my hand under her heinie every once in a while to make sure she hasn't wet the bed, working on my lists, shadowboxing, practicing my impressions and a couple of sure-fire jokes that are sure to get the crowd going before I sing the "Favorite Things" song that I'm going to perform for the talent portion of Miss America someday in honor of our father.

Birdie is positive that instead of the Lord showing up to return my soul to its heavenly home, Lucifer will appear in our room to stab my soul with his pitchfork and drag it down to his place. The reason I haven't been able to come up with anything yet to convince her that she's wrong is because she isn't. I was counting on her forgetting when

I told her, but for some unknown reason, she perfectly remembers that my filthy-with-sin soul hasn't been scrubbed clean in the longest time, since I stopped telling Father Ted my *real* sins in my *real* voice every week in the confessional and started telling him *fake* sins in my *Shirley Temple* voice, because for godssake, who wouldn't believe *anything* that tap-dancing, yodeling kid told them?

FACT: I got my reasons.

PROOF: Loose lips sink ships.

Sure, priests are *supposed* to keep what you tell them a secret, but it'd be pretty dumb of me to confess the whole truth and nothing but in my easy-to-identify voice to a regular at Lonnigan's Bar who is known to knock back way too many glasses of Communion wine.

Now, I'm not saying that I'm 100% sure that Father Ted would go blabbing my top snooping and blackmailing secrets to every Tom, Dick, and Harry in the parish. All I'm saying is that I need to BE PREPARED that half-in-the-bag priest could go blabbing my top snooping and blackmailing secrets to every Tom, Dick, and Harry in the parish. Gossip spreads faster around here than German measles and if our mother ever got wind of what my sister and me been up to, she'll get out one of the only possessions she hasn't given away of Daddy's to Goodwill Industries. His brown leather belt. Birdie and me wouldn't be able to sit down for a week. (That's what is known as an understatement. No joke.) Even worse, Louise *could* get so steamed when she heard about our detecting and blackmail shenanigans that she'd lock us in our room and telephone St. Anne's Home for Wayward Girls and the county loony bin and tell them to drop everything and come get the Finley sisters ASAP! (That's what is known as being screwed. Also no joke.)

"Please, honey," I say to my ants-in-her-pants sister, who could blow our caper at any second if she gets any more worked up. "You've gotta try really hard now to stop thinkin' about me kickin' the bucket in the middle of the night and going to Hell. Maybe . . . maybe you could think about something yummy instead! Something like . . ." I reach behind me and wave her favorite Red Owl grocery bag that's got the P B and M inside that I just realized sounds more like something you'd do on a visit to the little girls' room, and maybe Birdie, who I suspect can ESP my mind, just realized that, too, because she turns her nose up at the sandwich, which isn't like her at all. Not giving up, I bring up *another* one of her favorite subjects to convince her to chow down, which will keep her mouth busy with something other than squawking. "Remember how Daddy used to tell everyone up at Lonnigan's, 'Eat, drink, and be merry—'"

"For tomorrow we all could die."

"No, no, no, no, you're not remembering that right. What Daddy used to say is, 'Eat, drink, and be merry, for tomorrow we all could . . . ahhh . . . *spy!*'"

Feeling pretty good about that lie, I take one more look through the branches to make sure Gert is still on our back porch or on the way back to her house, but my sister must've moved around enough to draw her attention our way, because that old buffalo is stampeding straight toward the bushes we're hiding in with an I-got-you-now look on her ugly puss. Of course, she can't climb the cemetery fence to grab us, she's too decrepit, but if she makes it to the fence, she *will* be able to look through the black bars and down into the bushes.

"She's comin'," I squat back down and tell Birdie. "Quick. Get down on your tummy and back out very slowly, because if she catches us, she'll . . ." I don't want to rile her up worse than she already is, but what choice do I have? "She's gonna rat us out to Louise and ya remember what she told you this morning she was going to do if we got caught outside of the house doing something we're not supposed to?"

Luckily, a small part of Birdie's small brain *does* recall again that our mother threatened to take away her precious Three Musketeers bars, because she doesn't have to think long and hard about the answer to my question the way she does most.

She lickety-split drops to her belly, looks up at me with her run-of-the-mill blue eyes that have turned a steelier gray than the barrel of a gangster's gun, and says outta the side of her suddenly gone old-timey mouth, "Well, whatcha waitin' for, toots? An engraved invitation? Let's blow this pop stand."

8

UH-OH

Birdie and me are snaking our way through the familiar gravestones at our home away from home on our way to the biggest burial joint in the whole cemetery, which belongs to Mr. Gilgood. When he was still alive and kicking, the richest man in the neighborhood lived in a house that does not look like all the rest of our wooden houses. Mr. McGinty, who knows a lot about other things besides digging graves because he has a *World Book Encyclopedia* of his very own in his shack at the cemetery where Birdie and me visit him all the time, told me that Mr. Gilgood's place was so different because it was built by somebody name of Frank Lloyd Wright, who I think was one of the famous flying brothers because that house on 67th St. has always looked a little like an airliner to me.

I can only guess who or what my sister is thinking about on our trip to the scene of the crime—probably Daddy and Charlie and chocolate-covered cherries—but when we scoot past one of the graves that's blanketed in going-away presents on our way over there, what *I'm* wondering about for the umpteenth time is if I'm being a dope who is ignoring opportunity knocking loudly at my door.

I make an exception when it comes to the boxes of the Stover's candy that Evelyn Melman leaves once a week on Mr. Lindley's grave—why the wife of the hardware store owner is sweet on this dead plumber who got burned up in a house fire is one of life's little mysteries that I wouldn't mind solving when things die down around here. (Joke!) But if I didn't have the rule to steal only from people who have and never from people who have not, I could make such a killing at Louie's Pawn Shop with the parting gifts that grievers leave on the graves of their departed loved ones. Woolly teddy bears in vests, Christmas wreaths with silver bells that I can hear tinkling through the crack in our bedroom window at that time of year, flags waving on the Fourth of July, crocheted afghans during April showers—I guess to warm their departed's bones—and until recently, many of the tombstones had real gold St. Christopher medals hanging offa them. About the only person I can think of who has left something not so nice on a grave is Mrs. Eunice Hartfield. She propped a laminated picture on the tombstone of her deceased hubby that had a cigarette hole burned into the spot on his chest where his heart should've been after she heard at the church knitting circle that her best friend, Mrs. Dorothy Osbourn, was an even *best-er* friend with Mr. John Hartfield, so I guess that proves the famous saying "Hell hath no fury like a woman scored on" is true once and for all.

And, of course, the other thing I can't help but think about when my sister and me make our way to Mr. Gilgood's luxurious mausoleum is that we're breaking Louise's #1 Commandment—*The Finley Sisters Shalt Not Visit the Cemetery.*

Far back as I can remember, our mother hasn't wanted us to hang out here, but she's gotten even stricter since the day of our father's *pretend* funeral and burial that she wouldn't let Birdie and me go to. Because no matter how hard the Shore Patrol looked for Daddy's body after he fell over the side of *The High Life* the afternoon we went fishing together, they never found him. Not in Lake Michigan, and he never washed up on one of the beaches, either. So that's why his coffin that got carried out of the hearse by the six men named Paul was full of rocks and not Daddy's bones.

"Losing your father is a cross the three of us will have to bear, girls, but life goes on. Time heals all wounds," is the kind of bull hockey that Louise preaches to Birdie and me about every day. "We need to pull ourselves up by our bootstraps."

But I guess, like Mr. McGinty taught me, there are times that bull hockey isn't *always* bad. "Honesty *is* the best policy, Tessie, but it's got no business attending a funeral," is what he said. That's because our friend knows that if those sad people who've lost their most precious one were told the hopeless truth, which is that once they're done being numb they'll start feeling all the time like they got the worst thirst that *nothing* can quench and know deep inside of themselves that they're gonna spend every day of the rest of their lives looking for something precious they're never gonna find, no matter how many times the sun rises and sets, that would be pretty much the same as telling them, *You'll never hear your sweet one's voice, hug them, and laugh at their jokes again, so why don't you save yourself a lot of wear and tear and jump into that grave with them and get it over with?*

Why doesn't Louise feel that way?

She's got no trouble quenching *her* thirst up at Lonnigan's Bar with the guy she wants to replace our precious Daddy with. Sometimes I pretend that we need money so much that our mother is sacrificing herself by luring what's-his-name and his payroll check into her wedding web, but it sure seems to me that she's only thinking about herself. I have told her a million times that if she can't pay the electric or heating bill or buy more food, that's fine by us. Candles will do, and this winter Birdie and me can wear our coats and mittens in the house, and I can bring home school lunch in my uniform pocket for supper, but Louise won't listen to me.

But just because *she* doesn't care about Daddy anymore doesn't mean that Birdie and me don't and I had no problem telling her that. She had the worst tantrum I've ever seen the night I waited at the kitchen table for her to come home from Lonnigan's. I just couldn't take it anymore and she's not the only one with a temper around here, so I accused Louise of inflicting "cruel and unusual punishment" on Birdie and me because Daddy wasn't here anymore to protect us. She shook her finger in my face and screamed, "You want to see some cruel and unusual punishment, little girl? Try feeding two kids and . . . and paying bills and holding your head up high after your husband cheated and . . ." I hollered back at her, "Liar!" because Daddy would *never* cheat at cards, or approve of her keeping his two "babies" away from him, or want her to go on dates with what's-his-name. "You're the cheater and you will never be the boss of us! What he says still goes!" Louise slapped me across the face, which was something she had never done before, and in the morning she made French toast with cinnamon, just the way Daddy always made it.

Why can't our mother see that Birdie and me *need* the cemetery? It's not only our lifeline to Daddy, death is our #1 hobby, and her thinking that fads like Hula-Hooping or stamp collecting would be "healthier pastimes" and "less morbid" is so shortsighted. Death is never going to go out of style, and it's not a pain in the butt to chase down the block if it gets away from you, and it also doesn't make your mouth taste like glue.

And this is not even taking into consideration how in this beautiful cemetery that has so many trees and smells of flowers and just-mowed grass in the summer and at this time of the year burning leaves and sweet, ripe red apples, I have learned so much more than I *ever* have slouched over a desk in a stuffy classroom that reeks of chalk, kid sweat, and Fartin' Marty Larson.

Death is also very educational.

The tombstone that Birdie and me are strolling past now taught us that one job we should never get if we grow up is taxicab driving. Mr. McGinty told us that this poor man got killed by a passenger who took all his money and plugged him in the head with a .45.

DARGU MALISHEWSKI

JULY 10, 1911–APRIL 22, 1957

FARE THEE WELL

Something else I've also learned during the many hours we've spent in Holy Cross is that the Finley sisters really have to watch our steps. Not just grown-ups kick the bucket, kids do, too. Here and there and all over the place.

Cute little Jody Gersh choked on an apple. (A crying shame.) Three-year-old Bucky Martin drank lighter fluid. (Heartbreaking.) And two little girls named Junie and Sara who got murdered and left next to the Washington Park Lagoon are buried side by side under a white-trunked birch tree that shades their graves. (Worst way to go.) When I asked Mr. McGinty, who understands so much about life and death, why the girls from the next parish over weren't put in the ground near the pond, because I thought after the awful way they died they deserved to be set into the swankiest part of the cemetery, he set me straight. "The pond looks very similar to the lagoon, Tessie. When their families come to visit, it might bring back memories of where their children's bodies were found and that would be too much to bear. Grievers' hearts can only take so much before they bust into a million little pieces."

After he told me that, I surprised the hell outta the both of us when I swooned to the grass and burst into bawling because that was *exactly* the way I felt after Daddy died. Like my heart had done a cannonball onto a slab of granite and if I never saw Lake Michigan or any other lake as long as I lived it would it be too soon for me.

Birdie didn't feel as bad as me. Not at first, anyway.

No matter how many times I repeated what happened on the afternoon that Daddy died, she wouldn't believe that he wasn't *ever* coming back. That might seem like she was just being her weird self, but it was more than that. Unless you actually see someone die before your eyes, the way I did, I know from years of watching what goes on in the cemetery from our back porch that it can be *very* hard to understand that someone you loved with your whole heart, someone who inhaled your exhales, someone who you could never imagine living without, has ceased to exist. That's why God invented funerals and burials. As proof.

So when Louise refused to take Birdie and me to Daddy's pretend funeral and burial, and when she wouldn't show us where his gravestone had been sunk in Holy Cross, Birdie, who needs help understanding even the simplest things, had the worst time coming to grips with Daddy's demise. And after she saw the picture postcard in the rack at Dalinsky's Drugstore with the sunburned man on the front that I had to admit *did* look a lot like our handsome father holding up a fish with a pointy nose next to an ocean, my sister got convinced that Daddy *was* gone, but he was coming back. She 100% decided that after he hit his head on the motor and fell out of *The High Life*, he got amnesia and paddled to Boca Raton, Florida, and once she gets something stuck into her mulish mind, believe me, there is no budging it. From that day on, I lived in deathly fear that Louise would find out Birdie was thinking something so loonatic that could get her sent to the county asylum quicker than you could say *The Three Faces of Eve*.

Figuring the only way my sister would ever know for sure that Daddy was in a better position to do some deep-sea fishing than she'd let herself believe, I was positive that seeing his pretend grave with her own eyes would do the trick. Since our mother wouldn't help us out, I went to our friend, who also happens to be Birdie's and my godfather, by the way, Mr. McGinty. After I explained to him the awful pickle

I was in, I begged him to take me to where Daddy's casket had been sunk, but he told me that he was sorry, that it wasn't "his place," which really hurt my feelings, because if Holy Cross is *anybody's* place, it's his.

I spent every minute I could searching the cemetery for Daddy all by myself, but it's so big and very hard to find what you're looking for when your eyes are watering and the tombstones start to bleed together, so the Finley sisters were really down for the count. There Birdie was, feeling like her daddy would be home any second with a sandy tan and a pointy-nosed fish to fry up for supper, and I was feeling so sad and so bad about not saving him and worried to death about Louise finding out about my sister's undying belief in his Boca Raton amnesia that I was about two ticks away from saying goodbye cruel world and diving into the closest open grave.

But . . . see?

That only goes to show you how smart Daddy was when he'd punch his bag and make our basement floor slippery with sweat and tell me his most famous saying of all, "No matter how bad things get, Tessie, you gotta always remember, come Hell or high water, a Finley never, *ever* throws in the towel," because just when I was about to do just that . . . lo and behold . . . we found him!

EDWARD ALFRED FINLEY

REST IN PEACE

SEPTEMBER 2, 1931–AUGUST 1, 1959

Half-Irish kids like Birdie and me are only half-lucky, so us being led to his tombstone by a flock of fireflies during a crackling storm that lit up the night sky with so many lightning forks that it looked like God's silverware drawer, well, need I say more?

FACT: Miracles happen to Catholic kids.

PROOF: The Blessed Virgin Mary magically appeared to three shepherd children in a place called Fatima, Portugal, and she also stopped in to say hello to a girl named Bernadette in Lourdes, France, so fireflies showing up in Milwaukee, Wisconsin, one night to light up the way to our daddy's pretend grave is something that really could happen, and did.

9:51 a.m. When I see our all-time favorite tombstone in the distance, I get a good grip on Birdie's hand when she starts to veer that way, and tell her, "Honey, hold up," and then I remind her about how important good timing is and our life-changing, great-good-luck murder and our Mutual Admiration meeting. "Sorry, but before we go visit Daddy, we need to swing by the Gilgood mausoleum to look for clues like footprints or something like . . . ummm . . ." I probably shouldn't tell her that we might find Sister Margaret Mary's dead body back there. I'm not sure how'd she take that because she's so fragile and this has never come up before. "And what about Charlie? The poor guy is probably already sitting under the willow tree waiting for us to show up for our meeting." I swipe her too-long bangs out of her slightly bulging eyes that are looking a tad sad. "But I *sister*-promise, we'll pick up those chocolate-covered cherries offa Mister Lindley's grave and then we'll visit Daddy for as long as you want on our way home instead, s'awright?"

Señor Wences from *The Ed Sullivan Show* is another one of Birdie's favorite impressions of mine. She gets such a kick out of that little hand man that I was pretty sure she would do what she always does whenever I imitate him, because sometimes she *can* be predictable.

Sure enough, Birdie belly laughs and says, "S'awright, Tessie!"—thank God.

To get us where we need to be as soon as possible, I, the president of The Mutual Admiration Society, decide that it'd be a smart idea to take a shortcut to Mr. Gilgood's mausoleum, but I don't want to take a *completely* different route than the one I watched the murderer take last night. I don't want to screw up and miss any important clues along the way like broken branches or a torn piece of clothing, which are the first things Indians, the best trackers that ever lived, check for in the Saturday shoot-'em-ups when they're hunting down people with forked tongues.

I hold my hand up and tell Birdie, "Wagons, whoa," and spin back toward the house to look up at our bedroom window so I can get my bearings, and when I do, my Wigwam socks get almost clean knocked off!

I can perfectly see above the white towel Birdie hung out our window to let Charlie know the location of today's meeting and straight into our bedroom! Clear enough to count the daisies on our wallpaper and admire the paint-by-number picture I did of the sad hobo clown in honor of Daddy that's hanging above the Finley sisters' bed. What an eye-opener! I never thought for a second that when I watch what's going on in the cemetery, that someone could be doing the same thing to *me*.

"Look! The mausoleum!" my sister shouts. "Go, Bird, go!"

"Nooo," I yell when she whips her hand out of mine and rabbits off. "Come back here! I . . . I gotta tell you something really, really, really, really important!"

I just got a *very* bad thought.

Now that I know that looking out of my bedroom room is a two-way street, that means the villain I saw last night could have seen me seeing him wading through the very gravestones that I'm up to my waist in before he disappeared behind the Gilgood mausoleum with the limp body.

If I'd been staring out of any *other* upstairs window of the house, that dastard wouldn't have noticed me in the shadows, but dang that powerful nightmare-repelling night-light I stole for Birdie from the five and dime! It lights up our bedroom like it's the Miss America stage, and that murderer had a front-row seat!

Could *I* now be #1 on the perpetrator's hit list?

With a bullet?

Of course, the bad guy would have no way of knowing for sure that I saw his face, and I have no way of knowing for sure that he saw mine, but I got to BE PREPARED for the worst.

Too crafty to come out in the open to knock at our back door so he could kill the kid who saw him out of her bedroom window last night, if I was him, I would bide my time and hide behind Mr. Gilgood's final resting place and wait for me to show up to satisfy my curiosity so he could end my life before I could turn him in to the cops who would end his and . . . and my poor little sister is running straight into his murderous arms!

9

NO GUTS, NO GORY (NO JOKE)

I'm screaming, "Birdie! Stop! Stop! Stop! Stop!" but she keeps ripping toward the mausoleum that the kidnapping murderer could be hiding behind. I'm close enough to tackle her, but just like when I shove her through our milk chute to open our squeaky back door when Louise locks us out because she wants to have "a few minutes of peace," this is one of the times in life when my sister's featherweight tininess really pays off. The kid's got fancier footwork than Daddy's favorite boxer, Rocky Marciano. She's bobbing and weaving so fast through the gravestones that erupt out of the grass that I can't catch up to her until after she smacks the front of Mr. Gilgood's final resting place with both of her hands and yells, "I win!"

I do *not* tell her, "Congratulations," and dig a Hershey's kiss out of my pocket.

I slam the Red Owl bag down at her feet, stomp on it, grab her T-shirt in my fist, and quietly hiss out, "God*damn*it all, Bird," because the murderer could be right around the corner waiting to silence me for good. And then, of course, he wouldn't stop there, would he? He'd need to murder my sister next, because she eyewitnessed him offing me. Daddy would roll over in his grave, if he could, if I let anybody harm one blah-brown hair on the head of his precious tweetheart. "I'm warnin' you, ya run off like that on me again, cross my heart and hope to die, I'll . . . I'll . . ."

"You'll *what*, Tessie?" Birdie smarts back.

"I'll . . . I'll . . ." I'd die for her—might even be about to—but the only thing I want to do right this second is slap the smirk she's got smeared across her face all the way to 84th St.!

I'm *so* bent out of shape that I even forget about the danger we might be in, and I let my temper do the talking. "Say you're sorry!"

She sticks her tongue out at me, digs her hand deep into my shorts pocket, helps herself to a heaping handful of chocolate kisses, and singsongs, "I'm so, so, so, so sorry, Tessie, for not listening to you and running away," but believe you me, the kid is *not* sorry, not even a smidgeon. Usually meek and mild Birdie is looking about as repentant as the gargoyle that's glaring down at us from on top of the Gilgood mausoleum, because she is in the grips of #6:

SURE SIGNS OF LOONY

1. Seeing, hearing, and smelling stuff that nobody else can.
2. Acting more high-strung than a Kentucky Derby winner.
3. Wearing clothes that don't go together.
4. Not understanding what's going on in movies or television shows or the neighborhood.
5. Wetting the bed ~~all the time~~ sometimes.
6. Wild-streaking.
7. Extreme stubbornness.
8. Having a leaky memory and a drifting brain.
9. Not getting jokes and the ones they tell are lamer than Tiny Tim.
10. Murdering.
11. Drooling, when not asleep.

I *hate* it when she does this!

10:20 a.m. The famous saying "Life isn't fair" couldn't get any truer. Birdie is having a gay old time, throwing chocolate kisses up in the air and catching them in her wild-streaking smart-aleck mouth like they're salted peanuts at Lonnigan's Bar, and I'm left holding the bag in the graveyard, sweating bullets to come up with a they-went-thatta-way plan to escape a kidnapping killer who is probably already behind the mausoleum practicing his choking.

We could try to outrun him, but short-legged Birdie could never beat out a stork-legged man with murder on his mind, I don't care how Marciano her footwork is. We could scream, but a fat lotta good that would do us. Mr. Gilgood avoided people like the plague when he was alive, and he must've put it in his Last Will and Testament that he be buried as far away as possible from everybody else, because Birdie and me are on the very edges of the cemetery. Nobody would hear us yelp for help. Even Gert Klement with her powerful hearing aids would be, pardon my French, shit outta luck. Not that *she'd* come running to rescue Birdie and me, no way, no how. That bad Samaritan would just smile to herself and mutter, *My, oh, my. That sounds like the Finley sisters desperately yelling for assistance in the cemetery. I'd rush right over to save them, but they made their beds and now they can lie in them . . . at St. Anne's Home for Wayward Girls and the county loony bin*, and then she'd throw her head back, laugh evilly, and cut herself a great big piece of that devil's food cake.

I close my eyes and plead for help.

Q. O, dear Magic 8 Ball, what useful advice can you offer me under these life-threatening circumstances?

A. *Outlook not so good.*

Well, that's about as helpful as a rubber crutch.

What I need is some *useful* expert advice.

Wait just a cotton-pickin' minute.

What am I thinking?!

I do have some *useful* expert advice!

I haven't read any pages yet in *Modern Detection* where it's spelled out what a gumshoe should do if they find themselves trapped in this particular dangerous situation, but I'm 98% sure the New York City detective who wrote the book would recommend finding the nearest escape route, which, in Birdie's and my case, would be through the #1 spookiest spot in the whole neighborhood. Phantom Woods.

Should we tiptoe past the mausoleum and slip into woods that even the sun and the streetlights are too scared to shine into? Run through those trees whose branches are so black and twisted that they remind me of German children getting eaten by witches in the fairy tales written by those brothers who certainly were named correctly—Grimm? No. That plan is the perfect example of that famous saying "Jumping from the frying pan into the oven."

What else could I do to save our hides?

Chapter Thirteen in the modern detecting book covers a subject that especially interests me, so I paged ahead, and thank all the angels that I did, because I'm pretty sure that TIPS FOR ASSUMING A FALSE IDENTITY is about to come in real handy!

If only I had thought to bring along the disguises that are so near and dear to us. The black wigs and scruffy beards that Daddy bought Birdie and me at Kenfield's Five and Dime around this time last year so we could be hobos for Halloween. That was such a great night. After my sister and me counted up our candy and got out of our costumes, "Good Time Eddie" Finley couldn't wait to treat his babies to a gruesome bedtime story he called "The Butcher of Keefe Ave." After he got done giving us all the gory details and one of his tremendous good-night hugs and double Eskimo kisses, I got busy explaining to Birdie under our sheets that the story wasn't really true the way Daddy told us it was. "He was just having some tricky Halloween fun, that's all, honey." But my sister wouldn't quit whimpering, so I had to use my Roy Rogers flashlight to check under our bed for a butcher who escaped the insane asylum with a cleaver in his apron and . . . lo and behold! I know now that it was cows' brains, but I almost threw up when I saw the bloody, raw hunk of something dripping away under our bed that night! I yanked Birdie out of bed and we hightailed it down Keefe Ave. screaming like two little chickens, "The Butcher is on the loose! The Butcher is on the loose! Run for your lives!" It wasn't until we scrambled to hide under some bushes across the street that we heard our funny father laugh and shout off our front porch, "*Gotcha!*, girls."

Birdie and me still have those costumes. Sometimes we wear them to bed at night when we're especially missing Daddy, and we wear them most of the time when we snoop on neighbors who might recognize us. But because our black wigs and scruffy beards are balled up in the Radio Flyer in our garage with our other TOOLS OF THE TRADE, I'm going to have to come up with a different bright idea to get Birdie and me out of this fix ASAP! Something like . . .

Wait just a cotton-pickin' minute.

What was it that *Modern Detection* also mentioned in Chapter Thirteen? "If an operative should find themselves in a tight spot *without* their disguises, I highly suggest they use what is on hand to extricate themselves. *Improvise!* Assume an alternate identity!"

Now there's the ticket!

I got both of those helpful hints covered better than a coat of Sears and Roebuck paint!

And while I'm at it, what the hell, why not go for broke? Daddy would.

If the killer *is* behind the mausoleum and *if* he still hasn't peeked around the corner to recognize me, for all he knows, I could just be half of a pair of two *other* sisters racing around the cemetery on a not-a-cloud-in-the-sky beautiful Indian summer morning. Two *other* sisters like Barb and Jenny Radtke, who ran over to this mausoleum just for fun and not to investigate the crime he committed.

Boy, oh, boy, I'd sure love that tall, skinny guy to pay a visit to *one* of them sisters if he is on some kind of kidnapping murdering rampage, that'd be so great. That'd take care of #5 on my SHIT LIST: Brownnoser Jenny Radtke. I could run a line through her name with permanent ink. (Joke!)

All I gotta do now is hope that Birdie doesn't blow the roof offa my ruse and say something stupid like, *Who are you pretending to be, Tessie Finley, the kid who saw a kidnapping murderer sneak behind this mausoleum last night out of our bedroom window?* Because my sister adores game shows, I'm hoping to improve my chances of getting this trick past her by putting on a toothy grin before I announce really loudly in the voice of eighth-grader Barb Radtke, who everyone in the neighborhood knows has trouble saying words that start with the *s* sound, "Congratulations, Jenny Radtke, who was thleeping over last night at the white house behind the themetery and thaw a man murdering at twelve-oh-theven a.m. Unfortunately, due to thircumstances beyond my control, I've forgotten your prize for winning the race to this mausoleum this morning, but never fear! I'll award you your blue ribbon and cash prize after you're done practicing your thpelling words tonight. When you're completely alone and defenseless in the first-floor bedroom in the back of our blue house located at 7022 North Keefe Avenue, tho be thure to keep your eyes open for—"

"Land sakes, child," Birdie interrupts in a suddenly extremely polite, old-fashioned way. "While I generally find your voice characterizations delightful, may I remind you, and please feel free to correct me if I am in error, but I believe we've arrived at our current destination with the singular purpose of further pursuing pertinent clues in our ongoing criminal investigation. *Carpe diem!*"

Damnation!

Birdie has no idea of the danger we could be waltzing into. She doesn't have a clue that there's a fifty-fifty chance that Daddy could be signing one of us up for heavenly harp lessons in the next few minutes and the other one of us will be taking up handbasket weaving in Hades. But before I can get my jaw that dropped down to my knees snapped up and working again to warn off my wild-streaking, babbling-in-tongues, and definitely-going-more-old-timey-on-me-more-often sister, she melts behind the Gilgood mausoleum like freshly churned butter on a just-baked biscuit.

And that leaves me with no other choice but to swallow back the breakfast eggs and Spam that have come halfway back up my throat, pray that God is as big of a fan of Shirley Temple as I am, and prepare to rescue the kid who is now screaming at me from behind the mausoleum in her usual way of talking, "Come quick, Barb Radtke!"

Now she's figured out the improvised identity I was using to throw the kidnapping killer off our tracks?

Now?

Sometimes, like right this second, forgive me, Daddy, but I very much wish that I'd never stepped into your enormous shoes and made Birdie #1 on my TO-DO list. I've already had it up to here with her today and it's only 10:35 a.m.

In fact, my sister is getting on my nerves so bad that I'm tempted to let the murderer rough her up a little to teach her a lesson about how important it is to *never* forget that I'm the boss of the Finley sisters and always will be, but then, dang it all. No matter what Gert Klement tells anyone who'll listen, like it or not, I *do* have a pesky, chirping voice in my head that tells me right from wrong.

And right now my conscience is reminding me how 95% of the time, no matter how weird Birdie is, no matter how mad she makes me, no matter how many Tums I gotta eat because I worry about her getting *all* the numbers on the loony list, or how many tossing-and-turning nights I spend dreading what she might come up with when the sun does, if a genie magically appeared to grant me three wishes, not one of them would be *Please change Birdie into a normal sister.* To make a long story short, no matter how much I am currently despising her, I'm mostly willing to overlook her extremely short plus column because I love her with what's left of my heart. Warts and all. And if I don't rush behind the mausoleum to save her, the way I didn't save Daddy, I'll regret it for the rest of my life, and even after I die I'll be bawling so hard that my tears will put out the everlasting fire, which will probably piss Satan off so much that he'll send me to an even lower circle of Hell.

If I had Mr. McGinty's gun that's a souvenir of the war, I could shoot or bayonet the killer. If I had my double-Dutch jump rope, hog-tying would be good, and so would lynching him. With the saw I had to steal from Mr. Holland's gardening shed after I heard that he was planning to cut down the apple tree in his backyard that Birdie likes to pick from, I could cut off the murderer's feet to slow him down. But all I can get my hands on at the moment are Daddy's watch, my lists and detecting notebook, a stubby pencil, Hershey's kisses, and the lucky Swiss Army Knife. So, unless the murderer wants to know the time, is interested in snooping and blackmail secrets and lists, wants to write a letter, can't resist chocolate, or wants to add another murdering knife to his collection, what am I left with?

It looks like I'm gonna have to stab the guy with Daddy's Swiss Army Knife. Not just once, but many, many times. I found that out the hard way when #2 on my SHIT LIST, Butch Seeback, ambushed Birdie and me during the middle of a game of ghost in the graveyard a few weeks back. He jumped out from behind a tree, snatched Birdie, tucked her under his beefy arm, and ran off to the pond with me in hot pursuit. At the slippery edge, he threatened to throw my sister, who can't swim any better than me, into the deep end, if I didn't give him back the Oriental kitty that Mr. McGinty and me saw him try to drown in the same water that he was about to toss my sister. All the greasers push littler kids around. Trip them, pull their pants down, or throw their bikes off a bridge, that sort of thing, but Seeback? There's something *seriously* wrong with that boy. Never in a million years would I give him back the kitten we called Pyewacket after the one in the excellent movie starring Miss Kim Novak, *Bell Book and Candle*, so what choice did I have when that maniac hoisted Birdie over his head on that muddy bank to make good on his promise? I took Daddy's knife out of my pocket and flicked it open. Seeback sneered and said, "Whatcha gonna do, Finley?" *Hardy har har.* "Stab me?" I told him, "Looks like," and then I lunged at him and slid the Swiss blade in right above his knee, and when he dropped my sister, we took off to the sound of him squealing like a stuck pig, "I'll get ya for that, Finley, ya fucked-up little shit."

Lesson learned. One stab into the body of a despicable person isn't enough, so after I dig Daddy's knife out of my pocket, I'm ready to do an impression of Lizzie Borden when I come galloping around the corner of the Gilgood mausoleum to save Birdie from . . . from . . .

Damnation!

I *hate* it when she gets me all worked up like this over nothing.

She's kneeling in front of the ivy-covered back wall of the mausoleum, calmly sorting through a teepee-shaped pile of red and orange leaves. Mr. McGinty must've been doing some tidying. He takes good care of all the graves in the cemetery, because that's a part of his job that he takes *very* seriously, but I have noticed that he seems to take a little extra-special care of this mausoleum. I think it might be because he has shyness in common with the deceased hermit or maybe our friend is just very proud of this stone building that's the biggest in the cemetery, maybe in all of Milwaukee, I don't know. Whatever the reason, I'm not kidding, you could eat off the ground anywhere in Holy Cross, God knows my sister has, but Mr. Gilgood's tomb is especially tended to.

When I come to a heaving stop at her side, Birdie looks up at me and then down to my hand and says, "Whatcha gonna do with Daddy's knife?"

If I ever have to write a story in school about what the famous saying "Ignorance is bliss" means to me, I would use this *exact* moment as the perfect example. Instead of slowly explaining to her the horrible danger she *could've* been in, I do what I always do to protect what little of her mind she has left. I lie. Believe me, it's for her own blissful good.

I tell her, "You know how important it is that Charlie and me have things in common." *Good Housekeeping* sits next to *True Detective* in the magazine rack at Dalinsky's, so when I'm done reading about gumshoes and broads with big boobies in angora sweaters each month, I page through that ladies' magazine, too. There was an excellent article in the June 1959 issue called "Secrets of a Happy Marriage" that said it was *very* important that a wife have "shared interests" with her husband. "I got the knife out because I'm preparing to do a little whittling with him during our Mutual Admiration meeting."

I've found that visual aids always make whoppers more believable, so I snatch up a stick that's lying under the most famous oak tree in the whole cemetery and use Daddy's sharp knife to shave off some of the bark. The "Necking Tree" has had a ton of initials carved into its trunk by teenagers over the years—including Louise's and Daddy's. They come at night, because the graveyard is so pretty and peaceful, but mostly because it's closer and cheaper than steaming up their car windows at the Bluemound Drive-In movie theater.

FACT: I sneakily observe those hot-to-trotters outta my bedroom window rolling around in the grass, pawing at each other beneath the flickering streetlights. And at the Milky Way Drive-In, any idiot can see that the boys with their poufy, slick hair and Camel cigarettes stuck into their rolled-up T-shirt sleeves have got one thing on their minds, and believe me, it's not Orion onion rings.

PROOF: Dawn Jablonski was voted Queen of the Milky Way three summers in a row, so I guess the "exercism" that special priest performed to drive the devil out of her didn't work so good.

I stick the Swiss blade back into its red case, slide it back into my pocket, and ask my sister, "And what, may I ask, do you think *you're* doin'?"

"Lookin' for clues at the scene of the crime, a course." She's stirring the pile of raked up leaves she's kneeling in front of like they're a bowl of cake batter and her arms are Mixmaster beaters. "Isn't that what detectives are supposed to do?"

Oh, that's so, so, so, so heartbreaking.

Birdie wouldn't know a clue if it jumped up and bit her in her tail feathers.

On the other hand . . . she does have that super-duper smelling power. Could she be picking up on a scent that I can't?

Uh-oh.

What if it *wasn't* our friend Mr. McGinty who raked the red and gold leaves into the pile Birdie is searching for a clue in? What if the murderer I saw last night thought: *I could get caught if I stop to bury this body here at the scene of the crime, so I'll just hack it into little pieces and throw the bloody, disgusting parts into these pretty fall leaves, and then I'll rake them up nice and neat and make my getaway through these conveniently located spooky woods and no one will be the wiser.*

It's not like I'm a rookie in the corpse department. I've seen a boatload of stiffs during the Saturday afternoons I'm listening to Braves baseball games with Mr. Skank at his funeral parlor and he's teaching me about embalming and advertising and such, but all of those dearly departeds had their parts still attached to them.

"Stop digging!" I scream at Birdie. "There could be a dead body in there!"

"Don't be so thick, Tessie," she says with her spooky, wild-streaking laugh that always makes the hairs on the back of my neck stand at attention. "The pile isn't deep enough to hide a dead body."

"It is if it got cut into little pieces!"

Dear Jesus, what the heck have I gotten us into?

I know better.

Right around the time summer started, a burly guy with *MOTHER* tattooed on his right arm showed up at Lonnigan's Bar after closing time. I thought at first that Louise had sent the bruiser because she'd gotten tired of coming up to the bar to make sure Daddy wasn't playing cards and that gal can suck the fun out of just about anything faster than one of those Hoovers sold by Horace Mertz. But it turned out this galoot, name of Hall, was sent by his boss, Mr. Three-Finger Louie Galetti, which explains why he has to have someone else do his dirty work. Daddy told Hall very politely after he burst through the door, "Sorry. I'm a little short. Next week for sure." But Three-Finger Louie must've needed his money back ASAP, because that muscle man got the jump on the best fighter in the neighborhood and knocked him to the bar floor with a powerful right hook to his nose and then he emptied out the cash register. "Let this be a lesson to you, Tessie," Daddy told me when he was patching himself up in the GUYS bathroom after Hall left with the dough he stole. "Whatever you do, don't get in over your head."

What he was trying to teach me that night was that I was supposed to be very careful not to let my sister and me get into too much hot water and I am having a *very* bad feeling that's what I've done. I'm having so many grave doubts, in fact, that I'm about to cross out #2 on the list:

TO-DO

1. Take tender loving care of Birdie.
2. Solve whatever happened to Sister Margaret Mary for big blackmail or reward bucks.
3. Make Gert Klement think her arteries are going as hard as her heart.
4. Catch whoever stole over $200 out of the Pagan Baby collection box.
5. Practice your Miss America routine.
6. Learn how to swim.
7. Be a good dry-martini-making fiancée to Charlie.
8. Do not get caught blackmailing or spying.
9. Just *think* about making a real confession to Father Ted, before it's too late.

I'll do a 180 turn and tell Birdie I was dead wrong about what I heard and saw happening over here last night. That Louise's newest "gourmet" dish she served us for supper yesterday—liver with green olive frosting—must've given me some kind of brain poisoning that made me see things that weren't there. When my sister tells me, "Roger that, Tessie," we can run to Charlie at the weeping willow tree, have a quick Mutual Admiration meeting, and take out some of the treasury money we keep hidden in the trunk of the tree. And after we pick up the chocolate-covered cherries offa Mr. Lindley's grave—I *sister*-promised—we'll have a visit with Daddy, and then go straight home and get the red Schwinn out of the garage. I'll set Birdie on the handlebars and Charlie can hop on the back fender, and I'll pedal us over to the Milky Way Drive-In. Even though we've just eaten breakfast, we can always make room for their "out-of-this-world" food. I'll treat us to double Galaxy cheeseburgers and Pluto fries and we can slurp up a strawberry Mercury malt, three straws.

Yes, this is an excellent plan to keep us from getting in any deeper over our heads, because never in a million years would my almost-always-starving sister say, "No thanks, Tessie," to a visit to "The Milk" with Charlie. On this I am 100% positive.

"Tweetheart?" I say to the pitiful kid who's still kneeling in front of the leaf pile. "I'm sorry to have to tell you this, but I got you all worked up over nothing. Louise's olive liver musta poisoned my brain and made me imagine seeing a murder last night and . . . hey, speakin' of food, I bet you're starvin' from all the climbing and runnin' and leaf searchin', and I mighta accidentally stepped on that peanut butter and marshmallow sandwich I brought for you, so whatta ya say we just call it quits and—"

"Tessie!" she jumps to her feet and shouts. "I found a clue!"

10

A LITTLE BIRDIE TOLD ME

My sister may be acting like she's Charlie Chan, but believe me, whatever she found at the bottom of the leaf pile is *not* "inscrutable." It's probably a Juicy Fruit wrapper, which she likes to make necklaces out of, or maybe it's just one of those skinny balloons that are half-filled with what looks like Elmer's glue that, for some unknown reason, appear near the necking tree on Sunday mornings.

On the other hand . . . what if my idea about the killer burying a chopped-up corpse in the leaves was right? Could my sister have *her* hand wrapped around somebody *else's* hand or some other hacked-off body part? My tummy couldn't take seeing something like that. Just looking at the tongues in the window of Mr. Lebowitz's deli store that we have to walk past on our way up to the library, well, God Almighty. I have to do the same Helen Keller impression that I'm doing *now* whenever I need to get up to the Finney to tell Miss Peshong that I read a bunch more books so she can move me up on the Billy the Bookworm chart, because I'm going to beat brownnosing Jenny Radtke at her game of one-upping me or die trying.

"Quit groaning and open your eyes, Tessie!" my sister says. "Look . . . look . . . look . . . look at what I found!"

I'd really rather not, but when Birdie is on a wild streak, this normally mild-mannered kid can turn into a terrier dog digging for a bone. If I don't play along, she'll keep hounding me until I give in, so I have no choice but to peek from between my fingers at what she's unearthed and boy, oh, boy. I'm so relieved that what she's holding up with the tip of her pointer finger isn't the tip of a corpse's pointer finger that I'd shout *Hallelujah!* if I wasn't feeling so sorry for her.

How awful it must be to be Robin Jean "Birdie" Finley. To feel sure you have the answer to a problem only to find that you can't put two and two together time and time again. To get called Loonatic and Tweetle-Dumb and Birdbrain. To drift away to parts unknown. To have a memory that has more holes in it than the cemetery. To have your mother look at you most of the time like you're a stone around her pretty neck. To believe you found a clue to a kidnapping murder when you've done nothing of the sort.

Q. What was all-loving, all-knowing, all-mighty God thinking when He gave my little sister the short end of the stick?

A. *Reply hazy try again later.*

"Nice try, honey," I pat her back and tell her, "but from here on out, you better leave the real detective work to me."

"What do you mean I should leave the real detective work to you?" she says. From running around in the Indian summer heat and all the chocolate kisses Birdie has stuffed in her mouth, she looks like a fugitive who just got done robbing Dalinsky's Drugstore's candy aisle. "You always tell me that we're partners in crime."

"We *are* partners in crime. It's just that . . ."

Shoot.

Even during a wild streak, a time when my sister's delicate feelings are not as breakable as they usually are, I still have to be careful to put her down gently.

"I wish what you found *was* a clue. I really do, but . . ." I point at the chain she found in the leaf pile that's dangling from her finger. "This is just one of those St. Christopher medals visitors leave on the gravestones so their loved ones have a safe trip to the Great Beyond." Birdie *knows* that. She just forgot, that's all. "Please don't feel bad. We can't all be as excellent at detecting as I am. Many are called, but few are chosen." I switch gears and bring up what I tried to tell her before she found this so-called clue, which is something she really *is* good at. "So like I said, how about we forget all about this stupid kidnapping and murdering business, go grab Charlie, get those chocolate-covered cherries, say hi to Daddy, and then the three of us can head up to the Milky Way. Yum-yum."

I'm so sure my little chowhound cannot resist that offer that I don't even wait for her answer. I start off toward the weeping willow tree, but before I can go two full steps, Birdie grabs on to my hair and yanks me to a stop.

"You're wrong, Tessie. *This* medal *isn't* the kind people leave on tombstones so their loved ones have a safe trip to the Great Beyond," she announces to my back like she is the end-all and be-all on the subject of metal-medal identification.

"Yeah, it is!" I'm twisting like a fish on the end of a line, but she's got her fingers hooked around my ponytail but good.

"No, it's not!"

"Is, too!"

"Is not!"

"Let go of me, for crissakes!" I shout.

When she loosens her grip, I spin around and automatically go into the boxing stance my Golden Gloves champion father taught me to go into if anybody dares to put their hands on me—up on my toes, fists held high, and ready to throw the first punch. But just as I'm about to clean my little cuckoo's clock, it hits me that no matter how mad I am at this kid who may have the footwork of Marciano and the strength of new world heavyweight champ Floyd Patterson, when it gets down to it, Birdie Finley is a featherweight and it wouldn't be a fair fight. Daddy wouldn't like that.

"Okay, fine." I drop my hands back to my sides, rock back on my heels, and say *exactly* as 100% ticked off as I feel, "Why *isn't* the medal you found in the leaf pile one of those have-a-safe-trip-to-the-Great-Beyond medals, Birdbrain?"

She doesn't seem to notice that I've lost my temper and called her that mean name, because if she had, she would've gotten that crushed look on her face and given in to me, not thrown back her shoulders and cleared her throat like she's a contestant on her favorite quiz show who's about to give the answer to the big prize package question of the day. Ha! The only game show this twerp could ever win is *Queen for a Day*. The audience would pin the applause meter after they heard her sob story. Hmmm. Maybe I should put on my TO-DO list: Write to master of ceremonies Mr. Jack Bailey and enter Birdie on his show. Daddy never got around to fixing ours, so we really *could* use a new washing machine, and I think the winner gets to keep the mink cape they wear at the end of the show and that would be a big help if our heat gets turned off, and Birdie could give the shiny crown to Louise as one of her special gifts and maybe that'd make our mother love her a lot more than she does.

"Well, Tessie," my sister answers, so snooty, "this *is* a have-a-safe-trip-to-the-Great-Beyond medal, but not the kind grievers leave anymore on the gravestones of their loved ones." She holds it up higher so I can take another gander at it. "I guess you musta forgot that they started leaving the cruddy dime store medals after kids started stealin' the really nice ones on dares." Birdie swings what she found into the palm of her hand and holds it about three inches away from my face with one of her irresistible smiles that the army could use to make enemies surrender, that's how bad it can bring me to my knees. (No joke.) "I think *this* medal I found is made out of *real* gold, but, of course, far be it from me to second-guess an expert such as yourself."

If it sounds like she knows what she's talking about, it just so happens that this time she does. Times two.

#1: Kids *were* sneaking into Holy Cross and stealing the real gold medals in the middle of the night and they don't do that anymore and I'll never, ever forgive them.

After watching those thieves tippy-toeing out of the cemetery from our bedroom window, the Finley sisters would track them down and start charging them a pretty penny to keep our pie holes shut. Believe me, if there weren't so many of them, and if some of them kids weren't stealing the medals on dares they were forced into by my confidential informant, Kitten Jablonski, I'd put 'em all on my SHIT LIST.

#2: Birdie might know a lot about Atomic Fireballs to Wax Bottles and every candy in between, but *I* know what I'm talking about when it comes to jewelry.

I have spent many hours drooling over the diamonds and going rabid for the rubies at Howard's Precious Gems and Jewelry store on North Ave. in case I have to heist it someday on our way out of town.

But even though my sister got lucky on those two facts, I'm still positive that she's speeding the wrong way down a one-way street and I'd do just about anything to get her moving in the right direction, which is toward the weeping willow tree, where, hopefully, my darling Charlie is still waiting for us.

Unfortunately, I can't put that A+ plan into action until I examine the St. Christopher medal that Birdie found or I'll never hear the end of it, so I snatch the chain out of her hand to give it a quick look before we get under way.

"*Is* it real gold?" she asks me four times before I even have a chance to examine the medal, because she really stinks at waiting. During our peeping stakeouts, she always wants to catch someone in the act now . . . now . . . now . . . now! It's gotten so bad that I have to keep a sock in our Radio Flyer wagon that I can stick in her mouth. "Is it a clue? Is it a clue? Is it a—?"

"Will you wait just a cotton-pickin' minute!?"

When I study the medal closer, against all odds, I know right off that my sister just might be on to something. This St. Christopher does *look* like it's made out of pure gold, but to be sure, I better do what jewelry man Mr. Howard Howard makes young lovers do when they stop into his shop to buy their gold wedding bands. After he gives the young lovers a misty-eyed lecture about the sanctity of the holy sacrament of marriage and how their rings will always be a symbol of their everlasting and eternal love, because he misses his one and only wife so much he has to dab at his eyes with a hankie before he sets a cheap wedding band down on the counter, unlocks the big case, and removes one of the high-quality rings that are nestled in black velvet. He wants to teach the engaged kids the difference between cruddy imitations and the real deal, so he says to them, "The rings may look similar, but all that glitters is not gold. Hold the bands in your hands. Compare the heft."

"Before I can tell you for sure if this *is* a clue or not," I tell Birdie, "I need to check it against the medal I gave you. Turn around and lift your hair."

When I unhook the St. Chris I had to steal from the five and dime from around her going-green neck because he's the patron saint of travelers and she needed some divine intervention to keep her from falling off our bike every five minutes, my uncoordinated sister doesn't give me any guff, which is usually the first sign that her wild streak might be petering out, thank God.

"Well?" Birdie asks as I hold the two medals in my hand, side by side.

"Mmm . . ."

'Cause the massive mausoleum is casting a shadow over us, I take a step away from the shade toward a patch of sunlight that's skirting the edge of Phantom Woods so I can get the best look at them. Whoever is the owner of the medal Birdie found wore it a lot, because St. Chris looks pretty tired of holding up Jesus, who looks more like a hump on his back than a holy baby, but I can tell by how heavy it is and how shiny it is compared to my sister's cruddy one that . . .

Oh, boy.

Birdie, up on her toes and the edge of her seat, comes so close to me that I can smell Louise's Evening in Paris perfume wafting out from behind her ears and the chocolate on her breath when she insists, "Tell me!"

I really, really, really, really don't want to.

I'm not proud of that, but her beating me out in anything other than card games and cat's cradle doesn't happen very often and it's very discombobulating. It's like a bear getting eaten by a chipmunk or . . . or a Model T winning against a Corvette Stingray in a drag race. That's just not normal.

But I, the president of a detecting and blackmailing society, have sworn to do my best to solve any and all mysteries that come my way, even if they *are* against the laws of nature, so I got no choice but to tell #1 on my TO-DO list, "Bingo!"

"Bingo?!" she says, very put out. "This is no time to play games, Tessie!"

"For Pete's sake, Bird. I don't wanna play a game. *Bingo!* is a famous saying that means"—this is killing me, it really is—"that you're a hundred percent right, okay? The medal you found *is* nicer than the usual cheap ones people hang off the gravestones. It's real gold."

"Geronimo!" she whoops. "*Woo . . . woo . . . woo . . . woo . . .*"

I knew she'd do that. She always goes loco like this after she beats me at something other than races. (I still haven't added her repulsively-poor-winner problem to my list of BIRDIE'S NOT-SO-GOOD QUALITIES, but the second I get the chance, believe me, I'm going to write down: #47. She lords winning over me. #48. She couldn't do a decent Apache impression if her scalp depended on it.)

Once Birdie gets the *woo . . . woo . . . woo*–ing out of her system, she points down to my hand and says, "Did you notice that the clasp is bent? I bet that's why it fell offa the neck of the killer or the limp body he was carrying around last night."

This is the very last straw.

"So what if the medal *did* fall offa one of their necks?" Who in the hell does she think she is, anyway? She finds one dumb clue and all of a sudden she's Heap Big Chief Birdie and I'm General Custard? "How is knowing that gonna do us any good? Huh? Will it narrow our suspect list down?" I am going to give her both barrels. "For your information, that's what clues are supposed to do. Point a detective toward an alleged perpetrator and finding this medal doesn't do that. Everyone and their brother has one of these. Ya think you're so smart, go ahead. Name one person in this neighborhood who doesn't wear a Saint Christopher."

"Mister Johnson wears a deer tooth," Birdie says, very sure of herself. "And . . . and Mister Lebowitz!? He wears something called the Star of Dave at his deli store and . . . and Missus Pitts who owns the pet store, she's a prostitute who doesn't wear nothin' at all!"

She's right about Mr. Ernie Johnson. He's something called a taxidermist and the only person on Keefe Ave. who *doesn't* show up at St. Kate's for Mass or every Saturday night to play bingo or for potluck suppers, either. I am very suspicious of him, because he's always in his basement stuffing God only knows what, which is what I guess Lutherans do for a good time.

She's also right about Mr. Lebowitz, who is a Jewish man who doesn't eat fish sticks on Friday. For some unknown reason, he eats locks and beagles.

She's only half-right about Mrs. Pitts.

"Big deal!" I tell my getting-entirely-too-big-for-her-britches sister. "That's only three people outta . . . outta hundreds in the neighborhood! Those are chump odds! And . . . and you're not even totally right about Missus Pitts. She doesn't wear a Saint Chris medal because she's a *prostitute*, she doesn't wear one because she's a *Protestant!*" I know the difference between the two, thanks to Father Ted and Kitten Jablonski, but obviously, Birdie doesn't. "So what do ya suggest we do to find *Catholic* suspects? How about we stare at everyone's open shirt and blouse collars when they're standing in the Communion line this Sunday to see if anyone is missing theirs?" I can just picture the two of us hanging over the edge of a pew during Mass. "We go eyeballin' people's necks like that and mark my words, Bird, somebody's gonna start the rumor that the Finley sisters aren't only ghouls, but . . . but vampires!" Every Sunday those hypocrites got no problem kneeling down at St. Kate's Communion railing to drink the blood of Christ, but they're always more than happy to throw the first stone. "And the second Mass is over, they'll mob around Father Ted and beg him to command Louise to ship us outta the parish to homes or . . . or . . . maybe they'll get so worked up that they'll take matters into their own hands!" This is probably going a little too far, but I'd say and do anything at this point. "You've seen what ticked-off villagers do to vampires in the movies after they hunt them down." I place the whittling stick I picked up over my heart and pretend to pound it in with my fist. "And if they don't kill us by driving stakes through us, you're gonna wish they did. Every single one of them will be gossiping about us and that's gonna screw up Louise's chances to win that stupid election, which will make her so furious that the next time you wrap your lips around a Three Musketeers bar will be in Heaven!"

That last crack was a *very* low blow, but I'm so desperate that I don't care, and weirdly, it doesn't seem to faze my candy-worshipping sister, either.

"Maybe you should flip the medal over and see if there's any writing on the back, the way there is on the heart necklace that Daddy gave Louise for her birthday," she says with a lot of zing. "A name would be a great clue that could narrow our suspect list down."

She's making me want to pull every hair out of my head, or hers, but all of a sudden, I find myself feeling a little less thirsty for a strawberry

Mercury malt and a lot more interested again in solving THE CASE OF THE MISSING NUN WHO MIGHT BE KIDNAPPED AND MURDERED, because Birdie is *almost* right again. Finding a name on the back of the medal wouldn't be a great clue. That would be an excellent clue that really *could* narrow our list down:

QUESTION OR SURVEIL
1. Mr. McGinty.
2. Kitten Jablonski.
3. Butch Seeback.
4. ~~Mr. Johnson.~~
5. Suzie LaPelt.

But when I flip the medal over, I don't see nothin', so paying a visit to the Milky Way sounds like a much better idea again.

"That's the way the cookie crumbles. Better luck next time, kiddo," I tell her, but honestly? I'm not sorry at all. Her coming up with another clue in our case of the missing nun is starting to turn into a really bad habit. (No joke.)

But halfway to handing the medal back to her that I was going to let her keep as a shiny prize that she would probably gift to Louise tomorrow the way she gifted the pink, heart-shaped fake ruby ring this morning, the sun hits it in a way that . . . I still don't see a name on the back of it, but there *are* some squiggles way down on the very bottom. I hold the medal up close to my eyes, move it back a bit and then forward again, tilt it. If only I had my magnifying glass on me, but it's in our Radio Flyer wagon with our hobo disguises and all the rest of our spying **TOOLS OF THE TRADE**, hidden under some boxes in the garage so Louise won't find them.

"I'm not sure," I say, "but I think there might be some letters down on the bottom."

Birdie sticks out her grubby hand and says, "Gimme."

I don't usually trust her to handle evidence of any kind, but she *can* see so much better than me that I'm going to make an exception to that rule, even though I'm not so sure how much help she'll be. She recognizes small words like *so*, *the*, and *be*, and also *mom* and her name and mine and Charlie's and Daddy's, but her bad reading is one of the reasons she keeps getting held back to the third grade.

Because Birdie studies the medal for only a few seconds with her slightly bulging Indian eyes, I take that to mean that she can't make the squiggles out, either, so I'm surprised when she breaks into what can only be described as, pardon my French again, a shit-eating grin and tells me, "It says, 'To J. M. from M. M.'"

That can't be right. "One more time?"

"It says, 'To J. M. from M. M.,'" she repeats with a lot of gusto.

Is she trying to be funny again? She keeps this up, I might have to cross #9 off the SURE SIGNS OF LOONY list: Not getting jokes and the ones they tell are lamer than Tiny Tim.

"Are you pulling my leg?" I ask her.

Birdie looks down at her hands and my right gam like they might be doing something she doesn't know about and says, "No, I am not pulling your leg, Tessie."

Sure seems like she might be, because I know who those initials belong to and it's just out of the question those two would be over at the cemetery together in the middle of the night. And even more far-fetched to think that one of them did not live to see another day. Birdie must've gotten the letters mixed up, she does that sometimes. Flips them. A *w* can turn into an *m* and a *j* into a *g*, a *b* into a *d* and whatnot.

"How sure are you," I ask, "that you're seeing J. M. and M. M.?" I hold my thumb and pointer finger close together. "Just a smidge? Or . . ." I open up my arms as wide as they go. "Heaps?"

"Heaps and heaps and heaps and heaps."

Oh, boy.

I sure didn't see *that* one coming.

11

EVERYTHING COPACETIC?

Modern Detection says, "When searching for possible suspects in a murder case, start with the people who are the most emotionally involved with your victim, i.e., wife, husband, sister, brother, and girlfriend, etc. Statistics show that the closer the relationship a person has with another, the more likely they will be to kill them."

My statistic-loving fiancé, Charlie, loved that quote, but I dog-eared that page of the book and had to read it over around ten times. Stating that the more a person loves someone, the more likely they are to murder them? That seemed flat-out wrong.

On the other hand . . . if an important detective like Mr. Lynwood "My friends call me Woody and my enemies call me their worst nightmare" Bellflower of New York City, where there is more crime than he can flash his badge at, says that's a fact, who am I to question him?

Of course, I immediately recognized the initials on the back of the medal—J. M. = James McGinty. M. M. = Sister Margaret Mary—because I am very well acquainted with the two of them. But why our shy, soft-spoken, caretaking friend would be "emotionally involved" enough with our nasty, screeching principal to be considered a suspect in her murder is completely beyond me. And how could M. M. know J. M. good enough to give him this expensive gold present? You wouldn't gift something this special to just anybody. You'd have to *really* like a person, maybe even love them.

Uh-oh.

Could those two be doing what the Polack kids in the neighborhood snigger and call "the horizontal polka?" Oh, my Lord. No. That's not only disgusting, it's impossible. When you become a nun, you're married to God and the only way you're supposed to dance the polka is on your own two feet. Once *any* Catholic gets hitched, they're not supposed to shout, "Roll out the barrel, let's have a barrel of fun," with anyone other than the person they said "I do" to. Marriage is 'til death do them part.

That's the rule a Mr. and Mrs. are *supposed* to follow, anyway, but some of the ones in our neighborhood do make exceptions.

Evelyn at Melman's Hardware leaves the heart-shaped box of Russell Stover chocolate cherries on the grave of a man *she* wasn't married to, and Mrs. Nancy Tate waved her pom-poms in her rumpus room for Mr. Horace Mertz when her husband was recovering in the hospital from a broken leg, and as much as I like Miss Peshong from the Finney Library, she nibbles on the neck and the chocolate chip cookies of the husband that belongs to her heavy-sleeping next-door neighbor, Mrs. Maccio, when he gets off his Wednesday shift at the Feelin' Good factory.

"Bird?" I poke her in the ribs to get her attention. "You're not gonna believe whose initials these are on the back of the—"

"Mister McGinty's and Sister Margaret Mary's." That she figured that out completely surprises me, and I'm about to give her a pat on the back, but she doesn't give me the chance. "Shhh." Her head is cocked, and she goes stiff as a stiff when she whispers, "Ya hear that?"

St. Kate's church bells are announcing that it's half past the hour, the kids down the block are still shrieking out names during their Red Rover game, the same dog is barking two streets over, and much, much closer . . . someone is listening to the radio during their visit to a grave and, hopefully, not dancing on it. The Everly Brothers are wailing "Wake Up, Little Susie." That song was one of Daddy's all-time favorites. He'd sing to barmaid Suzie LaPelt—"Oo . . . la-la"—every single time it came on the jukebox at Lonnigan's. That's why I put her on my people to QUESTION OR SURVEIL list. Not because I think Suzie's guilty of something or should be shadowed. I really and truly miss spending time with the gal that almost all of the other gals in the neighborhood call "That French Slut," none louder or more often than our own mother.

"Wake up, little Susie . . ."

This is very bad timing for the missing sadness to spring back up. Hearing that tune and remembering how Daddy would get that cute twinkle in his eye when he'd sing it to Suzie . . . my heart just can't take it.

I stuff the St. Christopher medal in my shorts pocket, brush off the tears, and clear the ache out of my throat so I can tell my sister, *I need to go see Charlie*, but she cuts me off at the pass when she says, "Someone's comin' out of Phantom Woods."

And that's when all the other sounds fade away and I hear what she's been hearing.

The rustle of fall leaves. Not made by squirrels scurrying around for nuts. It's the crunch of human footsteps, getting louder by the second as closer . . . closer . . . and closer whoever it is comes stomping toward the Finley sisters, who are standing behind the mausoleum like sitting ducks.

Is it the kidnapping murderer?

Instead of hiding behind the mausoleum the way I thought he might be, could he have been watching and waiting this whole time behind one of those twisted tree trunks in Phantom Woods until the time was right?

I have to let my sister know that we could be in mortal danger, but when I open my mouth to scream, nothing comes out. Something's gone wrong with my breathing, too much out and not enough in and my eyesight isn't working too good, either. The cemetery is going fuzzy around the edges and my knees have gone wobbly, and before I can steady myself, I land in a heap on top of the leaf pile my sister was digging through. The leaf pile that could still contain a corpse casserole that very soon Birdie and me could become ingredients in.

FACT: Time can fly faster than Dracula, but it can also stagger like Frankenstein.

PROOF: It seems like I'm waiting for an eternity, paralyzed with fear on top of the leaves, before the owner of those footsteps appears on the edge of the woods.

My eyes are still blurry, but I can tell who it is. He's a few inches taller than the graves he digs, with a face that reminds me of one of those salt maps we made in geography class, that's how craggy it is from working so many years in the cemetery in all kinds of weather. His eyes are round and cow brown and his nose runs on the big side, too. If he was a kid, he'd get a nickname like "Elsie" or "Shnoz." The rest of him looks like a capital T. Drinking straw skinny below the waist, but strong in the shoulders from shoveling and the one hundred push-ups he does every morning after he eats his "breakfast rations." All in all, if you are looking at him from a distance, sideways, the way I am, I think our good friend Mr. James "Jimmy/Good Egg" McGinty is a fine-looking fellow with a good job and to the best of my knowledge, he is not, I repeat, *not* a murdering monster.

That's how come I suggested to Louise that she should go on a date with him before she started canoodling with what's-his-name. If Birdie and me *had* to have a new daddy, I thought our godfather would do nicely. But when I suggested to our mother that the two of them go on a picnic and even offered to make the sandwiches so she wouldn't give him stomach poisoning, she said, "Jimmy McGinty? No, thanks. I already have enough on my plate."

I think that might've been a nasty crack about the plate Mr. McGinty got in his head after he stepped on a land mine in the war, but it was also a huge Louise lie. We aren't doing that great in the food department around here, so her plate and Birdie's and mine are never full. She probably just didn't want to admit the *real* reason she wouldn't go on a date with Mr. McGinty is because he's Scottish.

We got so many different kinds of people in the neighborhood who came to the Land of the Free and the Home of the Braves from their old countries. The Hungarians are big eaters, of course, their name gives that away. Germans drink their beer out of steins and love bratwurst. The Polacks brought their hilarious jokes and the "horizontal polka" along with them on the boat. Micks have the worst tempers, can drink anybody under the table, and love blarney. 100% English people, like Gammy and Boppa, Daddy, and my Charlie, drink tea with stiff upper lips. The wops think they're the best thing since sliced garlic bread, because all of us are *Roman* Catholics and Rome is the city where the headquarters of the church is located. And Gracie Carver, who I can't wait to get back from Mississippi, is the only Negro we know, and she doesn't actually live around here. For some unknown reason, that's not allowed, she has to stay with "her own kind," which is such a pity, because if other colored people are as wonderful as Gracie that would make the neighborhood a lot more fun. She takes the #1 bus up North Ave. five mornings a week from a town called The Core with her best friend, Ethel, who is a helper to an old lady near Mother of Good Hope Church. Gracie is also not a Catholic who likes hymns, she is a Baptist who likes the music of Billie Holiday, keeping the church really clean, and like me, she likes poetry, but not by Dr. Seuss. (That Grinch book of his just slayed me.) Gracie likes some guy name of Langston Hughes, who I told her I will check out some day at the library when I get the chance. She also thinks The Mutual Admiration Society are the only ones around here who got any "snap" to 'em, but she gets a charge out of Kitten Jablonski, too. (Even though Gracie's not here right now, I mention her because she's such a good friend of ours that for a long time I was planning on Birdie and me running away to live with her, before she put the kibosh on that idea. "You'd get found right quick, Sugar. You and your sister'd stick out in my neighborhood like two marshmallows in a cup of hot cocoa," she said with one of her Southern laughs that I really love the sound of, it's very relaxing.)

And then we got the people like Mr. McGinty. The ones who play bagpipes at funerals, eat something called *haggis*, which they tell everybody is a "delicacy" on potluck night up at the church, so the Scots must also be known for being born without taste buds besides being famous for holding their purse strings *very* tight. Louise could probably overlook the awful music and their horrible taste in food—takes one to know one—but she could *never ever* put up with a skinflint. Getting a pile of money is #1 on our mother's TO-DO list.

FACT: The relief that flooded through me when I first saw our Scottish friend come out of Phantom Woods instead of an unknown raving murderer has suddenly dwindled to a dribble.

PROOF: This is a very terrible thought that I feel very terrible about having, but I'm 95% positive that the medal Birdie found in the leaf pile belongs to Mr. McGinty, which means he *was* at the scene of the crime and could be the guilty murderer.

And when he wildly waves his glinting-in-the-sun sharp gardening shears and shouts at us, "Where ya been, girls? I've been looking everywhere for you," my tummy must be thinking the same thing because it goes as hard as an arithmetic problem that doesn't add up.

It's awfully far-fetched to think he could be a killer, but . . . what if he is, and he's rushing toward the Finley sisters not to shoot the breeze with us, but for some other very scary reason?

Q. Was he *really* surprised when he came out of the woods and spotted Birdie and me behind the mausoleum? Or was he just *pretending* to be surprised? Did he figure we'd show up here this morning because he saw me watching him at 12:07 a.m. out our bedroom window lugging around a victim that he was "emotionally involved" with, the nun who gifted him the expensive gold St. Christopher medal? And isn't it mighty strange that during the millions of talks we've had over the years that he never said one word about how him and the principal of St. Kate's were so palsy-walsy, especially since I complained about her so much?

A. *Ask again later.*

As far back as I can remember, Mr. McGinty has never been nothin' but nice and thoughtful to Birdie and me, but in my experience, people and things can change for the worst, mostly when you least expect it. So, it's always better to be waiting for the other shoe to drop than to get caught off balance, because take it from me, something like that can just about kill you.

My boxing daddy also taught me, "Stay on your toes. You don't want to get sucker punched." And those words of wisdom are echoed in the pages of *Modern Detection*, too. Mr. Lynwood "My friends call me Woody and my enemies call me their worst nightmare" Bellflower says, "*Anyone* is capable of murder, given the right circumstances. Stay on your toes at all times."

Are *these* the right circumstances?

Gosh, I sure hope not.

REASONS WHY I DON'T WANT MR. MCGINTY TO BE THE GUILTY PARTY

1. I'd like my sister's and my head to stay where they are and not snipped off with his sharp gardening shears.
2. We can kiss good-bye to the reward bucks I thought we'd be making by solving the murder, because if he doesn't

decapitate us with his **Tools of the Trade** in the next few minutes, I could never blackmail Mr. McGinty, even *I* got my limits. And I don't want the reward I'd get for turning him in to the cops, either. That'd be blood money.

3. If he gets sent to the Big House, I'd miss watching our red bobbers in the cemetery pond during our late-night fishing trips. When he first invited me to join him, I told him no, because that's what Daddy and me were doing the day he died and I was scared I wouldn't be able to stand remembering how I let him down and the horrible missing sadness would come over me and make me feel like I was going under for the third time. But Mr. McGinty finally convinced me that fishing again could be another way to honor Daddy, like me singing for him at the Miss America contest the "Favorite Things" song, and that it might actually help me feel a little better, and he was right. I like watching the fireflies switching off and on under the reflection of the moon that disappears in ripples when frogs chase a fly, but mostly I enjoy the talks Mr. McGinty and me have about everything under the sun after we throw in our lines because sometimes I pretend that it's Daddy at my side instead of his old friend.

4. Birdie wouldn't miss reeling in a bluegill or those pond talks under the stars with our godfather if he gets electrocuted for murder because I make sure she's deep asleep when I crawl out our bedroom window and meet up with him. My little animal lover has always hated fishing, which is why she wasn't out on the boat with Daddy and me that afternoon. What *would* bother my sister is that we wouldn't be able to visit with Mr. McGinty anymore in his cozy shack that's another home away from home for us. She just can't seem to get enough of beating him at gin rummy, and, of

course, being the excellent caretaker that he is, he always has windmill cookies and cold Graf's root beer at the ready when the Finley sisters drop by.

5. We wouldn't be the only ones who would join the Lonely Hearts Club if Mr. McGinty got sent up the river. Charlie will be so sad to wave good-bye to our friend who taught him about birds and whittling, and believe me, my fiancé doesn't need another person he cares about leaving him in their dust-to-dust.

6. And what will become of our tan and black Siamese that Mr. McGinty dove in to save after that maniac kid, Butch Seeback, threw her in the cemetery pond? Unlike tail-wagging Birdie, I haven't fallen hook, line, and sinker for Pyewacket, but she loves running her little hand down the cat's back and purring along with her, and . . .

Wait just a cotton-pickin' minute!

There I go assuming again.

There's still a chance that dead Sister Margaret Mary didn't give the gold medal to Mr. McGinty. There's gotta be other people in the neighborhood who have M. M. and J. M. initials. Like . . . ah . . . or . . . well, just because I can't think of anyone right this second doesn't mean there *isn't* anyone. Just the same, until I can get things sorted out, to stay on the safe side, maybe Birdie and me better keep our distances from Mr. McGinty.

FACT: There is nobody I know that takes the famous saying "There is a place for everything and everything has a place" more seriously than he does.

PROOF: Because I'm not where I'm *supposed* to be—standing upright, instead of still laying on top of the leaf pile—after our neat-to-the-hilt friend comes to a halt in front of my sister and me, he starts acting more fidgety than Suzie "That French Slut" LaPelt does in the

Communion line when all the gals in the parish train their Sunday eyes on her.

Ex–army soldier Mr. McGinty is on high alert this morning, but he is most of the time. I swear, if there ever was a contest that awarded a blue ribbon for The Most Jumpy Person in the Neighborhood at the Fourth of July picnic at Washington Park, he would win with his hands tied behind his back. Because he hates loud noises, the other contestants wouldn't have a chance after he heard that starter gun go off. Mr. McGinty despises *Gotchas!* That's why I have to signal him with my *woo . . . woo . . . whoot* whistle whenever I get within striking distance. If I *don't*, he rockets into the air and reaches for his knife that he, like me, is never without. Only mine isn't a switchblade that can flick open fast enough to slit the throat of a Nazi. Or a nun.

"Why on earth are you down on the ground, Tessie?" he asks in his voice that sounds so rich and creamy. Birdie almost always goes hungrier when she hears him, because he sounds very much like Mr. Ed Herlihy, the man who does the commercials for Kraft cheese on the television set and Velveeta is her favorite food next to candy. "Everything copacetic?"

If he *is* the murderer, I don't want him getting more riled up than he already is, so I use the sturdy mausoleum wall and the whittling stick I picked up to help me get back on my feet. "Oh, yeah, I'm very copacetic, Mister McGinty." I reassure him with fake smile #3 and then, because it can't hurt to remind him that I got a deadly weapon on me, too, I open up my hand to show him my most prized possession. "Daddy's *very* sharp Swiss Army Knife fell out of my pocket, that's all. I was just lookin' for it in the leaf pile."

Unlike me, of course, sweet-hearted Birdie isn't thinking ugly, suspicious thoughts about our friend.

She right away holds out her little paw and says, "Charmed, I'm sure." She loves to shake hands. She'll hug people, too, or if she gets really excited, she'll give a person a juicy smooch or a lick on their cheek, if they don't turn tail when they see her coming, which I completely understand. I don't go in for that sort of sentimental sloppiness, either. Unless a person has the same blood as me running through their veins, stiff-arming is my policy. (I, of course, make an exception to that rule for Charlie.)

But Birdie's being more affectionate than a pet-store puppy never seems to bother Mr. McGinty, even if he is so shy. Like always, he grins down at her—he's got fantastic choppers—gives her little hand a few pumps in his big one, and then he gets busy wiping his fingers off with his hankie, refolding it, and putting it back in his gray shirt pocket just so, because gray is the only color of clothing he wears when he's on the job. "Going about my business wearing a sunny-yellow or sky-blue shirt, even a leaf-green one, would appear too cheerful to grievers. They might think I don't care that the world as they knew it will never be the same for them," he explained to me during one of our fishing nights after I asked why he always dresses so ho-hum. "It's more respectful to blend in with the gravestones."

His thoughtfulness and cleanliness-next-to-godliness routine are two of the main reasons I'm having such a hard time picturing him killing somebody. In the movies, blood and guts leave an ungodly mess and Mr. McGinty is *always* spit and polished. He keeps his shack spotless, too. A quarter bounces about a foot offa his bed and my finger comes off cleaner when I run it across the tops of the beautiful framed pictures of woods and birds that he's got hanging on the wall above his brown sofa and dust bunnies run for the hills when they see him coming.

On the other hand . . . I got medal evidence. And tall and thin Mr. McGinty matches the description of the guy I saw under the flickering cemetery lights last night. He also had the *opportunity* to kidnap and kill Sister M & M, because he lives right down the road from the scene of the crime. And he had the *means* to wring the life out of her, because I bet he could beat Samson in an arm wrestle.

But what in the heck would his *motive* be to snatch and snuff out a nun? Not killing anybody is the #6 Commandment on God's TO-DO list and Mr. McGinty is the most religious person I know, even worse than Gert Klement. He's front and center at Mass every single morning, faithfully confesses every week, actually looks forward to saying the Stations of the Cross, and one of his hobbies is collecting holy cards, for godssake! (I thought he was going to start crying when I gifted him the card of St. Michael, the patron saint of soldiers, for Christmas a few years ago.)

Q. Isn't it just a little suspicious that this military man who spends half his nights prowling around Holy Cross for "intruders" hasn't already said something about the commotion that he must've heard at 12:07 a.m. last night? Should I just go ahead and ask him if he heard the yelling and screeching? Or would that be doing the famous saying "Stirring the pot?"

A. *Cannot predict now.*

Slightly more relaxed, now that he knows I'm okay, Mr. McGinty smiles and says, "So what's cookin' this morning, girls?"

"Nothin' is cookin' this morning, Mister McGinty," my sister answers in a huff. "Campfires are *not* allowed in the cemetery, isn't that right, Tessie."

Even though I'm still scared because we're standing here chatting with a possible murderer, I can't help but answer, "That's right, Bird," with a little relieved smile on my face, because her saying something goofy like that means her wild streak is finally over, which is gonna make getting her to do what I want a whole lot easier.

Because he has known my sister for her whole life, Mr. McGinty doesn't circle his finger around his head or roll his eyes the way other people do when my sister says stuff like that, he just asks his question in another way, one he knows she'll understand. "What are you two doing this morning, Birdie?" He usually finds us at Daddy's pretend grave or the weeping willow tree having a Mutual Admiration meeting, so I understand why he's suspicious, especially if he's the guilty party that I'm beginning to think he is.

"We're doing . . . um . . ." Birdie swivels her head around in a what-the-hell-just-happened way, which is normal after one of her streaks is done and dusted. "What *are* we doing this morning, Tessie?"

"Remember, honey?" I think fast and wave around the whittling stick I found under the necking tree. "We came over here this morning to gather these for Charlie's hobby." I lied, because a detective such as myself knows that it'd be very stupid to say that we're looking for clues in a kidnapping and murder investigation in front of an armed and very strong suspect.

Of course, someone as nice and religious as Mr. McGinty cutting the heads off the Finley sisters in broad daylight is still pretty hard for me to picture, but Mr. Lynwood "My friends call me Woody and my enemies call me their worst nightmare" Bellflower, a detective for over thirty years in New York City, also writes in his excellent book, "You must suspect *everybody* during an investigation. Do *not* allow yourself to be swayed by appearances or personal relationships. Leave no leaf unturned." And it cannot be a coincidence that is exactly what Birdie did. She turned over all the leaves in the pile behind the mausoleum to find our first piece of evidence, which is pointing straight at the guy standing in front of us, which means it's time for the Finley sisters to make like bananas and split.

"Hey, it was great seein' ya, Mister McGinty," I say, "but time is a-ticking." I reach into my shorts pocket where I keep Daddy's watch to prove my point, but when I do, I can feel that the Timex has gotten tangled around the St. Christopher medal. *His* St. Christopher medal? I can't tip my hand until I know for sure, so I leave both of them where they are. "We got a long TO-DO list this morning."

I wish he wasn't so dang blasted tall. I'd love to get a good look at his neck before we take off, because if his medal *is* missing in action, that'd be such a great clue. It's to him what Daddy's Swiss Army Knife is to me. Holy lucky. He'd *never* let that medal out of his sight on purpose. He loves it so much that if it ever broke, he would not drop everything and run up to Mr. Howard Howard's jewelry store on North Ave. to get it repaired. He would drop everything and if his red-and-purple-scarred shrapnel leg wasn't aching too bad, he'd run over to the equipment shed where he keeps his shovels, shears, hedges, mowers, and whatnot to fix the medal himself at his wooden work table. "I'm beholden to Saint Christopher for saving my life countless times during the war," he told me once during a game of checkers we were playing on the card table in his shack. "I believe it was his divine guidance that helped me come back"—he knocked his fist against his head that's got the plate in it—"mostly in one piece." And then he hopped over two of my red checkers with a winning grin. "Christ the King me."

"What's this?" Mr. McGinty says when his eye catches something and he bends down to pick it up out of a low branch of the bush that Birdie is standing next to. It's a gold candy wrapper from a Rolo. He despises littering, but he could have that frown on his face because he thought he'd found his golden medal that he lost last night when he was up to no good.

Needing to get as far away as possible from him while the going is still good, I put my arm around my sister and hold her to my hip, so when I turn around to leave, she's gotta turn with me. "You go right ahead and straighten things up, Mister McGinty. Like I said, we need to get to work, too, right, Birdie?"

"Roger that, Tessie, but . . . I need to tell Mister McGinty something before we—"

"No, no, no, no honey, we don't have time." I can't risk that the "something" she wants to tell him is, *We found your medal and Tessie and me think you might be the culprit who kidnapped and killed Sister Margaret Mary*, so I say to her the only thing that I'm sure will make her leave the scene of the crime. "But I *sister*-promise we'll come back tonight and you can eat windmill cookies and pet Pye and talk all you want, okay?" But when I try to pull her in the direction of the weeping willow and Charlie, Mr. McGinty takes a giant step, blocks our way, and says in his commanding Velveeta voice, "I understand that you're on a tight schedule, Tessie, but I have a matter of the utmost importance to discuss with you and it shouldn't be put off until tonight."

Uh-oh.

Because I'm almost positive that he wants to army-interrogate me about what I saw out the bedroom window last night, I think this might be one of those desperate measures times that Daddy used to tell me I had to always BE PREPARED for, which I am. I don't even have to put a fake terrified look on my face when I point to the side of him and yell, "Holy Mother of God! Run for your life, Mister McGinty! Look out! It's a bee!" and with my other hand reach around and pinch Birdie on the heinie really hard.

"It got me!" she screams. "Ow! Ow! Ow! Ow!"

Thank goodness that the caretaker is as impressed as I am by my sister's big-lunged, operatic performance. He's windmilling his arms and frantically backpedaling, which is exactly what I hoped he'd do, because believe me, getting the third degree from a guy who is deathly allergic to bees, but who might be very copacetic when it comes to kidnapping and murder, that's the kind of close call I'm 100% positive the Finley sisters can live without.

12

THE DEAD MAN'S FLOAT

After Birdie and me make our getaway from Mr. McGinty, we stop on top of the steep, grassy hill that overlooks the cemetery pond, because even as desperate as I am to see my fiancé, the Finley sisters need to take a breather before we head over to our Mutual Admiration meeting. We gotta recombobulate ourselves.

"It's very important to always look your best when spending time with the man of your dreams," was another suggestion from that *Good Housekeeping* magazine article, and I'm pretty sure after chasing Birdie around during her wild streak, collapsing in a pile of fallen leaves behind Mr. Gilgood's mausoleum, and making a break for it from Mr. McGinty, that I don't look shipshape. More like "The Wreck of the Hesperus." (Joke!)

My already wavy hair has gone springy, my tan T-shirt has come untucked from my shorts, I'm drenched in Indian summer sweat, and Daddy's little dreamboat isn't anything to write home about, either. One of her pigtails got undone, her mouth that's ringed in chocolate is clashing with her cheeks that are pinker than a bubble gum cigar, and her shorts have a new grass stain across the seat in the shape of our state.

"Tessie?" she asks me as she rolls around on the ground.

"Yeah?"

"I been thinking."

That's *never* a good sign.

"Mommy named you after Saint Theresa the Little Flower," Birdie says, "so shouldn't bees come after you more than they come after me?"

Naming me after that sainted gal was just wishful thinking on my mother's part. "Like I told ya all the other times you asked me, the reason bees are attracted to you more is because you're a sweeter kid than me, honey, and you gotta remember not to call her Mommy."

"Roger that, Tessie," she says, and goes back to rolling around on the ground to try and locate the imaginary stinger I made her think she has in her heinie, which is fine by me. I need some time to pull myself together the best I can for Charlie. He better still be waiting for us at the weeping willow tree next to the pond that most cemetery visitors find such a lush oasis in the middle of row after row of unending sadness.

Staring down at the water from up here, I'm remembering how Mr. McGinty told me a long time ago that the pond was dug in the first place because "Beauty can help fill the cracks in people's hearts and comfort their souls."

There *was* a time not that long ago when the sweet smell of flowers drifting over from the graves, songbirds in the trees, and the feel of the pond mud oozing between my toes with someone I love and who loves me back *did* make my heart and soul feel good, but those days went away when Daddy did. I still *do* get a little glimmer of hope when I fish with Mr. McGinty, skim rocks across the pond with Charlie, or pick wildflowers that grow along the bank with Birdie, or if we have a really great Mutual Admiration meeting under the weeping willow, because sometimes, just for a minute or two, the crack in my heart *does* feel like it's getting just a little sealed up with hope. But most of the time, when

I stare at the furry cattails alongside the water, the missing sadness and an awful wave of black guilt washes over me.

Ever since I let Daddy drown, I have been blaming myself on two counts. And I'm not the only one. I've come to learn in *Modern Detection* that not diving in after him is known in the eyes of the law as "accessorizing after the fact." And in the eyes of the Almighty, sitting on my hands and laughing my head off while my father sunk to the bottom of Lake Michigan because I thought he was playing a *Gotcha!* joke on me, instead of at least *trying* to save him, makes me guilty of committing a sin of omission.

Hey, Tessie, who's next on your list to let down? Birdie? Charlie? Your dear old grandparents?

No way. No how. Cross my heart and hope to die.

I've been trying to teach myself how to swim in our bathtub. Soon as I can figure out how to do more than just the dead man's float, I'll be able to dive to any depth to save my loved ones. And I suppose I'd have to rescue Louise if she was going under for the third time, too. It would look too suspicious to the cops if I didn't.

What was that? There! That rustling in the weeping willow branches? Charlie? Boy, oh, boy, I can't wait to behold the look of amazement on his face after the three of us get seated in a circle beneath the flowing green branches that are long enough to keep us from getting noticed by cemetery visitors who might stop by the water to refresh their thirsty, sad hearts.

After I call our meeting of The Mutual Admiration Society to order, I'll first tell our Sergeant of Arms, who doesn't even know yet that we've taken on THE CASE OF THE MISSING NUN WHO MIGHT BE KIDNAPPED AND MURDERED, about the scrapes the Finley sisters had with Louise and Gert Klement and Mr. McGinty this morning. He's gonna get such a kick out of that.

Charlie may be a kid whose smile went rusty after his mother suicided herself, but he can't help but grin when he's got a good adventure or mystery story in his hands. That's another important something we have in common. We both love checking out books from the Finney Library that he sometimes joshes should be changed to the "*Finley* Library," because I really *do* believe the famous sign that's painted on the wall behind the checkout desk—KNOWLEDGE IS POWER.

"My heinie hurts, but I don't feel nothin' stickin' in me," Birdie sits up and says. She's stopped rolling, and now she's bouncing her bottom up and down on the grass. "Ya sure you saw a bee, Tessie?"

"Ummm . . . I guess it coulda been a hornet or a wasp. Ya better keep at it."

I want to keep her busy a little longer while I go on searching for more signs of Charlie, who is sure to peek his head out any second to check for the hundredth time if Birdie and me are coming his way, because he knows how important good timing is to me and we're so late for the meeting. But unfortunately, other than seeing tan and black Pyewacket streak out from beneath the green branches of the willow, all seems quiet down there and that can mean only one thing.

"God*damn*it all, Bird!" Before I even know what I'm doing, I reel around and knock her down on her back, straddle her, and shake my fist in her face. I'm not sure if we would've been on time for the meeting if she hadn't run off, but chasing her around the cemetery didn't help. I know it's not her fault when a wild streak comes over her, but I can't help it when my beastly temper comes over me, either. I am Big Bad Wolf mad! "Looks like Charlie got tired of waiting for us to show up, and guess whose fault *that* is?!" Before Birdie can say something dumb like *I don't know, Tessie. Whose fault is it?* I tell her, "Yours!" That's not completely true, either. Bumping into Mr. McGinty slowed us down, too, but my temper doesn't care about facts when it gets a grip on me, it has a mind of its own.

"I'm so, so, so, so sorry, Tessie."

Birdie didn't singsong that apology the snotty way she did when I asked her to give me a *mea culpa* during her wild streak, she really does mean it now that she's back to her old weird self. But instead of her whimpering making me feel righteous the way it should when you put somebody in their place, I'm all of a sudden feeling like I'm doing an excellent impression of that maniac Butch Seeback. *Whatcha gonna say and do next, you mean bully? Call your poor, half-witted sister Tweetle-Dumb and roll her down the hill?*

FACT: It's not my fault that I can be the worst big sister in the world, just the pits.

PROOF: Everybody knows that nasty tempers go hand in hand with red hair and I inherited the both of them from my mother.

Wait just a cotton-pickin' minute.

Why am I getting so lathered up and assuming again?

Charlie could still be at our meeting spot. I just didn't see him, that's all.

Shoving my temper to my back burner, I kneel next to whimpering Birdie, pry her too-long, blah-brown bangs off her forehead, and tell her in a less-boiling-mad way, "If ya wanna make up to me for all your screw-ups this morning, then right after I get you cleaned up"—she's a sweaty, wet mess. Tears are trickling out of the corners of her eyes and snot is gushing out of her too-upturned nose—"I want you to use your Indian vision and check for Charlie around the willow."

Sliding my arms under her arms, I get her to her feet, pull the rubber band out of her remaining messy pigtail and finger rake her hair into a ponytail like mine, hook her bangs that I was counting on Charlie to trim with his sharp whittling knife during the meeting behind her ears, then I lick my finger and rub off the dirt streaks on her knees and the chocolate ring around her mouth.

"That's better," I step back and tell her when I'm done spiffing her up. "You look so, so, so, so beautiful. You remind me of Ida Lupino."

"Thank you, Tessie," she tells me four times with a wink, and then I wink back at her, and then she winks back at me and that can go on forever, so I put a halt to it by asking her, "Ya ready to look for Charlie now?"

"Roger that, but before I do"—she spins around, lowers her shorts and undies down to her knees, and moons me—"can ya see the stinger?"

There's a red mark on the heinie cheek where I pinched the heck out of her, but, of course, I have no intention of owning up to that. I just pretend to pull something out and say, "There you go, good as new."

"Ship . . . ship . . . hurray!" Birdie says when she nuzzles her damp cheek—her face one—against my neck, and then because she is not an Indian giver in her words *or* her deeds, she tugs her undies and shorts back up to her round tummy and gets to work straightaway looking for Charlie at the willow tree with her red-man-looking-for-settlers-to-scalp stare.

When a few minutes pass by and she doesn't say anything, I ask her, "Well?" because waiting for the verdict is just about killing me. I can't remember a time that I felt more desperate to see my fiancé. "Ya see him?"

"Who am I lookin' for again?"

"Charlie!" And before she can ask me *which* Charlie, I spell it out for her. "Not Charlie 'Dogbreath' Bennett, not Charlie 'Booger' Hawkins, and not Charlie 'Four-Eyes' Arnold. Do you see Charlie 'Cue Ball' Garfield down there? You can't miss him. He's got a bald head!"

She looks a few more seconds, then turns back to me and says, "Nope. Nobody with a bald head down there. I'm hungry. I want some Velveeta."

Damn Mr. McGinty's Kraft-cheese-sounding voice!

Because I stomped her P B and M to oblivion, her tummy, which has a *lot* better memory than she does, is complaining to Birdie that it didn't get its usual morning snack. I was counting on all the Hershey's kisses she stole out of my pocket during the wild streak tiding her over to lunchtime, but there I go again, being a big assuming dope.

The safest thing to do would be to hustle us straight home so I could make her another sandwich pronto, but I can't do that. Birdie is *not* going to forget my *sister*-promise. So before we can climb back over the black iron fence, what we need to do is swing by Mr. Lindley's grave to get those chocolate-covered cherries before we go visit Daddy. If I don't put more food in front of my sister's face by the time St. Kate's church bells clang twelve, believe me, things will go from bad to worse around here in a hurry, which reminds me. How much time do I got left before Birdie starts flapping her arms, squawking, licking her lips, and staring at me like that famous saying "You look good enough to eat" is one she wouldn't mind putting to the test?

Daddy's Timex is still really tangled up with the St. Christopher medal in my pocket, but I have no problem seeing that it's 11:41 a.m.

Uh-oh.

"I'm hungry," Birdie repeats three more times.

"I know you are, honey, but . . ." I show her what I'm working on. "I just need to straighten these out real quick and then off we'll go to get ya something good to eat."

The Finley sisters need all the luck we can get and leaving Daddy's watch and the St. Christopher medal in a twisted mess feels to me as unholy lucky as drawing a mustache on the pretty blue Virgin Mary church statue like some kid did last week. (The Mutual Admiration Society is already on THE CASE OF THE BLESSED MUSTACHE. We have it narrowed down to two possible culprits. Butch Seeback, because he's *always* the most likely suspect, but it could also be Chuckie Jaeger, the kid who connects my freckles with a ballpoint pen when I fall asleep at my desk. He's a nincompoop, but he's also the best artist in school and that mustache on the Virgin statue was *very* lifelike.)

"Okay, Tessie, you straighten them out, but hurry. I'm really, really, really, really—" Birdie stops chomping on the bit long enough to point down at my busy fingers. "The medal for sure belongs to Mister McGinty, ya know."

"Remember, honey? We still don't know that this is his medal, we only strongly *suspect* that it is." I'm having a tough time separating it from the Timex and I can feel my temper starting to simmer again. "The only way we could know that this medal is his for sure is if I checked to see if his was missin' from around his neck and the only way I coulda done that is if I was wearing stilts."

"Well, then . . ." she says with a cock of one of her pale eyebrows. "How wonderfully fortuitous that when the gentleman in question bent down toward the bush that I was standing next to when we were behind Mister Gilgood's mausoleum that I availed myself of the opportunity to inspect his neck."

Oh, brother.

I have no idea what my suddenly-gone-old-timey-on-me sister is trying to pull, but she *couldn't* have thought of inspecting McGinty's neck to see if his medal was around it in a million years. Pyewacket the cat could think of doing that before she could.

From years of experience, I know that I shouldn't get into a sparring match with her when she's hungry, but between my frustration at getting the watch and the medal free from one another and my worrying about what's gonna happen next if I don't get some food into her and that smooth, superior tone she's using on me that sounds a lot like the one Louise uses when she thinks she's got the upper hand, I can't help myself.

"You didn't inspect Mister McGinty's neck," I tell her, snippy. "You're making that up."

"Well, I never." She crosses her arms across her chest and stomps her little foot. "For you to suggest that I'm prevaricating is nothing short of an outrage!"

PreWHATacating?

Talking gibberish is a *very* bad sign that I should put on the LOONY list when I get the chance, but . . . geez, I don't know. Long shots *do* come in every once in a while. I guess Birdie's attention *might've* been pulled in the direction of Mr. McGinty's neck. Not because she's smart enough to think of looking to see if his medal was missing on purpose, but because she got a whiff of what he was picking out of the bush. She could've whipped her head toward the leftover smell of chocolate and caramel that'd been wrapped in the gold Rolo wrapper and *accidentally* got a look at his neck.

"So you're tellin' me that something like this"—I hold up the free-at-last St. Christopher medal—"wasn't hanging around Mister McGinty's neck when he—?"

"Would you please kindly lower your voice?" Birdie says with a scowl. "I have abnormally sensitive hearing and you're aggravating my condition."

I know this is no laughing matter, but honestly, even when I'm as ticked off as I am, my sister just slays me. "Oh, ya got a condition that I'm aggravating, huh?" I say with a chuckle. "Well, I got a condition that you're aggravating, too, missy, and it's that you better be tellin' me the truth about what you saw, or didn't see, around Mister McGinty's neck."

She squares her shoulders, lifts her chin, and places her right hand on her heart. "I can unequivocally state that the caretaker's neck was completely . . . oh, my, dare I say . . . *bare*?" she *does* dare to say with cheeks the color of her freshly pinched heinie.

What the heck?

The kid who will pull her pants down and moon not only me, but just about anybody in the neighborhood, including Father Ted if the spirit moves her, is suddenly too prim and proper to say the word *bare*?

"And before you can question the quality of my eyesight again, young lady," Birdie says, Sunday school teacher snooty, "let me *also* assure you that my verification of the identity of the person that I observed in the vicinity of the willow tree a few moments ago is absolutely accurate as well."

The identity of somebody? At the willow tree? Is she . . . is she talking about my Charlie?

Wait just a cotton-pickin' minute.

I think I might've caught my sister telling me a coupla bald-faced, old-timey fibs.

"But when I asked you a few minutes ago to check for Charlie," I say nice and slowly, so there can be no confusion on her part or mine, "you told me that you *didn't* see him down there. And just now you told me that your verification was absolutely accurate." I hitch up my shorts and do my Sheriff of Dodge impression that she loves. "Sounds to me like you're changin' yer stories, little lady."

"I most certainly am *not!*" Birdie says, not charmed, I'm sure. "After you asked me to check for your betrothed beneath the weeping willow, I stated quite clearly that I didn't see anyone *bald* in the vicinity. Not that I didn't see *anyone* at all."

Well, that empties all the bullets outta my six-shooter right quick, because that's exactly what she *did* state, quite clearly.

Could she be telling the truth after all? On both counts?

I don't care so much about the Charlie situation anymore because I'm pretty sure I know where we'll find him, but I *do* care about the Mr. McGinty situation. If Birdie is right and this *is* for sure his medal I'm holding in my hand, then I'm almost positive that he's the kidnapping murderer.

FACT: "The road to Hell is paved with good intentions" is a very true famous saying.

PROOF: This is *not* at all what I wanted to happen when I thought it was a great-good-luck moneymaking idea to show up in the cemetery this morning to investigate what I heard and saw last night.

"I'm really, really, really, really hungry. I'm really . . ." drones my sister, who has suddenly returned back from her trip to the Wild West hungrier than she was before she left.

I *have* to get those chocolate-covered cherries into her gullet before the bells at St. Kate's start clanging to let her and everyone else in the neighborhood know that it's high noon.

Wait just a cotton-pickin' minute.

What's wrong with me?

I just remembered 12:00 is when Mr. McGinty told us that Mrs. Peterman decided to hold her husband's funeral so the workers he bossed around at the Feelin' Good factory could attend on their lunch break, which is the worst possible timing that could put the Finley sisters in grave danger—no joke—because the box of Stover candy that Mrs. Melman leaves on Mr. Lindley's final resting spot is not too far away from Mr. Peterman's new hole that most of our neighbors will be gathered around. If we're sneaky, we should be okay, but only if Birdie doesn't give us away. I so wish I had a gag on me like the sock I keep in the Radio Flyer wagon, because—

Clang . . . clang . . . clang . . .

Anybody who came to say their final good-bye to Mr. Peterman is about to be treated to a concert of hideously loud starvation squawking when those bells reach twelve. And, of course, one of them is bound to call our mother at the Clark station to tell her about the ruckus one of the Finley ghouls caused in Holy Cross during the funeral.

"*Señorita* Birdie!" I turn to tell her in my sure-to-please Zorro voice. "*Vamanos* to those chocolate-covereds!"

Clang . . . clang . . . clang . . .

Unfortunately, she wants those runny cherries in her tummy even more than I thought she did. Before I have the chance to get a good grip on her hand, she *vamanos*-es down the side of the hill yelling . . . yelling . . . I have no idea what the hell she's yelling. I caught the words, "*sister*" and "*run*" and "*tree*," but she might've yelled, "*mister*" and "*fun*" and "*free*," for all I know . . . no . . . no . . . no . . . no!

For some unknown reason, is unpredictable Birdie listening to her big heart instead of her big stomach? Could she be yelling at me, her *sister*, that she feels so bad about not seeing Charlie earlier, the way I wanted her to, that she's going to *run* down to the weeping willow *tree* to check for him in person? That wouldn't be great, but it wouldn't be the end of the world, either, because I keep a stash of emergency candy in a hole in the willow along with our Mutual Admiration treasury money.

But what if Birdie is listening to another part of her weird brain and she's yelling on her hustle down the hill that she's going to look for *Mister* McGinty at his shack because she thinks it'd be *fun* to play a game of gin rummy with him? And because she doesn't know any better, when she's done eating her *free* windmill cookies and drinking her *free* root beer, she's so proud of the clue she found that she just might brag to him when she's shuffling the "52" that she dug his St. Christopher medal out of a leaf pile behind the mausoleum where a murder was committed last night. And that right there? That could be a life-ending decision. The poor kid doesn't understand what could happen if she told already very jittery Mr. McGinty that we got proof that he was at the scene of the crime. Our armed-to-his-beautiful-teeth friend, who I'm now 95% sure murdered our principal, really, really, really, really wouldn't like that *Gotcha!*

Clang . . . clang . . . clang.

13

WHY . . . WHY . . . WHY . . . WHY?

From hanging out at Lonnigan's Bar with the best bartender in the neighborhood since I only came up to his knees, I have a bigger vocabulary than most kids, especially when it comes to cuss words, and I'm using every single one of them while I'm running after my sister down the side of the cemetery hill. Cussing and chasing after Birdie, I swear, if I could get paid for them, we'd be rolling in more dough than Meuer's Bakery. (No joke.)

"Don't run to the willow tree and don't run to Mister McGinty's shack. Go to the chocolate-covered cherries!" I'm shrieking between the clanging church bells that are telling my sister that it's feeding time. "Turn right at the bottom of the hill! Right! That's . . . that's the hand you deal cards with!"

Birdie doesn't slow down, turn around, and give me an A-okay sign, but she *must've* heard me, because just after St. Kate's bells finish sounding noon, she makes a sharp turn toward Mr. Lindley's grave, thank God.

We should be home free now because after she gets some of the oozing cherries into her, I'll honor my *sister*-promise to go see Daddy, and then the Finley sisters will climb the cemetery fence and make our way to Charlie's house, which is where I'm pretty sure he'll be whittling away on his back porch and full of questions. During our meeting, I'll spill the beans about THE CASE OF THE MISSING NUN WHO WAS KIDNAPPED AND MURDERED BY MR. MCGINTY. The Finley sisters might be in way over our heads, but Charlie will know what to do, I know he will. He's a very level-headed fiancé.

When I finally catch up to Birdie after her record-breaking race down the hill, she's not lounging around Mr. Lindley's grave stuffing her face. She somehow managed to snag the heart-shaped box of Stover chocolates that *were* sitting on top of it—thank you, Mrs. Melman— and flew straight over to the nearby marker that is our most favorite in the cemetery to stuff her face:

EDWARD ALFRED FINLEY

REST IN PEACE

SEPTEMBER 2, 1931–AUGUST 1, 1959

I wasn't BE PREPARED.

Usually, I feel like I'm coming home when I catch sight of his gorgeous, speckled, polished gravestone, but this morning, seeing it is sucking every ounce of strength out of me. Between dealing with Louise and Gert, and Birdie's wild-streaking ways, her everyday weirdness, and her new old-timey-ness, and . . . and wearing Daddy's big shoes, and not seeing Charlie, and worrying about how Mr. McGinty is looking so guilty of kidnapping and murdering Sister Margaret Mary that he's probably going to get the electric chair, I am knocked down to the grass next to Daddy's pretend grave for the count.

Of course, there's always the chance that Birdie didn't *really* see what she thought she did, which isn't far-fetched, no matter how positively old-timey she sounded up on the hill. Trusting her without grilling her further, well, that'd be dumb. And it just so happens that Mr. Lynwood "My friends call me Woody and my enemies call me their worst nightmare" Bellflower agrees with me. "When considering evidence or information gathered during the course of an investigation," he wrote in Chapter Five of *Modern Detection*, "it is absolutely crucial that you weigh the dependability of your sources."

Now, I love my little featherweight to death and back and all the stops in between, but "dependability" is not one of her best qualities.

"Bird?" I say to my partner in crime, who is pressing her cheek against Daddy's tombstone—that's the closest she can get to him, so she really is in hog Heaven.

"Yes, Tessie?" she says with cherry juice dribbling down her chin.

"Ya remember how you told me a little while ago that you were absolutely positive that Mister McGinty didn't have his Saint Christopher medal around his neck when we were behind the mausoleum with him?"

I'm praying that fact has slipped her mind forever, that she's about to say something like *What are you talking about, Tessie?* but God must be out to lunch or something, because Birdie shoves another chocolate in her mouth and nods four times with a lot of enthusiasm, poor thing.

All she knows is that she found a clue in a leaf pile and that Mr. McGinty's medal was not around his neck. That's the 1 + 1, but she's not smart enough to come up with what that equals. She doesn't understand how guilty that makes him. *We* figured out this case and I'm not so bigheaded to think that eventually the police won't. When they question everyone in the neighborhood about the disappearance of Sister Margaret Mary, Gert Klement will step up to point her finger at me. Tell the police what a banshee I am and how I don't have a conscience and that everyone in the parish knows how much I hate our principal for holding Birdie back in school. Of course, I wouldn't tell the coppers a thing when they dragged me down to the station house and gave me the third degree, because I *do* hate Sister M & M and I'm very willing to let bygones be bygones when it comes to Mr. McGinty murdering her. But my sweet-hearted, overly friendly sister? Even if I reminded her four thousand times to keep her mouth shut, she'll forget. She'll tell the police whatever she remembers about me hearing the yelling in the cemetery the night Sister Margaret Mary disappeared and about how she found Mr. McGinty's medal behind the mausoleum, and before we know it, the cops will come to pick up our godfather in a paddy wagon and tell him, *All aboard for the gas chamber*.

I tell Birdie, "I'm really sorry to have to break this bad news to you, honey." I have to prepare her. She is going to take this very, very, very, very hard, but the sooner I get it out of the way the better. "But . . . well . . . it looks like Mister McGinty is guilty of kidnapping and murdering Sister Margaret Mary."

Whatever Birdie is trying to tell me, she jammed her mouth so full of gooey chocolate I can't understand a word of it. Could be that she didn't understand what I said and wants me to repeat myself or maybe she *did* understand and she's too frozen with shock and sadness to throw herself down on top of Daddy's pretend grave and turn on her waterworks, which is what I thought she'd do considering how much she's always liked Mr. McGinty as much as me, and as much as our dear daddy did.

Our mother enforcing her #1 Commandment—*The Finley Sisters Shalt Not Visit the Cemetery*—is nothing new. She's always frowned upon Birdie and me wanting to head over here bright and early to watch Mr. McGinty dig fresh graves or mow the grass or plant trees and flowers, but "Good Time Eddie" Finley? He *never* gave his "babies" a hard time about spending time in Holy Cross. He would laugh and joke at the breakfast table, "Get off the girls' backs, Lou-Lou. Jimmy's brain might've gotten a little scrambled when he stepped on that land mine, but he's still the good Scotch egg he's always been. Ha . . . ha . . . ha."

That wasn't only a great Daddy joke, it was a true one. And even if it turns out that he *is* a kidnapping murderer, Mr. McGinty will always be a good egg in my book, *and* recently I have discovered that he's not one of the stingy kind of Scots. Unlike most everybody else around here who can't wait to brag about their charitable acts, our shy friend would *never* toot his own horn. That's how come I only found out last week that he did what he did.

Birdie and me were hanging out with him, playing with Pyewacket and checkers and cards, the way we usually do, because his shack is our other home away from home, when he suddenly remembered that he'd forgotten to sharpen his **TOOLS OF THE TRADE** in his shed. Once he left, my sister did, too—she took one of her trips to parts unknown, because petting Pye always derails her brain—so I took the opportunity to go scrounging through his desk drawer. I was looking for an envelope so I could send off for this booklet in the back of the Superman comic book that'd teach me "How to Become a Ventriloquist"—**Throw Your Voice! Fool teachers, friends and family**—because that'd be such a handy talent to have in my line of work. That's when I came across his checkbook in his desk drawer. Of course, I know that I shouldn't have, but what choice did I have? It's not my fault that it's my second nature to snoop. I peeked at the part in the front where he writes down what he's been spending his money on and boy, oh, boy! You'd never guess it by looking at him or the way he acts or the rusty Ford he drives, but Louise really missed out on a *huge* payday when she wouldn't put Mr. McGinty on her plate. He could afford to take her to the Taj Mahal for supper!

FACT: Our friend has got $201,789.05 keeping itself warm in the vault at the First Wisconsin Bank.

PROOF: He wrote check #2315 to secretly pay Mr. Patrick Mullarkey & Sons, whose business it is to carve cemetery markers, to create the beautiful and *very* expensive one Birdie is currently loving on.

So right about now, our dearly departed father is probably not looking down from Heaven and giving his "babies" two thumbs up while we're sitting on top of his pretend grave talking about how guilty Mr. McGinty is. No, I'm positive that Daddy wouldn't want Birdie and me to continue solving the crimes that are going to make his old and good friend since they played on St. Kate's basketball team together get sent to the Big House to die. The old and good friend who's also our godfather who's been treating Birdie and me like we're his real daughters since Daddy's been gone.

And just when I didn't think my heart could feel any more ganged-up on, I notice that the flowers Birdie and me placed last week against this gorgeous tombstone that Mr. McGinty secretly gifted to us have seen better days. I need to add on a #10 on my TO-DO list: Stop at Bloomers for a pink rose bouquet. Daddy never said, but I think they must've been his favorites. They're what he always brought Louise after they'd have a screaming match over his drinking—he was a bartender, for crissakes!—and his card playing—what's wrong with having a hobby?—and also when our mother would get her Irish up over him spending too much time with Suzanne "That French Slut" LaPelt—she was his barmaid!

Any idiot knows that leaving *kaput* flowers on a grave is the same as rubbing a departed's nose in the fact that they're dead, but I have no clue when I'll have the time to fetch fresh ones, so God forgive me, I reach over and grab a few of the fresh, fluffy white ones that are lying on top of the grave of Daddy's next-door neighbor, who Mr. McGinty told us was a carpenter:

DENNIS MARK WILLIAMS

MARCH 2, 1898–APRIL 11, 1940

MAY HE SLEEP IN THE ARMS OF ANGELS

So I guess now, on top of my already long list of sins, I can go ahead and add grave robbing. Covering up evidence, too. Because when I placed the white flowers I stole from Mr. Williams on top of Daddy's pretend grave, I spotted something buried deep in the grass next to one of the hawk feathers that Birdie finds and brings to him because she can't leave them anymore in his pants pockets. It was an L&M butt. That's the kind Louise Mary Fitzgerald Finley smokes, because those are her first two initials. Charlie, who keeps track of these sorts of things, told me that L&Ms are the most popular brand around here, but *this* coffin nail belongs to our mother. I recognize her Revlon red lip prints on the filter, I've seen them a million times. Louise misses Daddy, too? Enough to visit him? That's just too hard to believe on a morning when everything has been just too hard to believe. And if she *does* stop by here, I'm sure it's not to honor her wonderful husband or pay her respects. She probably just comes to tap one of her cigarettes over his pretend grave and say, "Ashes to ashes."

I know I *should* tell my partner in crime what I found, but because Birdie won't reach the same conclusion I have, I bury it deeper in the grass. If I showed that evidence to her, ya know what she'd do? She'd take it as proof that Louise is not as crummy of a mother as I tell her she is and that would be disastrous. If we have to run away, the tighter she's tied to our mother's apron strings, the harder it will be for me to convince her to take off for California.

This is all my fault.

If only I'd minded my own beeswax, our friend wouldn't be in this hot water. I'm so very sorry, Daddy, but when I started this investigation, how was I supposed to know that Jimmy "Good Egg" McGinty might turn out to be guilty and that your kid, the one who I'm supposed to be giving tender loving care to, might wind up being the key witness for the persecution, who would make sure that your best man paid the price for his crimes?

Wait just a cotton-pickin' minute.

155

I'm assuming again!

The only thing *really* written in stone around here are birthdays, deathdays, and heavenly hopes. And while it *is* looking very bad for Mr. McGinty, *Modern Detection* warns all the time in the same chapter that warns all the time about assuming, "If an investigator jumps to a final conclusion without clearly establishing means, motive, and opportunity, their entire case could be in jeopardy."

FACT: We got the medal evidence, but Birdie and me only got *two* of the three main ingredients that a gumshoe is supposed to have before they hand a suspect over to the cops on a silver platter!

PROOF: Mr. McGinty's *means* are his strong arms, and he had the *opportunity*, because he hardly ever leaves his post at Holy Cross at night, except to play bingo every Saturday and to eat his supper at Fish Fry Friday, and today is Thursday. But what would his *motive* be? Like my sister would say, *Why . . . why . . . why . . . why?* would he do our principal in?

This is very unprofessional conduct for the president of a detecting and blackmailing business to admit to, but ya know what? I honestly don't give a crud *what* evidence Birdie and me have found out about Mr. McGinty so far, and my tummy, for once, agrees with me. *Modern Detection* does, too. "Perhaps the most vital of all the TOOLS OF THE TRADE an investigator possesses is his gut instinct." Until we discover the *why* of the crime, Mr. McGinty is only around 66% guilty, so that's at least a little ray of hope at the end of the tunnel. If we keep our noses to the grindstone, The Mutual Admiration Society could find *another* person who we don't like so much that we could blackmail for $$$$ or earn a big reward for when we turn him in to the cops for kidnap and murder.

Q. Could we still get one of those and-they-all-lived-happily-ever-after endings to this case, instead of one of those really Grimm ones?

A. *Without a doubt.*

14

A TURN FOR THE WORST

Well, like a famous guy named Johnny whose hobby it was to roam around America planting fruit trees might say, *How do ya like them apples?* (Joke!)

Things are really starting to look up around here, which is a nice change of pace. Of course, I know that just because I'm hopeful The Mutual Admiration Society won't ever find out *why* the caretaker of the cemetery isn't guilty of those crimes, doesn't mean that we *won't* and that he *isn't*. The time might come that, like it or not, we'll have to face the music and admit to ourselves that Mr. McGinty *is* the kidnapper and murderer after all.

But until then, I'm praying that after Birdie, Charlie, and me talk to a few other people in the neighborhood, we'll come across a *different* bad guy to pin the crimes on. One who has *all* the ingredients we need to prove that he's the guilty party, including the motive, which means that Birdie and me gotta chop-chop and get to work. Only we can't do that until she's done with her visit with Daddy, because that'd just be asking for her to go unruly on me again if I bug her when she's hugging, kissing, and whispering into his gravestone, and that's fine. I don't mind waiting a little longer, because it'd be much better to explain my new plan to search for another suspect later, during our Mutual Admiration meeting. That way I won't have to repeat myself to Charlie.

We don't have time anymore to get together in his bomb shelter, which is the other location where we conduct our business, and that's a crying shame. It's cool and soundproof and Birdie likes it down there, too, because there are a lot of canned goods. But as *Modern Detection* states: "It's important for a detective to remain flexible during an investigation, for you never know what challenges might arise." Daddy agreed with him. "Ya need to roll with the punches, kiddo," he used to tell me, so that's what we'll do. Get together for a very quick meeting on Charlie's back porch about what's already happened this morning, and then we have to be on our way up to St. Kate's, so I can confess to Father Ted before his 1:00 p.m. quitting time. I'll fill the both of them in on my brand-new plan on the fly, and once I get my confessing out of the way, the three of us will roll up our sleeves and get busy working on THE CASE OF THE MISSING NUN WHO MIGHT BE KIDNAPPED AND MURDERED BUT BY SOMEBODY WHO IS NOT MR. MCGINTY.

As the president of our society, I feel it's my responsibility to come up with a few names to toss into the ring before the meeting, but all I can think of is one. #2 on my SHIT LIST.

Q. Is it asking too much to make Butch Seeback be the one I saw skulking around the cemetery last night with the dead body?

A. *Signs point to yes.*

Of course they do, because as much as I'd love to get that vicious kid sent out of the neighborhood and straight over to the House of Good Shepherd Reform School until he can be permanently sent to prison—mark my words, someday he will end up committing even worse hideous crimes than skin upholsterer Ed Gein—there is no denying the facts:

1. Butch isn't as skinny as the guy I saw last night. The high school dropout is built more like the safe at the First Wisconsin Bank on North Ave. (Another spot I might have to heist someday.)
2. The initials on the back of the St. Christopher medal are J. M. and his aren't. (Almighty God bestowing upon that turd the initials of B. S. only goes to prove once again what a great sense of humor He has, which is exactly what I'm banking on when I step into the box at St. Kate's to do my Shirley Temple confession.)
3. Seeback definitely wasn't the one who shouted out, "I'm warning you! Watch yourself! You're treading on dangerous ground!" last night. (His voice is as recognizable as mine.)

While Birdie finishes up visiting with Daddy, instead of trying to keep everything that I gotta do in my head, I take my stubby pencil and my navy-blue detecting notebook out and use the back of the gravestone Mr. McGinty bought for us to update my list. Daddy won't mind. In fact, I'd bet my allowance, if I got one, that he's feeling a whole lot better about the direction the investigation is going now, which is good, because I don't like to picture him rolling over in his grave, if he could.

QUESTION OR SURVEIL
1. ~~Mr. McGinty.~~
2. Kitten Jablonski.
3. ~~Butch Seeback.~~
4. ~~Mr. Johnson.~~
5. Suzie LaPelt.

Whenever someone says that famous saying "Killing two birds with one stone," it reminds me of my sister and I gotta reach for my Tums, but it seems to me, that's what we have to do next.

Killing bird #1. After the very short Mutual Admiration meeting, the three of us will race over to St. Kate's before Father Ted leaves to go to Lonnigan's for his lunch of Jameson's neat.

Damnation!

I hate the hoops this mother of mine makes me jump through. It would save so much time if I could just sign the book in the church lobby as proof that I went to confession, but I tried that once already and it didn't work. Louise outfoxed me. She checked with *her* biggest confidential source in the neighborhood who she can always count on to rat me out—#5.

SHIT LIST

1. Gert Klement.
2. Butch Seeback.
3. Sister Margaret Mary.
4. The grease monkey who fixes cars at the Clark station and tries to peek in the little girls' room window when you got to stop to tinkle because your sister can't make it home from the Tosa Theatre after she drinks a large root beer.
5. Brownnoser Jenny Radtke.
6. What's-his-name.

Radtke, the kid who is always the only one left standing next to me during a spelling bee, was only too happy to snitch to Louise last week that she saw me "loitering around the Milky Way with Birdbrain and Cue Ball" during the time I was supposed to be loitering around the confessional with Father Ted. (I got off easy, because Louise doesn't know that making me go to bed without one of her "gourmet" suppers is *not* a punishment.)

Killing bird #2. When I'm at church, it's going to cost me, but I'll have the chance to question Kitten Jablonski. She'll be there, without a doubt, because same as me she's always one of the last kids to confess on Thursday and she always saves me a spot in line. I'm hoping that my confidential source will be able to give me some names to add to a new list that I'd love to make in my navy-blue detecting notebook: VERY LIKELY SUSPECTS THAT AREN'T MR. MCGINTY.

Long as I got my pencil out, I remove my most important list from my shorts so I can add on the new #10 and #11 and change #2.

TO-DO

1. Take tender loving care of Birdie.
2. ~~Solve whatever happened to Sister Margaret Mary for big blackmail or reward bucks.~~
2. Hope we don't find out *why* Mr. McGinty kidnapped and murdered Sister M & M and concentrate on finding someone else who did.
3. Make Gert Klement think her arteries are going as hard as her heart.
4. Catch whoever stole over $200 out of the Pagan Baby collection box.
5. Practice your Miss America routine.
6. Learn how to swim.
7. Be a good dry-martini-making fiancée to Charlie.
8. Do not get caught blackmailing or spying.
9. Just *think* about making a real confession to Father Ted, before it's too late.
10. Stop at Bloomers for pink roses for Daddy.
11. Think up a catchy slogan for Louise that might help her beat Mrs. Tate in the election so she doesn't blame Birdie and me when she loses.

After I make sure the updated list is safely tucked back where it belongs, I crane my head around the corner and say to Birdie like I'm walking on eggshells, because ya never know with her, "Honey? I'm sorry, I don't want to rush you, but—"

"It's okay, Tessie." She stops patting her sticky hands against Daddy's gravestone and polishes it back up with the bottom of her T-shirt. "I know we gotta have our meeting with Charlie now."

"Good remembering!" I pull her up to her feet and give her four pats on the back. "And right after our meeting, we need to . . . ummm." That was a close call. I almost reminded her about #9 on the TO-DO list, the making-a-real-confession-to-Father-Ted one, and I don't want her to go very hellfire on me again. "We need to get the latest gossip about Sister Margaret Mary's disappearance offa Kitten. But . . ." I take her face into my hands. "Before either one of those things can happen, we got one more really important caper to pull off first, Bird."

"What one more really important caper do we have to pull off first, Tessie?"

"We gotta climb back over the black fence."

Having good timing has never been more important, so I almost cry with relief when she turns back to the magnificent gravestone, and says, "Roger that, Daddy. Tessie and me have to go now, but we'll see you tomorrow, same time, same station."

The chocolate-covered cherries and the chat Birdie had with our father must've been an even bigger shot in the arm than it usually is, because she's doing a great job of imitating me—monkey see, monkey do—when we scurry away from our most favorite place in Holy Cross to weave through the tombstones toward our final destination—Charlie's house.

We've done a great job so far, and we'll be home free once we get past the grave of Mrs. Elizabeth Hughes April 16, 1923–January 31, 1957. She got murdered by Mother Nature. A giant icicle cracked free of Mrs. Hughes's roof and dive-bombed her head when she was shoveling her front porch during the bad storm two winters ago.

Wait just a cotton-pickin' minute.

What are all these cars doing here?

Damnation!

Birdie's bad memory must be rubbing off on me or something, because I forgot all about Mr. Peterman's funeral *again*.

Because we can't reach the cemetery fence until we get past the mourners that are gathered around the hole, I grab Birdie and pull her down behind Mrs. Hughes's tombstone and tell her, "Stay put and keep your lips zipped. I gotta surveil."

Just like I knew it'd be, the service that the old priest at St. Kate's is presiding over today is already in full swing and very crowded, because so many of the fathers in the neighborhood are chocolate chip cookie makers at the Feelin' Good factory that Mr. Peterman was the foreman of. The deceased to exist was also head usher at church, which is also a big muckety-muck deal. I bet more people showed up for Daddy's pretend funeral, but there's gotta be at least a couple hundred visitors bunched around the open grave like a big black bouquet. Of course, most of them are gals, because they don't have jobs. Other than her friend Mrs. Jablonski, who had to start handing out shoes at Jerbak Beer and Bowl after her husband never came home from the Red Owl with a gallon of milk, Louise is one of the only mothers in the neighborhood that has to work for a living.

Birdie tugs on my T-shirt and says with a teasing smile, "Betcha a quarter that Father Joe croaks before he gets to *the valley of the shadow of death*," because that's what we always bet one another after we find out that he's the one saying the funeral service when we're sitting out on our back porch and watching the goings-on over here.

Boy, oh, boy, it really *would* be so helpful if Father Joe, who rumor has it said Mass on the *Mayflower*, got called back to his Maker in the next few minutes. Him keeling over into Mr. Peterman's grave would create such a great distraction, the kind that *Modern Detection* mentions in one of the chapters. It says that gumshoes should come up with something big and flashy if they need to take people's minds off *them* and put it on something *else*. Starting a fire, that's a good distraction, which I'd have no trouble doing if I had a pack of Lonnigan's matches on me, but they're back home in my nighttime sleuthing shorts.

On the other hand . . . when Father Joe says Sunday morning Mass, it's hard to hear his sermon over all the snoring, so maybe his mumbling long-windedness alone will be enough of the distraction Birdie and me need to get past the group of grievers, because everyone standing around the grave might fall asleep.

Once I do a little more surveilling and I'm sure of the safest route we need to take to the fence, I squat back down behind Mrs. Hughes's tombstone and tell my accomplice, "Okay. First we'll run and hide behind the hearse, then we'll cross the road, and then we gotta haul heinie into the bushes and crawl toward Charlie's backyard. Go low and slow, but not too slow, just . . . just go where I go, step where I step, and please, honey, whatever you do, don't make a racket."

While the Finley sisters are snaking from tree trunk to tree trunk before we make a run for the hearse, I'm not all that worried that someone at the funeral will hear Birdie if she does start singing or yelling out my name, because as usual, the neighborhood gals are making rackets of their own.

FACT: Most of them who are doing "Cry Me a River" scenes around Mr. Peterman's grave aren't *really* sad.

PROOF: Those gals have what are called "ulterior motives," which is nothing more than having a sneaky secret reason for doing something other than the obvious reason for doing something.

You get a lot of credit around here if you genuflect deeper than everybody else, sing hymns louder than everybody else, and push out more kids than everybody else, so the *only* reason most of the gals showed up at Mr. Peterman's funeral today is to grieve better than everybody else. Mrs. Ann Tracy is the parish's overall "Best Mourner," but Mrs. Sophia Maniaci is breathing down her neck because she's Italian. (Besides being the best cooks, the wops are the loudest people in the neighborhood and they wave their hands around a lot when they talk, so it's a very excellent show they put on.)

When Birdie and me reach the hearse that brought Mr. Peterman over from church, I stop us before we start running across the road toward the bushes so I can peek around the black fender to make sure one more time that nobody is staring daggers at us when . . . lo and behold, who should slip into the service but the biggest party pooper on the planet!

I'm somewhat surprised to see Louise, but not shocked. I'm used to her showing up whenever or wherever I least want her to. But why isn't she up at the Clark station answering phones or taking money or pumping gas or whatever else a cashier is supposed to do? And who is that guy holding her hand? I don't recognize him, so it's got to be what's-his-name. Well, if it is, the dollar signs in Louise's eyes must be blinding her, because even from where I'm standing, I can see that he is shorter than Daddy by a lot and not even close to as good-looking. He's got a weak chin and his ears stick out worse than mine. Did this numbskull leave his job at the American Motors factory assembly line and pick up our mother in his Chevy during his lunch hour so they could attend the funeral together because sometime this morning Louise realized that job or no job, she *had* to show up today so she didn't look bad in front of the other Pagan Baby gals? Or . . . did she get fired already? Our cupboards are already 90% bare, and if they go to 100%, that's not going to sit so well with you-know-who.

My sister with the Lassie hearing must've heard me gulp after I saw Louise, because she squeezes my hand and says, "You okay?"

I spin toward her and put my hands on her cheeks to lock her in place, and tell her, "Yeah, yeah, I'm fine and dandy." I *cannot* let Birdie look over her shoulder. If she does, she might shout out, *I love you, Ida Lupino!* because she would have no problem seeing Louise, who *really* stands out in the crowd in her fancy work clothes she left the house wearing, which is not going to go over so big. There's rules you gotta follow around here and our mother is breaking a big one. She should *not* have showed up to the funeral looking like Rita Hayworth on May Day when the rest of them gals are looking like Bette Davis on Ash Wednesday. That's a *huge* mistake on the part of a gal who wants to win votes in the Pagan Baby election.

Staring straight into the windows of my soul, Birdie asks, "If you're so fine and dandy then how come you're shiverin'?"

Of course, I can't tell her that I'm shaking in my boots because I'm scared our mother is going to catch us in the act of breaking her #1 Commandment, so I tell her, "I . . . I just got the willies being this close to the hearse 'cause . . . 'cause it reminded me that Sister Margaret Mary's rotting corpse might be lying somewhere around here, but I'm okay now, so . . ." I point in the direction I need her to go. "Run as fast as you can across the road and straight into the bushes over there." I'm hoping that the both of us can get up enough speed that even if someone from the funeral looks our way, we'll be an unrecognizable blur of arms and legs. "One for the money, two for the show, three to get ready, and . . ." I knit my fingers through hers, but instead of go, Bird, going, where I want her to, she starts tugging against me and tries to veer in the opposite direction. "Whatta ya doin'?" I whisper to her. "This way, honey, we need to go *this* way."

"No, we need to go *this* way, Tessie. Toward the hospital. You need a doctor, ASAP!"

"I need a . . . WHAT?" Of course, I have no idea why she would get this dopey idea into her head. "I don't need to see a doctor and we are not going to the hospital. Now, c'mon." She doesn't budge. "Did you forget the plan already?"

"No, I did not forget the plan already, Tessie, but you're *not* fine and dandy." If I don't keep my grip on her, this stubborn, wiry kid who is working herself into a tizzy could drag me down the cemetery road toward St. Joe's Hospital in front of our mother and half of the parish. "I think you're comin' down with the delirious flu again that made you talk so crazy last winter. Do you have a fever?"

When she raises her chocolate-covered hand and tries to press it against my forehead, I bat it away, because enough is enough already. "Why would ya think something dumb like, I mean—" At least she didn't go old-timey and tell me she thinks I got typhoid. "Why would ya think I'm sick?"

"'Cause when I asked you if you were okay a little while ago you said you were, but you made a big gulp like your throat was sore. And then you shivered really bad when you told me that the hearse was reminding you of Sister Margaret Mary's rotting dead body and that is such a delirious thing to say 'cause . . . 'cause"—her slightly bulging eyes are really bulging now, almost out of her head—"you *know* that we don't have the most important something we need to prove that she's been murdered!"

Now, if I didn't feel so petrified that we're about to get caught by Louise or another parishioner who's gotten bored out of their gourd listening to Father Joe's *valley of death* talk, I'd shout out, *Hot damn, Birdie!* and make a *very* big deal out of the fact that she just remembered, all by herself, that we *don't* have the motive for Mr. McGinty murdering our principal.

"*Sister*-promise, honey," I whisper to her, "I don't have the delirious flu or . . . or nothin' else delirious and . . . and . . ." I pull out Daddy's watch. It's 12:26 p.m. "We're runnin' out of time, so let's go."

Of course, because I gave her the promise of all promises, she had to believe me, even though she does not look at all convinced that I *am* the picture of health when we do the fifty-yard dash across the road. And by the time St. Kate's bells start nagging all the bad kids in the neighborhood that they better drop whatever mischief they got themselves into because they only have a half hour before Father Ted hangs out a **NOT IN SERVICE** sign outside his confessional, even though I've somehow corralled Birdie into the bushes that run along the cemetery fence, she keeps stopping to ask me every few seconds, "You still fine and dandy, Tessie?" and if I don't immediately say, "Yes, Birdie. I'm still fine and dandy," she tries to take my temperature again.

When we've made slow but steady progress and we're almost to the place where we'll monkey up the black iron fence and jump down into Charlie's backyard, I'm feeling happy but not thrilled beyond belief, because now we got a new problem. I wasn't born yesterday. I know this plan I came up with is not foolproof, and, as usual, it boils down to nothing more than bad timing.

There's gonna be about ten seconds or so that my sister and me will be on top of the fence, and even a guy holding onto the leash of a seeing-eye dog wouldn't miss us up there, for cripessakes. So could our mother and most of the parish gals, which includes the black evil lump that I spotted in the #2 position graveside, next to the widow Peterman. The veil on her black pillbox hat was thoughtfully hiding her ugly puss, but I'm sure it was Gert Klement. I know she would've much rather stayed back at her house, watching and waiting to swoop down on the Finley sisters, but she *had* to show up today. It wouldn't look too good if the president of the most powerful club at St. Kate's missed the funeral of the head of the ushers unless she had a very great excuse, like she was on her deathbed or something, which is too much to ask for.

So it looks like what I'm up against now is one of those six-of-one, half-a-dozen-of-another, flip-a-coin situations. Heads, Birdie and me stay hunkered down in these bushes until the service is over and it's too late for me to go to confession, which means that Jenny Radtke will tattle and we'll have to take our medicine when Louise gets home tonight smelling like red sauce and garlic after her date with what's-his-name. Tails, the Finley sisters risk climbing to the top of the fence where we could so easily be seen before we drop into the yard of my darling future husband, who I'm wanting to see so much that my heart feels swollen and ready to burst out of my chest.

Q. Is the famous saying "Love conquers all" really true?

A. *You may rely on it.*

Well, then. Tails it is.

15

PROVE IT

Of course, I'm not worried about anybody at Mr. Peterman's funeral catching sight of coordinated me on top of the fence before I drop quickly into Charlie's yard. But when spazzy Birdie is out in the open for those ten seconds, that's gonna take a real leap of faith. (No joke.)

I sweep her shaggy bangs out of her eyes and say, "You've done a pretty good job doing what I told you to and I need ya to keep up the good work. I'm gonna boost you up now." She can make it over without help from me, the way she did this morning, but it just about gives me a nervous breakdown when she does. "Remember to be really careful around the pointy spears, and . . . and please don't yell out Charlie's name four times the way you always do. They might hear you at the funeral."

Dear patron saint of pots and pans, just this once, could you help her keep a lid on it?

"Okay, Tessie. I'll be really careful around the pointy spears and I won't yell Charlie's name out four times the way I always do, Roger that," Birdie says. "But before I don't do those things, I gotta ask you an important question, then hope to die, I'll do whatever you tell me to." She makes a big *X* over her heart and then she points to the top of her shorts, which is where she stuck the Stover box when she needed her hands free to crawl. "Did you hear what I yelled when I was runnin' down the top of the cemetery hill toward Mr. Lindley's grave to get these chocolate-covered cherries?"

This is an example of the famous saying about water being under the bridge, because who cares what the hell she loonatic-yelled now? She made the right turn. "Just because I forged a card that says I am, and just because I pay deaf Jeffy Lanfre a quarter to teach me to read lips, that doesn't mean that I'm *really* deaf," I remind her. "So yeah, of course, I heard what ya yelled when you were runnin' down the hill. Now would you please put your foot in my hands and—"

"Prove it."

"Prove *what*?"

"Tell me what ya heard me yell when I was runnin' down the hill."

Damnation!

Because she was moving so fast, I didn't catch all of it, so I'm just going to tell her what I *did* catch and hope that's good enough. "At first I thought you mighta yelled *sister* and *run* and *tree*, but now I'm pretty sure you yelled *mister* and *fun* and *free*."

"Aha!" Birdie says, like she's Sherlock Holmes who just solved the mystery of the turn of the century. "Just as I suspected!"

"Okay, good, that's a load off." I bend my knees with a grunt and get ready to give her an alley-oop. "Remember, you hoped to die if I answered your question, so unless you wanna croak in the next few minutes, ya better put your foot back in my hands so I can boost you over this fence!"

But again, instead of doing what I need her to do, the kid goes toe-to-toe with me and says, "For your information, I *did* yell *sister* and *run* and *tree* and something else that is really, really, really—"

"That's great, even more terrific than Tom. Now—" I'm feeling so fed up that I might throw *myself* on the fence spears and commit Harry Cary the way the Japs do in the movies with Audie Murphy when the war isn't going their way. "God*damn*it all, Bird!"

She looks down her too-upturned nose at me like *I'm* the Finley sister who was born with a defective brain, then says with a sigh, "I'm so disappointed in you, Tessie. Knowing *everything* I yelled when I ran down the hill is so important to our investigation. A real detective would want to know that information so bad that they'd beat the truth out of me if they had to."

Don't tempt me, sister.

Q. Does Zorro have to deal with this kind of orneriness from his sidekick, Bernardo? Does Groucho have to take this kind of guff offa George Fenneman? How about Edward G. Robinson? Does he have to put up with back talk from Dirty Rat?

A. *My sources say no.*

All *I* want to do is get over this fence safely and see my Charlie and have our meeting and get up to church before confession ends and spend the rest of the day proving that Mr. McGinty is innocent of a kidnapping murder after we grill the other people on the QUESTION OR SURVEIL list, and all my sister is doing, as usual, is gumming up my well-thought-out plans!

I lose my temper and tell stubborn Birdie in a very snotty voice, "Go right ahead. Tell me *everything* you yelled when you were runnin' down the hill. Every teeny-tiny, itsy-bitsy word because we have all day to sit here and have a coffee clutch." I puff out my cheeks like Dinah at the diner. "How do ya take your joe, kid? One cream, twenty sugars?"

Birdie gives me one of her irresistible grins—she's got cherry bits stuck in her teeth—and says, "I yelled that we can't prove that Mister McGinty murdered *Sister* Margaret Mary, because—"

171

"I don't know what I'd do without you," I say, forcing myself to sound nicer than I feel, because even though I want to throttle her, from years of experience, I know that when it comes to getting her to do what I want her to do, I'll always catch more flies with sugar than vinegar. "Thanks so much for remindin' me that we need a motive to prove that he didn't do Sister M and M in."

"What's a motive?"

Oh, for godssakes.

"A motive is the *why* somebody would do a crime. Now, if you love me, I'm begging you—"

"I love you more than you will ever know, Tessie," Birdie says, so heartfelt. "And you're right. Knowing the *why* of the crime would be important to have in our murder case, but only if we had an even more important something."

Well, this is going about as well as the Scarecrow's search for a brain. (No joke.)

She's about to tell me something really dumb, but if I don't want to stand around in these scratchy bushes with her 'til the cows come home, I have to say, "Fine. What is the more important something we need in our murder case that we don't have?"

"A dead body."

See? Dumb with a capital D.

"We got a dead body!" I tell her. "The corpse of Sister Margaret Mary that I saw getting carted behind the mausoleum last night! Remember that?"

"And do *you* remember when you asked me to check for Charlie from the top of the hill that I told you I didn't see *him* near the weeping willow tree but that I saw somebody *else*?"

I don't care if she saw someone like a griever rushing to Mr. Peterman's funeral, so I fire back, "And do *you* remember that I don't got holes in my head the way you do? Of course I remember. My brain is a steel trap!"

"Then you better let what you caught in there out, because"—Birdie rocks back on her heels with the same pleased smile that Pyewacket the cat gets when she remembers that she's got nine lives and she can afford to play a little fast and loose—"the somebody else I saw was *Sister* Margaret Mary *run*ning past the weeping willow *tree!*"

"You . . . you . . . WHAT?"

Oh, no . . . no . . . no . . . please, God, no.

FACT: Seeing a dead nun running through the cemetery is very bad. *Very* Virginia Cunningham loony.

PROOF: My poor little sister has finally lost every single one of her marbles.

Could this really be the awful moment I've been dreading?

I've always pictured this kid with the screwed-up brain and messed-up memory who really loves Daddy and Louise and quiz shows and me and Charlie and candy and playing cards and cat's cradle and belly laughing at all my impressions and drifting away to parts unknown turning into a 100% raving loonatic on a dark and stormy night, not on a cornflower-blue-sky-as-far-as-you-can-see day. She's not even doing #11 on the LOONY list—drooling, when not asleep. And she hasn't murdered anyone, either, unless she did it during one of her wild streaks, so I can't cross #10 off, either.

We got to hurry back home and pick up our plaid running-away suitcase, and the second thing we got to do is hit the road to California ASAP! But before those chips can fall into place, I have to get Birdie to play along, so I tell her in the voice that I've practiced many, many times in the middle of the night to BE PREPARED for when this day would come, "You're safe with me, honey. Just come along quietly and nobody will get hurt."

When my sister throws back her head, I'm sure she's about to start raving crazy things the way a person would if they went from minor-league cracked to major-league cracked, but she surprises the heck out of me once again. Instead of letting loose of a loony-sounding, unhinged laugh like the movie gals who are locked up in padded cells make when it's their turn to get dragged down to the steaming hot baths, she does one of her regular old belly laughs.

"That's a very good impression of the head doctor in *The Snake Pit* movie, Tessie," Birdie says, "but I got news for you. *You're* the one that's gotta screw your head on straight. I *sister*-promise that Sister M and M is not dead. Now"—she slips her little foot into my cupped hands—"what say we climb this fence, have a quick meeting with Charlie, and then we'll all go up to church so you can confess to Father Ted in your Shirley Temple voice and question Kitten Jablonski to see what she can tell us about Sister's disappearance."

I don't know, ya know?

It must be the Indian summer heat getting to me, because just for a second, I swear I saw something so smart beaming out of Birdie's eyes that it made me doubt everything I ever thought about her, because never before have I heard her say so many smart things all at the same time.

Q. Could I have been wrong about her all these years? Maybe it's not the size of a kid's brain that makes them an egghead. Maybe a kid's heart can make them really smart, too?

A. *Ask again later.*

Naw, that'd be a waste of breath, because my sister gives me the answer to those questions when I crouch down even further to give her a better boost over the cemetery fence and say, "Ready for the old heave-ho?" and she licks my cheek and says, "Ready, Frank!"

16

A MATCH MADE IN HEAVEN

12:36 p.m. Well, that just goes to show ya once again how life can change on a dime. If you would've asked me a few minutes ago what the chances would be of my sister stumbling across *another* piece of evidence, I would've laughed and launched a loogie at you from the top of the cemetery fence.

FACT: Sister Margaret Mary is *not* dead.

PROOF: Normally I take everything that comes out of my Birdie's mouth with more grains of salt than a box of Morton's (Joke!) but she *sister*-promised that she saw the missing nun alive. (Obviously, it crossed my mind that what she saw was a zombie, which is a person who *is* dead, but still gets around. But Birdie told me that she saw our principal *run*ning near the willow tree and in every movie about zombies I've ever seen at the Tosa Theatre, they are a *very* slow-moving people.)

Of course, it's a huge relief to know now that Mr. McGinty isn't guilty of killing, but he isn't completely in the clear yet of performing *any* criminal activity. His initials are still on the St. Christopher medal I got in my front pocket, so even if he didn't murder M. M., I still might've seen him kidnapping her outta my window last night. For all we know, what Birdie witnessed at the willow tree was our principal escaping from J. M.'s shack this afternoon, where she was being held prisoner for ransom. That nun might at this very minute be back at the convent already dialing up the cops at the Washington St. station house to report that she got snatched by our friend and that they better arrest him ASAP, but she'll be shit outta luck in that department. According to the ton of gangster movies I've seen, kidnapping is known as a *federal* case and believe me, G-men are no laughing matter. They got worse senses of humor than my mother.

On the other hand . . . the ex–army sergeant who is always on high alert for intruders can be very fast on his feet, because he dodged all but one of the land mines he came across during the war. He would have no problem catching up with his escaped prisoner. Sister Margaret Mary could at this very minute be strapped with tidy but tighter knots to one of Mr. McGinty's folding chairs at his card table.

But on the other, other hand . . .

FACT: My brain feels like a beehive buzzing with a million *on the other hand*s and that's not the way a trained investigator should be feeling if they want to hunker down and solve THE CASE OF THE MISSING NUN WHO MIGHT BE KIDNAPPED ~~AND MURDERED~~ BUT NOT BY MR. MCGINTY.

PROOF: *Modern Detection* says, "An investigator should *always* remain clearheaded. During the course of an investigation, you must not falter or doubt yourself. You must stay firm in your convictions."

Easy for him to say.

I'm ashamed to admit that my mind is murky, and that I *am* faltering and doubting myself worse than Thomas, and I feel about as firm in my convictions as one of Gert Klement's triple chins. I'm the president, for godsakes, and I don't have a clue where I should lead The Mutual Admiration Society next, other than up to church so I can Shirley-confess and talk to my confidential informant, Kitten Jablonski, the way Birdie said we should after she performed ESP on me to learn my new plan. (Maybe her Indian vision is so good that she saw straight into my mind, because believe me, it'd be impossible for her to think up all those smart ideas all at the same time all by herself. After I tuck her in tonight, I'm gonna think of a number from one to ten and see if she can guess it, because her being able to mind read, well, as you can imagine, that would be a real moneymaker.)

Yes, if I'm being truthful with myself, our case has come apart on me. I have too many questions and not enough answers. The only something I'm feeling even a tiny bit good about at this point in the investigation is that there's a chance that The Mutual Admiration Society might strike blackmailing pay dirt *if* Sister Margaret Mary is still kidnapped and *if* we can find out who did it. As long as it's anybody but Mr. McGinty, we are in for such a windfall and I know exactly how I'm going to spend it, if we don't have to use it to pay for Greyhound bus tickets so we can run away.

SHOPPING SPREE

1. Stick some money in Louise's hiding place in the pantry behind the soup cans so she can pay the bill for the house that still smells like Daddy in its nooks and crannies.
2. Buy Birdie a lot of food.
3. Pick out bird-watching binoculars for Charlie at the pawn shop.
4. Pay for some advertising.
5. Order the X-ray glasses from the back of the Superman comic book.
6. Give deaf Jeffy Lanfre money to buy me some hearing aids at St. John's School for the Deaf.
7. Talk to Mr. Yerkovich and his best friend, Terry, at Bloomers about giving me a break on a lifetime supply of pink roses for Daddy's pretend grave.

Almost all of that list is written in blood, sweat, and tears, but I'm still working on my pro and con list for #4. If we're successful solving our current case, The Mutual Admiration Society has got to find a way to let everyone know what hotshots we are.

But if we pay for some advertising, I'm not sure if we should buy a billboard like Mr. Art Skank did or if dotting our front lawn with signs like the election ones his sister, Mrs. Nancy Tate, has got stuck in hers would do the trick. Either way, those advertisements would only mention our detecting abilities, because we can't broadcast the part of our business that charges to keep secrets secret. "The Mutual Admiration Society Is Our Name, Blackmailing Is Our Game" is a *very* catchy slogan, but that would be like that famous murderer and skinner coming up with—"Stop by Gein Upholstery Tonight after Midnight! Ask for Ed! Come Alone for a Life-Changing Deal!"

I adore them all, but #5 on my SPREE list is the one that curls my toes the most. I have been waiting *so* long to order a pair of those **X-RAY SPECS for $1.00** that they got in the back of Superman comic books— **Look at your friend. Is that really his body that you see under his clothes?** After we get our blackmailing payoff from whoever kidnapped Sister Margaret Mary, I plan to stick a buck in the envelope I borrowed from Mr. McGinty's desk and run to the mailbox faster than a speeding bullet! (Joke!) And on the day the package lands on our front porch, I'll rip it open with more power than a steaming locomotive! (Another one!) And after building inspector Mr. Hopkins figures out that it was nothing more than Beans and Wienies Wednesday that was causing it to reek so bad in the school basement, I'll show up the first day back with those cardboard specs in my navy-blue uniform pocket. And then I, Theresa "Tessie" Finley, blackmailer extraordinaire, will use those X-ray glasses to look through the Peter Pan blouses of the eighth-grade girls who stuff their boulder holders with socks every morning before they walk to school. Believe me, those boobie fakers will fork over their babysitting money so fast to keep me from announcing over the school's loudspeaker that they're *not* traffic-cone pointy under their white blouses, but flatter than Keefe Ave. The Mutual Admiration Society would make so much moola that we could laugh in the face of *The Millionaire* if he came knocking. This investigating business is turning out to be so much trickier than I thought it'd be, so boy, it'd feel good to pull off something I'm already great at, ya know? Something easy I can wrap my hands around. Something like fake boobies. (Somebody call the doctor, my joke department is having triplets!)

But for now, between being terrified that someone from the funeral might have seen my sister and the only reason they didn't shout, *Look at the top of the cemetery fence, everybody! It's one of the Finley ghouls!* is because they didn't want points taken off for rowdiness while they were participating in the "Best Mourner in the Parish" contest, and my worries that I'm not going to make it up to church in time to confess, but also knowing that I'm finally about to see my fiancé, when I part the bushes in his backyard, I feel like I'm being attacked from every direction.

Birdie is jacked up, too. My little live wire is squiggling, struggling to break out of the half nelson I got her locked in so she doesn't escape from these bushes and bolt toward my Charlie, which would scare the living poop outta him, because he, well, he is not the strong and silent type. Charlie is only the silent type. And he is not much to look at, either. If he rode past someone when he was delivering newspapers that person would never think, *Gosh, what a handsome kid.* Once they got a load of his head that all the ringworms ate the hair offa what they would probably think is, *That kid just reminded me that I haven't gotten up to Jerbak's Beer and Bowl to play a game of snooker in a while.* Charlie "Cue Ball" Garfield is also the runt of a family that is famous for rough-and-tumble sons who wrestle in state championship matches and win. But believe me, what my fiancé lacks on the top of his head and in his muscles, he more than makes up for in his heart and soul.

FACT: The two of us are one in a million. A match made in Heaven.

PROOF: I always thought since second grade when Charlie sat in the desk next to me that he was the cat's meow, but he didn't return the favor.

We didn't become engaged until a month ago, and I think I owe that good timing to my daddy and Charlie's mom, Frances "Franny" Garfield. To make both of their kids feel better about having to live without them, I strongly suspect that our passed-away parents got together to hatch a plan, because I don't care what the priests say about suicided people not going to Heaven. If her son can forgive his mother for committing the worst mortal sin then it doesn't make sense that the Son of God, whose job it is to be all-forgiving and all-loving, would send Mrs. Garfield to Hell for ending her life before He could. That's nothing but all-sour-grapes in my book.

The night Charlie showed up to throw pebbles at my bedroom window, I slid down the double-Dutch rope to ask him just what the heck did he think he was doing disturbing me in the middle of practicing my Miss America singing routine. "You are one of *m . . . m . . . my* favorite things," he told me. And when he picked up my hand and pressed it against his soft cheek, I'm not kidding, I felt the earth move under my feet and I'm pretty sure I heard heavenly harp music.

But whenever I try to bring up the evening when he put stars in my eyes *or* the afternoon he became a motherless child, Charlie changes the subject to his newest whittling project (funnily, he's been trying to sell cue sticks to Jerbak's Beer and Bowl) or he starts talking about birds, blackmails, TV shows (*Zorro* is his favorite, just like it is Birdie's), movies, and books (the Hardy Boys float his boat). Or he'll just start reciting how many times people do things, which is another hobby of his, statistically speaking. I don't know why he won't talk about the night he showed up under my bedroom window, but I'm pretty sure that he won't talk to me about his mom because his father, who is very ashamed of his wife for doing away with herself, has absolutely forbidden any of his sons to speak her name again. (When I think about what mean Mr. Garfield would do if he ever found out that The Mutual Admiration Society takes the #23 bus every Saturday afternoon to the Forest Home Cemetery so Charlie can bring his mom a bunch of yellow daisies because those were her favorite and she couldn't be laid to rest in Holy Cross on account of it being sacred ground because what she did is the worst sin for a Catholic to commit, I break out in a clammy sweat and have to gobble down four Tums.)

Yeah, before Mrs. Franny Garfield closed their garage door and started up their Pontiac, Charlie could've won a Most Popular Kid in the Parish contest, but my boy is nowhere near being that outgoing anymore, which is why I'm desperately working on loosening up his English stiff upper lip in more ways than one, if you get my drift.

Some other helpful hints on how to take care of the man of your dreams in the *Good Housekeeping* article called "Secrets of a Happy Marriage" were: "A dry martini can work wonders" and "Be a good listener." Not to toot my own horn or nothin', but I'm pretty good at both of those things. Daddy taught me how to mix all sorts of drinks for customers when him and Suzie LaPelt would have to go to the back room together for the longest time to fetch more bottles of booze and peanuts. I got plenty of experience sliding drinks down Lonnigan's long mahogany bar, and over the years, I learned how booze of any kind can turn even the quietest people into real chatterboxes.

I figured what do I have to lose, so I offered to shake a dry martini up for Charlie after The Mutual Admiration Society had finished up one of our spy missions a few weeks ago. When we were putting away our TOOLS OF THE TRADE, I pointed to the bottles of vodka and vermouth I took out of our kitchen cabinet and stowed away in our garage and said, "Would you like a dry martini tonight, dear? They can really work wonders." He smiled and said, "Thanks, but no thanks," and then he nodded down at our Radio Flyer. "I'm on the wagon." (He can be a pretty funny sad kid sometimes.)

So for now, all I can do is grin and bear his silent treatment, which seems to be par for the course of love. According to the same *Good Housekeeping* magazine article, there are no matchups, not even the ones made in Heaven, that are not without "a few wrinkles that a wife will need to iron out after the honeymoon."

FACT: One of the other bones I got to pick with Charlie is that I'm not sure how good a breadwinner he will be.

PROOF: If he wants to be a first-rate private detective who holds up his end of our family business, he needs to keep his eyes peeled and BE PREPARED at all times, which he isn't.

Through the branches of his backyard bushes, I can see him studying the wild blue yonder along with Pyewacket, when what my fiancé *should* be doing is noticing me wrestling my sister around in the bushes. Of course, I could be mad, but as half owner of the Siamese and Charlie, I can't help it. It does my heart good to see them spending time together doing their shared bird-watching hobby. Pye is snugged-up in his lap, pretending to lick away at a huge, horrible burr in her fur, but I know that's a ruse. Because Daddy always said, "You can't kid a kidder," I know that she's really on the hunt. I haven't made up my mind yet to love her, but I *do* greatly admire this cat from the Orient for the way she moves so stealthily and her picky taste in people, but I am most impressed by her power to force me to give her windmill cookie crumbs with those spooky blue eyes of hers. (Knowing how to hypnotize people like that doctor in the *I Was a Teenage Werewolf* movie? That'd be so cool, daddy-o, cool. I'd make my sister listen to me at *all* times and I'd force Charlie to bare his soul to me, and if I could stand looking into Gert's face for a few minutes I'd make her hand over her hearing aids, and one morning at the breakfast table, I'd say, *Look into my eyes . . . look into my eyes, Louise Mary Fitzgerald Finley. When I snap my fingers, you will wake up and love Birdie and me as much as you did before Daddy died.*)

"Let go of me, Tessie!" Birdie says, strangled-sounding, when she's trying to worm out of the half nelson I got her in that has now become a quarter nelson. Because she's so damn strong and slick from the heat, and when she wants to see my fiancé, she *really* does, with one more wiggle and a twist, she slips out of my arms.

12:41 p.m. Watchful Pyewacket—she has staying on guard at all times in common with her other half owner, Mr. McGinty—immediately spots Birdie barreling toward the Garfields' back porch, so she hops off Charlie's lap and streaks past me on the way back to the caretaker's shack, but my future better half isn't so lucky.

"Knock it off, Bird," I say when I reach the two of them just in time to slap my hand over her mouth so she doesn't juicy smooch Charlie's cheek again, which he doesn't seem to mind sometimes, but this is not one of those times. His peepers are close in color to Birdie's and my birthstone, a light green, and the left one twitches like crazy when he's worked up about something, which makes it look like he's winking at me over and over and that's so adorable, I can't barely take it. I want to shout from the roof of his house, *I love you to death, Charlie "Cue Ball" Garfield and I can't hardly wait until the day we're standing at the altar together, even if you are the most wrinkly kid I know next to Birdie!* But I'm not sure how he'd take that, so I just peel my sister offa him, flip her into the deep leaf pile next to the porch, and tug my ninety-eight-pound weakling back up again.

"You okay?" I ask him.

He shakes his head, wipes off his slobbered cheek with the back of his hand, and tells me "M . . . M . . . Missus Klement told m . . . m . . . my dad this m . . . m . . . morning that Sister M . . . M . . . Margaret M . . . M . . . Mary went m . . . m . . . missing last night," Charlie struggles to say. Most of the time he talks like everybody else, but when he gets *really* upset, he starts talking with this cute little *m* stutter. (This is just a theory of mine that has not been proven, but I think the reason Charlie's tongue gets so twisted up on *m* words when he gets worked up is because that's the letter *m*om starts with.) "Ya know anything about that, Tessie?"

FACT: The famous saying "The course of true love is full of potholes," is so true.

PROOF: I'm having now what is known as mixed feelings. Because we both love Birdie, I thought Charlie and me had hating our principal in common, so I'm disappointed that he's got himself riled up about her disappearance. But at the same time, I'm feeling this rush of gushy love for him warming up my whole body and dang, I'm desiring very much to stick my finger in that dent in his chin and wiggle it around a little.

"Yeah, I know that Sister went missing and . . . and a whole lot more," I tell him, "but . . ." I'm saved from veering into a love spat by the clang . . . clang . . . clanging of St. Kate's church bells informing the neighborhood that it's 12:45 p.m. "I don't have time now to explain it all. I'll fill you in on our way to—"

"The train station," he says.

"The . . . the . . . WHAT?"

"Tell me the truth, Tessie." My fiancé looks over at Birdie like he doesn't want her to hear what he has to say, which he doesn't have to worry about. She's sitting in the middle of the red and gold leaves next to the porch that Charlie must've been raking before he started staring up at the sky, happily goofing around with her cat's cradle string and coming up with some newfangled pattern I've never seen before. "Did your not showing up for the m . . . m . . . meetin' under the weeping willow have something to do with Sister M . . . M . . . Margaret M . . . M . . . Mary disappearing?" Charlie says softly, because he hardly ever uses a loud, angry voice. His father does enough of that for the whole family. Birdie and me can hear Mr. Garfield going at his boys late at night, and it takes all I got not to jump out of bed, run over there, and give him a piece of my mind. "Ya didn't do something ya weren't supposed to, did ya?" Charlie's left eye is doing an impression of a Mexican jumping bean, and if he *had* hair, he would be raking his beautiful fingers through it. "If ya finally *did* do one of the terrible things to Sister M and M that you been promisin' to do . . ." He squats down, slides a wad of damp-looking dollar bills out of the side of his hightop black sneakers and presses it into my hand. "I grabbed our treasury m . . . m . . . money outta the tree hole just in case the Finley sisters had to m . . . m . . . make a break for it."

Oh, Charlie, my Charlie.

See why I can't help but adore him, wrinkles and all?

This boy . . . he *always* thinks the best of m . . . m . . . me.

184

17

STATISTICALLY SPEAKING

'Cause the three of us have lived in this neighborhood our whole lives, The Mutual Admiration Society knows all the best shortcuts.

We didn't have time for even a short meeting of the minds on Charlie's back porch, so when we're racing down the alley that'll take us the fastest way to church—Charlie is holding one of Birdie's hands and I got hold of the other to keep her from gallivanting into Mr. Holland's yard to grab ripe apples off his tree—I announce, "I hereby call The Mutual Admiration Society to order," and give Charlie the *Reader's Digest* version of THE CASE OF THE MISSING NUN WHO MIGHT BE KIDNAPPED ~~AND MURDERED~~ BUT NOT BY MR. MCGINTY as we bust through the crooked white gate in the Baxters' backyard, duck under the wash that's hanging on the Muldoons' clothesline, hop the rickety fence in the Winners' side yard, and run across 68th St. to our final destination—St. Kate's.

When we come to a stop at the bottom of the steps, Charlie grabs a hold of the metal railing and pants out, "I'm really glad that Birdie saw Sister Margaret Mary near the weeping willow, because that means Mister McGinty didn't murder her and neither did you, Tessie."

"Yeah, but just 'cause we know now that Sister Margaret Mary isn't dead, that doesn't mean—"

Wait just a cotton-pickin' minute.

What in the hell kind of cruddy president am I?

This is a *huge* something to miss that could really affect our bottom line!

"Maybe I saw some *other* person getting murdered in Holy Cross last night!" I shout as we climb the steps toward the big church doors.

"Ummm . . ." Charlie says, "please don't take this the wrong way, Tessie, but you do have a tendency to . . . ahhh . . ."

"Lie?"

"That's true, but what I was gonna say is that maybe your facts are right about what you heard and saw out your window last night, but you mighta just added them up wrong. Like that time you saw your mother drop something into your applesauce at the fish fry and you were so sure that it was curare or . . . or how about the night we were spyin' on Mister Johnson doing some stuffing in his basement and you immediately went positive that he was working on the head of a man with a thick tan beard."

"But . . ."

Okay, fine. It might've been a little too far-fetched to think that Louise dropped curare into my applesauce instead of mixing in that disgusting crushed-up iron pill that she's always trying to force down my throat, but I'd just seen a Sherlock Holmes movie at the Tosa Theatre where that deadly poison was a real problem for him and Watson. And I really resent Charlie bringing up that spying night over at Mr. Johnson's house. Didn't I right away admit that I might've jumped the gun when the Lutheran taxidermist reached for his beer and I could see by the light on his work table that the head he was working on really belonged to a deer and not a man with a thick tan beard? (We might not have caught him doing something bad that night, but I *still* think he's stuffing things he isn't supposed to in his basement.)

"But if I didn't see or hear somebody getting murdered," I say to Charlie in more of a henpecked way than a future wife maybe should, because if he thinks I am going to marry him if he keeps pulling the rug out from under me like this, he's got another think coming, "then what do *you* think I saw and heard last night?"

"The Gilgood mausoleum is near the necking tree," he says, like he has given this a lot of thought.

"Roger that, Charlie," Birdie nods and tells him with one of her irresistible smiles.

"So what you might've witnessed, Tessie, was two greasers having a screaming m . . . m . . . match about how many bases they should run and when the girl wouldn't do what the boy wanted her to do he punched her in the face and . . . and that's why she screamed and her body went limp, and then he took her back behind the m . . . m . . . mausoleum to kick her when she was down."

He knows a lot about what goes on under the necking tree because his four older brothers, when they aren't wrestling boys, wrestle with girls beneath its branches and they have no problem bragging about who they pinned. And even though his father is not a Golden Gloves champ, the reason Charlie started nervous stuttering is because he knows almost as much as I do about punching and knocking people out. His father used to do that to his mother. Mrs. Garfield couldn't hide those purple bruises under her eyes at Mass on Sunday no matter how much Pan-Cake makeup she piled on.

But even though what Charlie said *could've* happened last night, because those greasers do have hot-to-trotting and fighting as their two main hobbies, I'm not even close to being sold on that idea. So when my sister bats her slightly bulging eyes at him and says, like she thinks his idea is the best idea she's heard of since the invention of peanut butter and marshmallow on Wonder bread, "Charlie, that's such smart thinking!" I'm starting to feel like the odd man out around here, and like maybe I need to spend some time refreshing my sister's memory about which of us Charlie is engaged to.

My fiancé stops climbing and says to Birdie, "Thank you for the vote of confidence," but then he turns and says to me, "I really hate to break it to ya, 'cause I know how m . . . m . . . much you're counting on this now since she wasn't m . . . m . . . murdered, but . . ." Whatever he's about to tell me, isn't going to be good. "Sister M . . . M . . . Margaret M . . . M . . . Mary getting kidnapped by M . . . M . . . Mister Mc . . . Mc . . . McGinty or anybody else is very far-fetched."

That's such an awful thing for him to say that I'm too shocked at first to form words to argue with him, and if Birdie opens her mouth to agree with him one more time, I don't care if she *is* a featherweight, I'm going to smack her clean off this step!

FACT: The Finley sisters were in the cemetery all morning, so we've been out of touch, or what *Modern Detection* calls "*incommunicado*." You wouldn't believe what can go on in this neighborhood in a couple of hours. Babies get born every five seconds, Mr. Skank gets a new customer on his table, some kid breaks another kid's nose and sends him to the hospital, fires get set, windows broken, the gals have gab sessions over their backyard fences and hang out some other poor gal to dry.

PROOF: I'm getting a very bad feeling in my guts that Charlie is getting ready to tell me something he heard about our principal's disappearance that I don't want to hear.

Reaching into my pocket, I make a wish on Daddy's holy lucky Swiss Army Knife before I choke out the question Charlie better say no to, if he knows what's good for him, "Sister hasn't turned up, has she?"

"Not that I heard, but . . ."

O, thank you, St. Jude, patron saint of lost objects and persons, for sleeping on the job!

"What I mean is that when *I* heard Missus Klement tell my dad that Sister M and M had disappeared," Charlie explains as the three of us go back to hiking up the rest of the church steps, "I got some ideas about what mighta happened to her and kidnapping wasn't one of them. *Statistically speaking*, somebody getting snatched for ransom happens about as often as a triple play."

Charlie is on rock-solid ground now. Just like undertaking Mr. Art Skank, he knows a lot about Braves baseball and who swings and misses and how many bases get stolen and how often the Green Bay Packers win or lose, and it's not only sports he keeps track of. My fiancé marks down what flowers are the most popular at the cemetery, what people's favorite colors are, who dies from what disease or accident, which Masses get the biggest crowds, how many and what kinds of birds he sees, and I guess how often nuns get kidnapped. (He's never said, but I bet he even keeps track of how many mothers do away with themselves and how many times their sweet boys are the ones who find them in their garages.)

This constant recording of things is *not* one of Charlie's better qualities. This is one of his wrinkles I will have to iron out after our honeymoon in Wisconsin Dells. He's too black-and-white, too much like Joe "Just the facts, ma'am" Friday. I'd like him to spend less time noticing how often things *do* happen and more time thinking about what *could've* happened, because being able to picture a crime in your mind is a very important part of being a gumshoe, according to *Modern Detection*. "The ability to envision possible scenarios that may have unfolded during the commission of a crime is an essential skill an investigator must endeavor to achieve."

So with the words of famous Mr. Lynwood "My friends call me Woody and my enemies call me their worst nightmare" Bellflower still ringing in my ears, and because the "Secrets of a Happy Marriage" article said that even if a wife completely disagrees with their husband, sometimes it's better to pretend that you don't because that can cause fur to fly, I say to Charlie, "If you're so sure Sister Margaret Mary *wasn't* kidnapped, what other possible scenarios do *you* think unfolded to make her disappear?"

"*You* coulda unfolded on her, for one thing," he says adorably. "And accidents are always a major cause of missing persons. Maybe Sister went down to check the hole that Two-Ton Thomkins made in the basement steps and she fell in and nobody found her yet, the same way Timmy Martin is always falling into abandoned wells and doesn't get rescued until Lassie shows up. Or maybe Sister's disappearing wasn't an accident at all. She coulda done something on purpose."

"Like what, Charlie?" a practically drooling-all-over him Birdie asks.

"Well, she coulda run off to get married like that priest at Mother of Good Hope did, or maybe she quit her job like that gal in *The Nun's Story* did."

Well, isn't he just a little statistically speaking black cloud raining all over my private-dick parade.

But facts are facts, no matter how much I don't want to face them and my down-to-earth future husband might be on to something here. I was so sure that our principal had been murdered last night in the cemetery and according to my sister, I was wrong about *that*, so I guess Sister M & M might not have been kidnapped, either, and admitting that to myself has got my tummy more knotted up than the Boy Scout handbook. (No joke.)

What about my shopping spree?

All my BE PREPARED plans?

How about my idea to stuff our running-away jar so full of blackmail or reward greenbacks that if Gert Klement convinces Louise to send Birdie and me to our "homes" that we'll be able to run away in style to live in California and . . .

Wait just a cotton-pickin' minute.

Who's in charge around here?!

I put my foot down and tell Charlie, "You *could* be right that something else happened to Sister Margaret Mary besides Mister McGinty or anybody else kidnapping her, but then what about the Saint Christopher medal Birdie found in the leaf pile with their initials on it? How does that figure into all this?"

Charlie shrugs—he really loves to shrug—and says, "Ya got me."

You better believe I do, my match made in Heaven. Until death do us part, I want to say, but I'm not sure how he'd take that, so instead I clear my throat and tell him more businesslike, "As president of The Mutual Admiration Society, I hereby declare that we'll keep investigating Sister's disappearance like she *has* been kidnapped until we find evidence that proves she wasn't."

"Roger that, Tessie," Birdie says, and when Charlie pulls open one of the church's doors, he must be on board, too, because when he ushers the Finley sisters into St. Kate's, he bows his head and tells me, "Your wish is my command," and ya know what? If I didn't have serious detecting and confessing to do, I would very much like to pucker up and take him up on that offer.

18

DARING

There are times when I step inside our church that I can't help but fall down to my knees. Not in prayer, of course. I am not impressed with most of the malarkey the nuns and priests try to peddle us. You'd have to be as dumb as Birdie to fall for most of those tall tales the employees of God tell us during catechism class and Sunday sermons.

Take Noah and the Ark. All you have to do is spend an afternoon at the Washington Park Zoo to know how much animals poop and are at each other tooth and nail. Noah and his family would have to jump overboard because they couldn't stand the smell on that boat for forty days and nights *and* those wild animals would devour each other the second they had a chance, including the dove that showed up with the olive branch in its beak, it wouldn't have escaped the snarling jaws of death, either.

FACT: The Almighty could've saved Daddy from drowning or bestowed upon me a swimming miracle, so our on-again, off-again relationship spends a lot of time in the off position.

PROOF: I only pray because I need to keep all my bases covered and I only go to church to keep Louise from heckling me. But my soul? I think it must really like the beautiful interior decoration job that was done on St. Kate's, because like it or not, the place can make me feel like I'm having one of those holy times. Like the ones I have every so often when I'm at the cemetery pond and everything feels right with my world again for a minute or two.

The church smells of incense and floor polish this morning the way it always does, which is nice, but it's the way the sun is passing through the stained glass that's my favorite part. Especially the way it's slanting into the window that belongs to St. Joan of Arc. I admire that she was a fighter, but I can't help but wonder if being a French slut like Suzie LaPelt is why that kid *really* got turned into French toast, because I'm 100% positive Louise and the other gals in the parish wouldn't mind throwing Daddy's barmaid into a bonfire, either.

The rest of St. Kate's is also easy on the eyes. Very la-di-da luxurious. The main altar that's watched over by Jesus hanging on the cross is dripping with gold, there's a fancy carved wooden stand made out of some kind of special blessed wood where the priests try to scare us into being better Catholics, and the Communion railing is made of real marbles. The main altar is where the Tabernacle sits—the rumpus room for the white wafers the priests pass out that are the "alleged" body of Jesus. (Even though we're warned not to, I've chewed up a Communion wafer and it was boneless.)

On either side of the big altar, there are two much smaller ones that are not as lush but still quite nice. The one on the right belongs to the Virgin Mary. I can see that there's no mustache above her chipped pink lip anymore so it must've got scrubbed off this morning by the gal who is taking our friend and church cleaner, Gracie Carver's, place while she's in Mississippi nursing her sister back to health.

On the altar to the left, there's a statue of Charlie's and Birdie's all-time favorite saint. The same way our pal Mr. McGinty is *very* devoted to St. Christopher, the patron saint of travelers? That's how gaga those two go over St. Francis. Charlie adores him for two reasons. Frances was his mother's name and that saint also liked birds the same way my fiancé does. And, of course, that means my animal-loving sister also goes nuts for that olden-days holy man who has three cute sparrows sitting on his shoulders with little cocked heads like Birdie gets when she's hearing something nobody else can.

After The Mutual Admiration Society gets done dipping our fingers into the Holy Water font and crossing ourselves—Birdie splashes some on her face, too, she always does—and once my eyes adjust to the dimness inside the church, I easily spot who I'm searching for. Lighthouse-tall Kitten Jablonski towers above all the other kids waiting in the confession line, the ones who *always* show up at the last minute on Confession Thursday.

Charlie tells me when I complain to him about the stiff penances Father Ted doles out to me, "According to my most recent survey, when Father starts hearing confessions, the largest penance he doles out is three Hail Marys, but once the church bells clang twelve thirty, he switches over to the Stations of the Cross."

He's probably right about that, because not only does Charlie keep track of what he *observes* happening in the neighborhood and in movies and the sports page, etc., another hobby of his is going around the neighborhood with a clipboard and questioning people. He'll ask what cereal someone ate for breakfast or what television shows they like, their favorite colors, and whatnot. Charlie bugging kids like this is enough to make them say, "Ya writin' a book or something? Buzz off, Cue Ball." But to me? This is a lot like sweating the truth out of someone, so it might turn out to be a real plus in our family detecting business.

So, I'm going to consider confessing to Father Ted earlier from now on, because he *does* go very crabby and very thirsty for his Jameson's whiskey at half past noon and who can blame him?

I'd be raring to throw back a stiff one, too, if I had to sit around in a box that's hardly bigger than a coffin for two hours straight while every sweaty and farty kid in the parish files in to tell him their list of sins. Having to listen to what unholy screwups we all are week after week has *got* to make that priest feel like he's falling down on the job, which is probably why he drinks so much.

After I check Daddy's Timex, I tell the boy I'll be blissfully wedded to someday, "I only got nine minutes left. Give me the rest of the money ya took out of the willow and take Birdie over to St. Francis and trim her bangs, and whatever you do, I'm warning you, batten down your hatches, dear. Our little dreamboat has been a very slippery character all morning."

Soon as Charlie digs the last of our treasury bills out of his black hightop and says, "Good luck with Father Ted and getting the skinny offa Kitten," I take off toward the confessional on the other side of the church that the rest of the bad kids are standing outside of, including the worst of the worst, the delinquent who I wanted to see *least* of all today, the kid who's got me at #1 on his WANTED DEAD OR ALIVE list—Butch Seeback. It is my general policy to avoid him at all costs, but there is no getting around him this time. (Standing next to Kitten the way he is, Butch looks like a bowling ball about to knock down a pin.)

Moving within smacking distance of that maniac is not on my TO-DO list, so believe me, instead of weaving through these pews, I'd much rather turn tail and hide under our back porch, which I'd happily do *if* I hadn't already spotted #5 on my SHIT LIST, Jenny Radtke. The little brownnoser has probably spent the whole morning saying rosaries that I wouldn't show up so she could report me to Louise. She's sitting right across from the confession box with that sickeningly sweet smile she's always got glued on her face. As usual, her perfect blond pageboy that I plan to someday hack off with the dullest blade of Daddy's Swiss Army Knife after I slip a mickey into her punch during a sock hop is

Breck-shampoo perfect, and the spelling bee medal that once belonged to me and I vow will again, is hanging from her neck. She's fingering the prize, flaunting it in my face, when I slide through the pew in front of her on my way to the sinner's line and what I wouldn't give to flatten her already flat face even further.

And besides that little rat fink Radtke tattling to my mother, the other important reason I gotta stick around, like it or not, is because I have a presidential duty to uphold. If The Mutual Admiration Society is going to have any chance at all of figuring out just what the heck happened to our principal so we can clear Mr. McGinty's name, I can't lose what might be my only chance in the near future to talk to the #1 most up-to-the-minute, in-the-know kid in the neighborhood.

FACT: Looks like Kitten Jablonski and Butch Seeback have become an item.

PROOF: She's letting him snap her bra strap.

My confidential source and one of my worst enemies becoming a couple is enough to turn my stomach inside out and hang it out to dry, but it's not that big of a shock that Kitten thinks Butch is hot stuff. When her and me and Birdie go to the movies together some Saturdays, Kitten always roots for the gunslingers in the black hats and the monsters in the creature features.

FACT: Butch and Kitten are living proof of the famous saying "Love is blind."

PROOF: Love is probably also deaf, because that's the only explanation I can come up with for someone as on the ball as Kitten wanting to swap spit with a kid who looks like the bank vault at the First Wisconsin Bank but sounds like Lamb Chop on the *Captain Kangaroo* show.

When my confidential informant spots me hustling toward her, she shoves Freddie Beaudry out of the line of a dozen kids waiting to confess and waves me over. Not out of the goodness of her heart, mind you. Kitten is a very tough cookie who really isn't known for that. She is a smooth operator—her snitches report to her day and night—who never does nothin' or says nothin' for nothin'. There is *always* a price.

When I land at the spot she cleared out for me, Kitten says outta the side of her mouth *very* fast, like always, because time is money, "Cuttin' it pretty close today, Finley. What's shakin'?"

"I been busy all morning trying to find out what happened to Sister Margaret Mary," I say. "What'd ya hear?"

When she puts her hand out, I place two bucks in it—one for giving me skips and one for whatever she's about to tell me. "I know what you're thinkin', but Butch didn't have nothin' to do with it," Kitten says with her grin that always makes me miss July, because her teeth are so yellow and crooked that they remind me of the ears of corn that Louise won't buy at the Red Owl. "He was with me all night."

That's sickening, but not breaking news, because I already drew a line through Butch's name on my QUESTION OR SURVEIL list, but I'm not going to ask her for my money back, because she wouldn't give it to me.

"Tell ya what I'm gonna do." Kitten must be in a really good mood, because she has what *every* girl in this neighborhood wants, a steady boyfriend, even if he is repulsive, 'cause she tells me *much* more charitably than she usually would, "Gimme three more bucks and I'll give ya a big fat hint about Sister Margaret Mary's disappearance." After I happily hand over the cash, she makes a big show of sticking the bills down the front of her shirt, because she's one of the few eighth-grade girls who *doesn't* have to stuff socks into her bra every morning. "This morning, Sister Prudence found a note in Sister Margaret Mary's cell that told—"

"A note?!" This is such great news that if I was Birdie, I would do the *woo . . . woo . . . woo* Indian celebration dance right down the main aisle of church. Charlie was wrong and I was right! Sister *was* kidnapped just the way I thought she was!

FACT: Whoever snatched our principal *wasn't* Mr. McGinty.

PROOF: It just dawned on me that thinking this whole time that he was the guy who coulda kidnapped her was really, really, really, really stupid. Nobody goes around taking people just for the hell of it, they do it for the money, and our godfather is the last person in the neighborhood who needs bucks, so all is not lost! The Mutual Admiration Society could still find the much poorer guilty party and earn a reward from the cops or figure out some way to blackmail him, and what a feather in our detecting cap that would be!

I excitedly ask Kitten, "How much dough did the kidnapper tell the sisters he wants in the ransom note?"

She looks confused and says, "The *who*? The *what*?"

Because she's so tall, I figure she must not of heard me, so I stand up on my toes to repeat myself. I paid for this confidential information with hard-earned blackmail money and I don't want to share it with every other bad kid standing in this confession line, so I whisper close to her face, "The kidnapper," which goes to show how thrilled I am at this recent turn of events, because that's a very risky thing to do, considering her leprosy pimples and my future as a Miss America contestant. "How much ransom money does he want to return Sister Margaret Mary to the nunnery?"

Kitten snaps her head back and says, "What's wrong with you? Ya got the delirious flu or something, Finley? I didn't say nothin' about a kidnapping or ransom money."

"But . . . but . . . you just said Sister Prudence found a note and I . . . I . . ."

Damnation!

I assumed again.

If Kitten's information is correct—and I have no reason at all to doubt a kid that I've admired since kindergarten when she flicked a booger into Sister Jane's carton of milk and blamed it on Jenny Radtke—The Mutual Admiration Society is back to square one: THE

CASE OF THE MISSING NUN ~~WHO MIGHT BE KIDNAPPED AND MURDERED BUT NOT BY MR. MCGINTY~~.

I could kick myself *and* that lying Magic 8 Ball all the way down Keefe Ave.!

This hasn't been a life-changing day at all. This has been a life-wasting day. I could've been doing so many more useful things all morning, like . . . like spying on Skip Abernathy to see if it's him who stole over $200 out of the Pagan Baby collection box or I could have spent some time thinking up an advertising slogan for Louise's treasury election or taken a bath and practiced my swimming or worked on any of the other more useful numbers on my TO-DO list.

I have suffered such a blow that I desperately ask Kitten without thinking, "Are you *sure* Sister hasn't been kidnapped?"

Uh-oh.

That was a big mistake.

Kitten's got the business slogan "Satisfaction guaranteed," but if you ever *doubt* her information? Believe me, the only guarantee you're gonna get is that she'll give you the *worst* Indian burn you ever had in your life. I'm not kidding, Cochise would be jealous. (No joke.)

She's already put her hands into a grasping, twisting position. "Ya ain't doubting my information, are ya, Finley?"

I don't think she meant for Butch to hear that, but he did, because he belts out in his high-pitched lamb voice, "Ya hear that, everybody? The Finley snot just doubted Kitten's information!"

All of a sudden the kids that were ratting their hair and cracking their gum and making out in the confession line freeze in place, and even Mrs. Cumberland, who was practicing the organ in the choir loft, quits playing "Holy, Holy, Holy" in the middle of the chorus.

Of course, I didn't mean to ask Kitten if she was *sure* she knew what's going on in the neighborhood. It just slipped out. But doubting her information like that? Especially in front of all these kids? That was . . . that was like asking Mr. Skank if he knows how to embalm a body or . . . or asking Mr. Yerkovich at Bloomers flowers if he knows how to arrange a wedding bouquet or asking Mr. McGinty if he knows how to dig a proper grave. Those are their "bottom lines" and Butch is making it sound like I just crossed Kitten's!

I peek over to where I left my troop of two to see if they noticed how quiet it's gotten, and how I could really use some help, but it looks like I can't count on them to come to my rescue. Charlie's back is turned, and he's busy doing exactly what I asked him to do. He's got out his whittling knife and his determined look and is trimming Birdie's too-long bangs the way she likes them as they chatter away to one another, probably about what a great saint Francis is or something else dumb.

I have taken a long walk off a very, very, very, very short pier. And I'm positive that groveling is not going to get me out of the fix I'm in, but I give it a shot and try to tell Kitten anyway, "I . . . I didn't mean to doubt . . . I'm sorry."

If it was just the two of us standing here getting ready to confess, I'm pretty sure she'd just punch me in the arm and say, *Don't let it happen again, Finley,* because she knows how highly I regard her and I have never, not once, over all these years questioned how good she is at her job. But with all the greasers hanging on her every word and her new boyfriend egging everybody on, she's got no choice. She has to think of her reputation.

Kitten leans down, grabs my left wrist, and twists the ever-lovin' hell out of it, and fine, I guess I deserved that. But then, I don't know, ya know? Maybe she's showing off for Butch or maybe it's just that "time of the month" the eighth-grade girls talk about at recess or maybe I hurt her feelings or something, but Kitten grins with her corn teeth and says loud enough for all the greasers in the confession line to hear, "Finley here"—she hard-noogies the top of my head with her bony knuckles—"I guess she knows better than me and doesn't need my information." There's lots of laughing and booing and cat-calling from the crowd. "Sooo . . . go ahead, kid. Show us what ya got. Find out on your own what happened to Sister Margaret Mary." My wrist is burning and now I got a headache and I think I might toss my cookies, because I can tell that Kitten's not done humiliating me for doubting her by the look on her pimply face—I've seen this look many, many times over the years. She's about to growl out the dreaded life-changing challenge that no kid in the neighborhood *ever* wants to hear, "I dare ya."

That's when Mrs. Cumberland goes back to playing "Holy, Holy, Holy" on the organ, and the greasers go back to snapping their Black Jack gum, and Butch Seeback starts bleating, and brownnosing Jenny Radtke hyena-giggles because a dare is a *very* big deal around here. Especially one that comes out of Kitten Jablonski's mouth. She's dared kids to stay overnight in the abandoned haunted house on 70th St. where a murder took place or jump offa the roof of school or steal real gold St. Christopher medals off of gravestones when jumpy and armed Mr. McGinty is just a few yards away or slam back so many potato pancakes that they throw up on one of the nuns on Fish Fry Friday.

Now that I know that Sister Margaret Mary is *not* dead and *not* been kidnapped, that means that the only mystery The Mutual Admiration Society has left to solve is finding her, which I really, really, really, really don't want to do. For Birdie's sake, wherever our overly strict principal she is, I hope she stays there forever. But because of Kitten's dare, I really don't have any choice in the matter now, do I. Her legion of snitches will be spying on me from every street corner and alley and from behind every tree and garage in the neighborhood for the next three days, and if I don't look like I'm at least trying to find out what happened to our missing principal, those snitches will report back to her and I'll be so far up shit creek without a paddle that it won't be funny.

It's one thing to *try* and *fail* at a dare—razzing for a month or so, some sittings on the bubbler, gum in my hair, etc.—but if a kid doesn't give it her best shot, well. If Birdie and me don't end up running away, I'll never be able to leave the house or walk down the halls at school or the aisles of church or anywhere else in the neighborhood without some kid clucking and calling me a yellow-bellied chicken shit or throwing an egg at me. They inflicted so much cruel and unusual punishment on Mary Olson when she ignored one of Kitten's dares that her family had to move out of the parish. To another state.

So before I disappear through the red velvet confessional curtain to tell Father Ted my sins, I do what I gotta do. Trying to hold back my tears, I look up to Kitten and croak out, "I accept your dare," and then I spit in my hand and she does the same, and when we shake on it, my fate has been sealed.

19

CLOUD NINE

Maybe as a reward for letting Father Ted get out of the black box and over to his favorite barstool at Lonnigan's faster, and for not farting, he goes easy on me for a change. After I get done telling him a short list of some of my real sins that aren't that bad—being mean to my sister, not saying my prayers, only half following the Fourth Commandment to honor my father *and* my mother—he absolves me with the Latin forgiveness words and assigns me my penance. "Say three Hail Marys, Shirley," he tells me from behind the black curtain. "Send the Jablonski kid in, and tell the rest of those delinquents to say the Stations of the Cross," and then he slams the window shut in a *very* thirsty way.

I don't want to do what Father told me to do, but to keep my soul from getting any filthier than it already is, when I come back through the red velvet curtain, I dutifully tell Kitten, "You're up," and then I give his instructions to the kids still in line.

Of course, there's a rumble of grumbling and swearing, even though these greasers wouldn't dream of sticking around to say the Stations. They're only here today, same as me, because their mothers are probably paying Jenny Radtke a quarter to snitch on them, too. They'll hang around long enough until that blond rat with the spelling medal that is rightfully mine leaves, and then they'll all head up to the Milky Way Drive-In for a lunch of out-of-this-world burgers and to gun their engines and ogle girls and smear ketchup on one another and play mumblety-peg with their switchblades.

After Kitten enters the confessional, without her to stand between us, I can tell by the sneer on his face that Butch Seeback is itching to take a shot at me. I try to run, but in my weakened state, I don't get very far before the missal he took out of a pew hits a bull's-eye on the back of my head and almost sends me sprawling in the main aisle.

"Hey, Trigger, why the long face?" Charlie cracks as I squeeze into the pew between him and Birdie. "Did Butch threaten to rearrange your mouth to the back of your head again, or didn't Kitten have any good information?"

"You could say that." I rub the part of my head that got hit by Seeback's missal missile, tell my fiancé that my sister's bangs look very nice, and then I ask him to hold on for a second because I need to get my wits about me and update my most important list while everything is still fresh in my mind, or before I develop a case of amnesia from the noogie Kitten gave me and the smack on the back of the head that her new boyfriend treated me to.

TO-DO

1. Take tender loving care of Birdie.
2. ~~Solve whatever happened to Sister Margaret Mary for big blackmail or reward bucks.~~
2. ~~Hope that we don't find out *why* Mr. McGinty kidnapped and murdered Sister M & M and concentrate on finding someone else who did.~~
2. Try to do Kitten's dare and find Sister Margaret Mary.

3. Make Gert Klement think her arteries are going as hard as her heart.

4. Catch whoever stole over $200 out of the Pagan Baby collection box.

5. Practice your Miss America routine.

6. Learn how to swim.

7. Be a good dry-martini-making fiancée to Charlie.

8. Do not get caught blackmailing or spying.

9. Just *think* about making a real confession to Father Ted, before it's too late.

10. Stop at Bloomers for pink roses for Daddy.

11. Think up a catchy advertising slogan for Louise that might help her beat Mrs. Tate in the election so she doesn't blame Birdie and me when she loses.

Charlie knows how my temper flares if anybody interrupts me when I'm working on a list, so he slouches back against the pew, weaves his fingers together, and plays that "Here's the church, here's the steeple, open the door and see all the people" game with Birdie until I have my business squared away and I'm feeling less dizzy.

"So?" he asks. "What'd Kitten have to say about Sister Margaret Mary?"

"You'll be happy to know that you were right about everything. Sister M and M wasn't kidnapped and she didn't have an accident, either." I repeat to Charlie the exact words Kitten said before I cut her off at the pass: "This morning, Sister Prudence found a note in Sister Margaret Mary's cell that—"

"Let the nuns know where she was going?" Charlie says.

"I think so." I sigh stronger than Louise does when she stares at me like I'm a lost cause, and for once I'd have to agree with her. "But I thought when Kitten first mentioned that a note was found that it was a ransom note and when she told me it wasn't, I got so disappointed that I accidentally questioned her information and she . . . she . . ." When my lips begin to tremble, Charlie, who keeps close track of the who, what, where, when, and why goings-on in the neighborhood, picks up my hand, looks at my red wrist, cringes, and says, "She gave you this hideous Indian burn." He closes his eyes the way he does when he's feeling very sad or when he's trying to recall one of his statistics. "I know that hurts like the dickens, but look at it this way. Ya got off lucky 'cause she likes you and Birdie so much. If any other kid questioned her information in front of the other greasers like you did, she'd . . . she'd . . ." He opens his beautiful green eyes, sees the look on my face, and gulps. "Kitten dared you," he says with a groan, but Birdie doesn't. Not because she doesn't understand the hot water I'm in, but because she doesn't understand *anything* at this point in the game. My little dreamboat has hauled anchor and sailed off to parts unknown. She's rocking back and forth in the pew next to me, grinning up at St. Francis like the two of them are taking a stroll on the deck of a luxury cruise liner on the high seas.

After I tell Charlie what Kitten dared me to do, he says, "Oh, Tessie, The M . . . m . . . m . . ." He hates it when he nervous stutters, so he looks up to his favorite saint for a little help and his prayer is answered. "The Mutual Admiration Society will find out what happened to Sister Margaret Mary, we will." He picks up my hand and blows on my wrist to cool it down. "I know how much you were countin' on solving this case, but you gotta remember the encouraging words from the first chapter of *Modern Detection*. 'Don't give up. If the investigation you're working on isn't fruitful, try shakin' another suspicious tree.'"

I know that Charlie's trying to cheer me up by reminding me that I have the two people I love most in the world to lean on over the next three days and that we have so many bad apples in this neighborhood that we'll have no problem finding another case to solve, but after striking out all morning, I'm feeling more like gum stuck on the bottom of a shoe than a gumshoe.

"I wish you the best of luck," I tell Charlie. "I'm throwing in the detecting towel."

"Aw, c'mon, Tessie," Charlie says. "Don't be that way. You know that—"

1:24 p.m. "We gotta go," I say before he can tell me to keep my sunny side up. I love him *very* much, but this is one of the things we do *not* have in common. How can he be so cheerfully sad all the time? It's like being hungrily full or . . . or smartly dumb, which, well, I guess I am the perfect example of. "Louise wants us to clean up the house, and then I gotta get busy workin' on the dare."

When the three of us pass the pew Jenny Radtke is still sitting in, she's brushing her perfect little blond pageboy when she laughs and says, "The same way you've failed to beat me in the spelling bees, you'll fail to complete Kitten's dare, and then ya know what's gonna happen, ya loser? You'll be an even bigger laughingstock, which is going to wreck your mother's chances of becoming the new treasurer of the Pagan Baby Society."

I lunge at her and snarl, "Sit on a screwdriver and rotate, ya stupid little squealer," which wasn't half as much fun as something else I had in mind, before levelheaded Charlie planted himself between her and me so I couldn't commit spelling-medal strangulation.

"Hey," he whispers to my back as I tug my still-drifting sister down the main aisle of St. Kate's feeling lower than low, bluer even than one of Gracie Carver's Billie Holiday songs she likes to listen to when she cleans the church. "I'm going to stay and light some candles for my ma, but after ya get your chores done, we should go over to the convent and talk to Linda O'Brien. She got sentenced to work in the kitchen this week for telling her mother that she wouldn't know her ass from a hole in the ground, so she's probably the snitch who told Kitten about Sister Margaret Mary's note that Sister Prudence found. You could bribe Linda to tell you where Sister is with the rest of our treasury money."

That's very sweet of Charlie, but very dopey. First off, we only have three dollars left after I paid Kitten for information, and second off,

Linda O'Brien wouldn't tell us where our principal went even if she knows. She'd *never* risk that, not for all the money in the world. Believe me, *nobody* wants to double-cross Kitten. (There are stories floating around the neighborhood about kids who have that are too gruesome to repeat in mixed company.)

When we reach the church doors, gentlemanly Charlie opens them for Birdie and me, and I guess I must look pretty pathetic, because he finally does the something that I have been wanting and waiting for him to do for the longest time. He uses his mouth for something other than talking!

And then, I don't know what the hell happened, because I'm not kidding, the sweet peck on my cheek from his lips that are so much softer than I ever imagined drove any bad thoughts I was having out of my brain faster than St. Patrick drove the snakes out of Ireland.

I feel lighter than air! I'm floating down the steps of St. Kate's on cloud nine! I forget that I am a detective who was so positive that she had a kidnapping and murder case on her hands but was 100% wrong. I forget that I shook on a dare that could make my life, my sister's, and my mother's take a terrible turn for the worst. I even forget to miss Daddy.

It's my little dreamboat Birdie who brings *me* back to earth, for a change, after we make the turn onto our block and she docks herself in front of the Tates' house.

Birdie points and says, "Uh-oh."

She's talking about the new, huge sign our mother's opponent has sticking out of her front lawn. It's almost as big as the **WORKS OF ART** billboard her brother and my friend, "The Leonardo da Vinci of Undertaking," has on top of the old Goodyear tire store on North Ave.

TWO-FOUR-SIX-EIGHT!

WHO'S NEVER MISSED A PAGAN BABY MEETING?

NANCY TATE!

210

Maybe Louise was right after all and her opponent really *is* a lame duck, because she's wasted a piece of perfectly good poster board on a terrible slogan that isn't even true. The gal formerly known as Mommy has many, many faults, but to the best of my knowledge, the one and only time she ever stayed home on a Thursday night was when Doc Reynolds *made* her, because she had a strepped throat. So if Mrs. Tate is trying to convince the voters in the parish with her new advertising sign to make her the treasurer because our mother is an undependable meeting-misser, she's barking up the wrong—

Damnation!

Louise got so wrapped up in going out to dinner at Mama Mia Ristorante with what's-his-name after her first day at work at the Clark station that she completely forgot all about tonight's Pagan Baby meeting! Her not showing up at the school gym at 6:00 p.m. sharp to pack cardboard boxes with Ban deodorant, Ivory soap, Breck shampoo, and all the rest of the "gifts" a.k.a. "bribes" those gals send to the jungle will destroy her chances of being the new treasurer.

FACT: The patchwork quilts Mrs. Tate makes on her Singer sewing machine are packed in those boxes that are going to the Congo, too, but they're not bribes. If those natives don't right away stop voodoo worshipping and convert to worshipping Jesus, those quilts are used as torture devices.

PROOF: If the parents *don't* sign on the dotted line ASAP, Kitten Jablonski told me that Gert instructs the missionaries to roll them up in those patchwork quilts and keep them there until they agree to let the priests baptize their babes in the Amazon River.

That's how evil and eye-for-an-eye Gert Klement is!

And since she was the one who nominated Louise for the treasury job, if our mother makes her look bad in front of the whole parish by skipping the get-together in the gym tonight so she can go out for a fancy Italian dinner while all the rest of them are breaking their backs packing those boxes, mark my words, Gert will act *very* revengefully. In the name of the Lord, of course.

Mrs. Tate must've heard through the grapevine that Louise was going to be slurping up spaghetti tonight with Moron Gallagher instead of attending the meeting and she got on the stick and made up this huge advertising sign to spread the news. Or maybe it was Louise herself who smiled at the weak-chinned, shorter-than-Daddy lout at her side at Mr. Peterman's funeral and bragged about how she was going straight from work to a supper date after one of the gals asked her where she found the gall to show up looking like Rita Hayworth on May Day when all the rest of them were looking like Bette Davis on Ash Wednesday.

This is not looking good, unless . . .

Mrs. Tate wouldn't remind Louise about tonight's meeting for obvious reasons, but did Kitten's mother, Mrs. Doreen "Dory" Jablonski, happen to pull her best friend to the side at the funeral and tell her, *If you want to win that election, doll, you can't miss the meeting tonight. Ya better postpone your date to tomorrow night?*

Dang, I sure hope so, for more than one reason.

Even though I can't really spare the time because I am under so much pressure to complete the dare to find out where Sister Margaret Mary went, I have to keep my strength up. So tomorrow night, I'll bow my head and thank St. Peter, the patron saint of fishermen, the way I always do every Friday, for providing at least *one* meal a week that I don't have to spend worrying if Birdie and me are being food poisoned by Louise.

Wait just a cotton-pickin' minute.

Louise moving her date from tonight to tomorrow night could work out much better than I could ever have dreamed of! Friday Fish Fry would be the *perfect* place to act on one of these ideas I came up with for the guy who is trying to take Daddy's place. #4 is what I got in mind:

JUST DESSERTS

1. Find out where the numbskull lives and smear black shoe polish on his Chevy's whitewalls.
2. Put a bag of burning dog doo-doo on his porch, ring the doorbell, and run.
3. Call him at his "alleged" job at the American Motors plant and use that impression you learned from watching gangster movies where the wops are always threatening their enemies: *Dis is Three-Fingered Louie Galetti and you-a better stay away from that doll Louise Finley if you-a don' wanna be fitted for a cement raincoat, ya goomba.*
4. Doctor up his food, *if* you ever get to meet him face-to-face.

I guess Charlie's long-awaited kiss did not only fuel my heart, it must be fueling my brain with high octane, because on top of the genius revenge I'm already planning for Leon Gallagher, I've just had another brilliant idea! This one for my mother's opponent in the Pagan Baby election!

"Tessie?" Birdie tugs on the bottom of my T-shirt. "You seein' what I'm seein'?"

"Only if you're ESPing me and seein' the new sign I'm gonna stick in the Tates' lawn tomorrow night." I mad-scientist laugh, the way they do in the movies after they've dreamed up something *really* nasty.

"Hark!" Birdie shouts in her old-timey voice.

Still planning out what I'm hoping to pull on what's-his-name at the fish fry if the timing is right, and what I'm definitely going to pull on Mrs. Tate, I don't really pay attention to what Birdie is harking about. I figure it's probably just a *robin* redbreast sitting on a tree branch or something shiny she's found sparkling out of a sidewalk crack, until she elbows me hard in the side and says, "A certain unwieldy elderly lady who does not have our best interests at heart, sister dear, has returned from unfortunate Mister Peterman's funeral." She raises her arm and points up the block at the white Rambler with the little black flag waving off its antenna that's coming down Keefe Ave. "To avoid being thoroughly interrogated and enduring the subsequent consequences which are surely to be inflicted upon us after Missus Klement shares our forbidden location with our *mater-familias*, might I suggest that we return to our homestead *posthaste*?"

20

O, DIOS MIO, I AM SO
MUCHO TEMPTED

The Finley sisters are so used to running away from our putrid neighbor that it isn't until after we half tripped up our porch steps, yanked open the door of the house, and sagged onto the sofa huffing and puffing that we figured out that we didn't even need to *amscray*—another kind of Latin, this one pig—when we saw Gert's boxy car cruising down the block toward us. Louise *told* me to go to confession this morning before she left for work and that's exactly where Birdie and me were coming from.

So between the holy heavenly kiss from Charlie, my glorious new eye-for-an-eye plans, and for once, being where I'm supposed to be when I'm supposed to be, I'm feeling pretty dang cocky by the time #1 on my SHIT LIST stomps up our front porch steps. I am a big believer in the famous saying "Know thy enemy"—I got it in a fortune cookie from Men Hong Low Chinese Restaurant on Lisbon Ave., which has excellent chicken chop suey, by the way—so I 100% knew Gert would show up to check on us and I'm BE PREPARED.

I got the look on my face that the kid in *Old Yeller* gets on his when his dog gets rabies and he's got to shoot him when I answer her meaty knock on the front door. "Good afternoon, Missus Klement. Gosh, I was so heartily sorry to hear about Mister Peterman. I hope his funeral went as planned."

Those black painted-on eyebrows of hers inch up to the edge of her bone-colored hair when she grins with her fake teeth that she keeps in a glass next to her bed and says, like she's just so sure she's got me by the short hairs, "And how did you know that I attended the service if you stayed here in the house as you were supposed to, Theresa Marie?"

Geez, maybe listening to Father Joe's droning grave sermon about the valley of death *did* make her arteries go as hard as her heart, because she wouldn't have asked that question if she was thinking straight. Usually Gert is much wilier than that.

"When Birdie and me paid our respects to Mister Peterman from our *back porch*," I tell her, still looking very hang-dog, "we saw you standing next to Mrs. Peterman at the grave. Black really suits you, by the way."

When our enemy gets done *harrumph*ing, still very certain that she's caught us up to no good, she slyly says, "I came by earlier today, you and your sister must have heard me." We sure did, you Holy Water–wielding, *Dominos vobiscum*–ing, exercising-the-devil battle-ax. "If you were home and not out gallivanting, why didn't you answer the back door?"

Before I can answer, my sister, who is sucking the last drop of chocolate out of one of the Hershey's kisses I awarded her from my secret stash in the umbrella stand—for some unknown reason, old-fashioned Birdie is a faster runner than weird Birdie and she *actually* beat me in the race home when she saw Gert's car coming down Keefe Ave.—calls over from the sofa, "Hi, Missus Klement! We're so sorry we missed you this morning. We were probably down in the basement doing wash. Our machine hasn't been working right, so we can't hear anything when the clothes are spinnin' around, can we, Theresa Marie?"

I almost give myself whiplash when I jerk my head toward her and say, "Ahhh . . . no, we sure can't, Robin Jean."

Holy Jesus with a twist!

The kid who can't even remember to tinkle half the time or her address or how much her mother despises Ida Lupino just came up with almost the same gorgeous lie I was going to tell Gert! (I am *definitely* doing that ESP test on her tonight.)

"Did you need something else, Missus Klement?" I say, so very dutifully. "Because I really need to . . ." I bring out the feather duster that I've been holding behind my back, but then, like I just remembered something, I hit myself on the forehead and get ready to tell her the fib that, if I do say so myself, Mr. Howard Howard could sell in his precious gems and jewelry store in the fancy case. This fib is 24k. "Goodness gracious, I was so involved in my chores and praying that I almost forgot to give you a very important message!" Just in case her best friend *didn't* pull Louise to the side over at the funeral and remind her about the meeting tonight, this next bit should take care of that problem. "Our dear, very punctual mother, who works her fingers to the bone and will make such an excellent new treasurer of the Pagan Baby Society, was in such a hurry this morning to start her new job that she asked me to ask you when you came by to check on us if you'd call her this afternoon at the Clark station to let her know what dessert you'd like her to bring tonight." (Ever since Louise was the one and only suspect in THE CASE OF THE TROTS, she's only allowed to bring a sure thing to the Thursday meeting. So all of them gals don't have to stop doing what they're doing and run to the little girls' room every five minutes to deal with diarrhea, she needs to pick up a safe and scrumptious treat from Meuer's Bakery.) "So, could you please do that?"

My Moriarty, Kryptonite, and Ming the Merciless all rolled into one nods, but then gives me the worst watery evil eye, because she was so sure she caught us doing some shenanigans and she doesn't like being thwarted any more than I do. But believe you me, I know her, she won't give up without a fight. (Unfortunately, we have this in common.) She's still hoping to catch Birdie and me doing something, *anything* that she can tattle to Louise about when she calls her at work before she stomps off our front porch in a huff.

And sure enough, with another perfectly white, sneering grin—swear to God, next time I sneak into her house, I'm gonna steal those teeth—she asks me, "Did you go to confession today?"

"She certainly *did* go to confession today, Missus Klement!" Birdie shouts from the sofa. "You can even check with Jenny Radtke. And for the rest of the afternoon, when you come to check on us, if we don't answer the door"—Birdie magically makes her blue rosary appear in her little hands—"it's because we'll be in our bedroom doing more praying, isn't that right, Theresa Marie?"

Of course, I am feeling *very* proud and impressed by Birdie's excellent lies under fire, but I don't let that show when I tell Mrs. Klement to her face that's growing redder by the minute, which I heard is a sign of a stroke, so here's hoping, "That's absolutely right, Robin Jean." And as long as our neighbor is here darkening our door . . . this is such a long shot, but what do I have to lose? "And one of the people we'll be praying *for* all afternoon is Sister Margaret Mary, because we've been in the house all day and haven't heard one way or another if she's been found." Of course, Gert, being such a big-deal muckety-muck around here, she must've found out at the funeral that our principal still hasn't shown up, so I bet she also knows what was in the note the nun left that probably explains what happened to her. "If she *hasn't* turned up yet, does anybody have any idea where Sister might be? Robin Jean and me are so worried about her."

I thought Gert might show off and spill the beans, because she doesn't know about Kitten's dare, but after she gives me one more disgusting look, she makes her way over to her house muttering "banshee" and "eternal damnation."

And I, not slowly at all, rush to my sister's side to ask her how in the heck she came up with that great half fib about our loud washing machine that really does spin out of control so bad that it can chase Birdie and me halfway across the basement and corner us near the furnace.

"Honey!" I tell her. "I'm so proud of you. How in the heck did you think—?"

"Can I please see the evidence I found behind Mister Gilgood's mausoleum?" she says.

Still so impressed by her slick fibs, I don't question why she's in such a hurry to take a look at the St. Christopher medal, I just reach into my shorts pocket and hand it over to her.

"Now that we know for sure that Mister McGinty didn't kidnap and murder Sister Margaret Mary," Birdie says more soulfully than Mr. James Brown, "we need to take his medal back to him soon as we can. He must miss it so much."

She's right, of course, but we can't do that until Gert leaves for the Pagan Baby meeting. We snuck past her once today, so the odds aren't good that we'll be able to do it again. And considering the daring deep water that this nonswimmer is in, The Mutual Admiration Society really should spend all of tonight sleuthing and snooping around the neighborhood under the cover of darkness to try and find news about Sister Margaret Mary instead of climbing the fence to Holy Cross.

On the other hand . . . if we don't go visit Mr. McGinty tonight, I'd be breaking the *sister*-promise I made to Birdie this afternoon when I still thought he was a kidnapping murderer and I wanted her to go, Bird, go and she wanted to stay and talk to him some more, and I can't do that. Besides, I owe it to the poor guy whose holy lucky charm I've kept from him most of the day, and I owe it to myself, too. Suspecting that this old basketball-playing friend of Daddy's, my fishing pal, a wounded veteran of the war, teacher of whittling and bird-watching to Charlie, our godfather, who has been taking such extra special care of my sister and me since we lost Daddy, was a horrible criminal all day has really taken a toll on me.

Maybe we should divide the difference. Go see the caretaker the first hour we have free tonight when Louise and Gert are at the meeting, and for the second hour, The Mutual Admiration Society will start working on the dare. Tomorrow afternoon, *that's* when we'll really ramp up looking for information about Sister Margaret Mary. During the hours Louise is busy staring at her reflection in the Clark station's front window, Birdie and me can easily sneak out of the house to meet up with Charlie, because wretched Gert will not be around then, either, to keep us under her thumb. She'll spend the whole afternoon proving to everyone in the parish that there's nobody nearer to God than she by doing what she does *every* Friday afternoon starting at 1:00 p.m. She'll help the nuns at St. Kate's prepare for the fish fry in the school cafeteria with a more martyred look than St. Sebastian, who died from a very bad arrow attack followed by a clubbing to death, which, in my opinion, is a very good example of the famous saying—"Overkill." (Joke!)

Yes, that's a pretty decent plan, but I can't explain it to Birdie right now because working too far into the future confuses her, so I just tell her the part that will really excite her. "We can't go over to the cemetery right *now*, honey, because you-know-who's watchin' our every move, but after Gert leaves for her meeting tonight, just like I *sister*-promised you this morning, we'll go visit Mister McGinty and give him his medal back and you can talk to him and drink Graf's root beer and eat windmill cookies and . . . and pet Pyewacket, won't that be fun?"

I *can't* tell the caretaker how we hung on to his medal all day as evidence against him, because that would hurt his feelings, but, never fear, I already got another BE PREPARED plan that I'm 75% sure will work.

'Cause I can't trust my sister not to blurt something dumb out to Mr. McGinty, something like the truth, I'll have to wait until she gets some cookies and soda into her and gets busy purring along with Pye— they will take a trip to parts unknown together, they always do—then she won't be around anymore to deny the story I'm going to tell him after I take his medal out of my pocket and place it down in front of him. When he cries out *Praise be! I've been looking everywhere for it! Where did you find it?*, because I feel so wretched for thinking the worst of him, I won't even have to put on one of my pretend-sad looks when I answer him: *So sorry, Mister McGinty. I found it in Birdie's shorts pocket. She must've come across it this morning in the cemetery and picked it up, because you know how she can't resist anything shiny, and then she forgot all about it, because of her horrible memory, ya know? Please forgive her for she knows not what she does. And hey, by the way, why are Sister Margaret Mary's initials on the back of it?*

Being extra religious, our friend will especially like me using the famous saying that will remind him how Jesus asked His Heavenly Father to forgive the people who nailed His Kid to the cross, which was pretty damn All-Big of Him, if ya ask me. (Anybody crucified me or my sister or Charlie or my grandparents or Gracie Carver or a couple other people around here that I really like, believe me, they would be #1 on my SHIT LIST for all of eternity.)

"That plan sound good to you?" I ask my sister.

"What plan?" she says as she hops off the sofa and turns on the Motorola in such a goofy way that it's hard to believe that just minutes ago the kid told the smartest washing-machine and rosary-praying lies to Gert, but that's just the way she is. Unpredictable. Forgetful. With a tummy that never feels full. "I'm getting really, really, really, really hungry again, Tessie. Do we have any Velveeta?"

"Sorry, honey, we're out." Not only of cheese, but a lot of other stuff, too. Old Mother Hubbard would feel right at home in our pantry. "Don't you have any of the chocolate cherries left?"

She points to her protruding tummy and then down to the green shag carpet. The Stover box has been picked clean, which explains why the kid who always feels so much better when she knows where her next meal is coming from licks her lips and says, "Can I have my TV dinner now?"

Seeing my sister sitting there with her shorter bangs that Charlie cut for her sticking straight up in the air and beggar dirty while she waits for the Motorola's picture tube to warm up, I realize that we don't only have to clean up the house, we gotta clean up ourselves, too. After running and rolling around and sneaking and crawling and digging through leaf piles on this hot Indian summer day, the both of us are looking like something the cat dragged in, and that's not going to go over real big with Louise when she gets home tonight from her meeting. Once she gets a whiff of us, believe me, she will *not* get a nose-full of sugar and spice and everything nice. She'll figure out that we been out and about and up to no good.

"Tell ya what," I say to Birdie. "After I straighten up the house a little, let's take a bath and put on our spy clothes for tonight's trip to see Mister McGinty and then I'll stick your TV dinner in the oven." She adores bubble baths, so I'm sure she'll go for this idea. "You can finish watchin' . . ."—I turn around to check what show is beginning to show up on the TV screen, "American Bandstand"—"but the second it's over, you come right upstairs and get in the tub."

"Roger that, Tessie," she says with one of her irresistible smiles. "Now get outta the way, you're blocking Mister Dick Clark."

After I run the garbage out to the silver can—Gert's on her back porch, rocking away and watching our house like a guard waiting to catch escaping prisoners—I finish dusting and running the sweeper across the carpet, and peek in on Birdie to make sure she's where I left her, then I head upstairs to run the tub water. I squeeze in a few squirts of Joy soap to get it nice and frothy, and hurry into our bedroom to pick out what our mother has started calling "*ensembles*" out of the little dresser she wedged into our closet.

I've got to dig deep to find two *mostly* clean sets of navy T-shirts and shorts to wear on our trip over to Mr. McGinty's shack tonight and the snooping around we got to do for the dare, so I'm down at the very bottom of the bottom dresser drawer when my hand bumps into something sitting under the white paper Louise put in there with thumbtacks that are long gone.

"God*damn*it all, Bird!" I say, because I'm sure this giant lump must be covering up some food that she hid away for a rainy day and, of course, forgot all about. I've come across some very disgusting things growing here and there throughout the house and considering how bad a state my tummy is already in because of Kitten's dare, I don't want to feast my eyes on whatever leftovers Birdie stuck under the dresser paper, but what choice do I have? Who knows how long whatever she buried under here has been multiplying? We could wake up to The Blob breathing down our necks one of these nights.

So I push the clothes to one side of the drawer, breathe through my mouth, warn my gut that it's about to get some bad news, and slowly lift up the corner of the paper with the tips of my fingers. Sure enough, the wad is big and green and . . . and the worst horrifying, revolting *Gotcha!* next to the time I found the dripping, bloody cow's brains that Daddy put under our bed on Beggars Night last year, that I'm pretty positive I'm gonna throw up! And when I get done doing that, I will reach into my back pocket, take out my stubby pencil and my TO-DO list, and draw a line through #4. Catch whoever stole over $200 out of the Pagan Baby collection box.

Q. The culprit that I, and everyone else in the parish, have been looking high and low for, is *not* Skip Abernathy, but my very own sister?!

A. *Signs point to yes.*

Damnation!

Why . . . why . . . why . . . why . . . would she . . . ?

Wait just a cotton-pickin' minute.

Could this stack of cash . . . could it be one of Birdie's special gifts?

But it's not fluffy like the feathers she lays around Daddy's tombstone, and it isn't shiny like the ring with the pink, heart-shaped stone she rested against Louise's plate this morning, and the new nickel I found under my pillow when I was waiting for her to wake up so I could tell her about the great-good-luck murder. And they keep this dough in the collection box at church, so she didn't find it lying on the ground like she did those gifts. No, as hard as it is for me to believe, I'm 100% sure that Birdie stole these greenbacks right out from under St. Kate's nose.

Damnation times ten!

"Tessie?" My sister isn't calling to me from the living room, but the bathroom down the hall, so "American Bandstand" must be over. "I'm getting in the tub now just like you told me to and yes, I turned off the water."

I can't let her know that I stumbled across the worst piece of evidence that could get her sent away, *not* to jail, but to a "home," because she is an innocent who cannot be held responsible for what she does, so I steady my voice and call back to her, "Did you remember to take off all your clothes including your undies, honey?"

"Yes, I remembered to take off all my clothes including my undies, honey."

The poor kid couldn't have known what she was doing when she took the money from the church box, and she's probably already forgotten that she did. I'm not sure that she even has a conscience—that annoying, chirping voice might be located in the part of Birdie's brain that she didn't get because she came out of Louise too early—but what I do know is that no matter how hard I try to hide it, my sister, who I love and know best of all and who loves and knows me best of all, is gonna figure out how scared I am if I run into the bathroom and present this stolen wad of bills to her and tell her what she's done. Her eyes will bulge bigger and then her little face will crumple and she'll start flapping her arms and squawking and yelling with her big opera lungs how sorry she is over and over and over and over and then she'll ask if I still love her so many times that I almost don't anymore and . . . and Gert won't even need to turn on her powerful hearing aids to know that it's time to call Louise, who I'm pretty positive would send my little sister away to the loony bin if she finds out what Birdie's done, which she won't, if I have anything to say about it.

Never in a million years would I let #1 on my TO-DO list, who I promised Daddy I would take tender loving care of, live the rest of her life in a padded room.

Because I wasn't BE PREPARED for something like this to happen, I've got to come up with a plan ASAP! I'd normally spend hours puzzling over a new list, but I don't have that luxury right now. I've got to act fast, but my usual genius brain is so shocked and stunned that it can only think of four solutions to our predicament off the top of my head:

1. Stick some of this money in my shorts pocket and the two of us could run away right now to California.
2. Bring the stolen loot to Mr. McGinty's shack tonight and beg for his help.
3. Follow the original plan I had when I found the culprit to stick the money under some bushes at the church and then come across it after Mass this Sunday so I can be a big hero.
4. Sneak out of the house and return the money to the collection box tonight all by myself.

I reach for my Magic 8 Ball that I keep hidden from Louise in the closet behind a shoe box because it is a sin to ask questions about your future to anybody but all-knowing God.

Q. Which plan should I pick? #1, 2, 3, or 4?

A. When I turn it over, *Reply hazy try again later* floats up. Damnation!

We need to act *now*, not *later*, and I've just about had it up to here with these watered-down answers.

"Tessie!" Birdie shouts from down the hall. "Come practice your dead man's float!"

Please, Daddy, please help me know what to do . . . what to do . . .

1. I like the idea of making a run for it, but first I'd have to talk Birdie into it, and that could take forever on account of how much she loves Louise, and I would really miss Charlie so much.

2. If I involve Mr. McGinty, that could make him guilty of the crime of accessorizing after the fact, the way I am, because I let Daddy drown, and I wouldn't wish that awful feeling on anybody, except for Jenny Radtke and Gert, and, of course, Butch Seeback, but he probably wouldn't even feel bad because he has the mind of a maniac.

3. Hiding the money under the bushes at church and then pretending to find it this Sunday after Mass is too risky. Somebody, say Gert Klement, would start telling everybody how suspicious she thinks it is that Theresa Marie Finley, of all people, was the one to find the stolen money. *Dog smells its own dirt first* is probably what she'd say.

4. Yes, returning the money tonight to the collection box when Birdie and Louise are snoozing seems like the best idea.

Thank you, Daddy. Amen.

"Tessie . . . Tessie . . . Tessie . . . Tessie!" my sister calls from the bathroom.

St. Kate's keeps its doors open all through the night so the workers at the Feelin' Good Cookie factory and American Motors can stop by when their second shift is over to do their praying, so not getting noticed by one of them is going to be *very* tricky. I'll wear my hobo disguise or pull one of the black stockings over my face, and then, when the time is right, I'll . . .

"What's takin' you so long?" the little thief says from right behind me.

I gasp and jump about a foot because I was so caught up in trying to form a plan I didn't notice that I wasn't hearing her splashing in the tub anymore. I try to slam the dresser drawer shut so she doesn't see the money, but one of the T-shirts I piled to the side has gotten caught in the runner, so all that's left to do is try and shield the drawer with my body.

I very carefully wiggle around to face her, then I say, with a huge smile, "That was a great *Gotcha!* honey. I think you mighta even scared some poop outta me, ha . . . ha . . . ha!"

"Thank you, Tessie. I wanted to show you my bubble beard!" Birdie strikes a movie-star pose. "Do I look like Burl Ives?"

I don't know why she loves that movie star so much, but she does. "That's a doozy of a Burl beard, honey, but you can do better."

"Can I?"

"Yes, lots, lots, lots, lots better. So you should hurry and get back in the tub and work on it a little more before all the bubbles are gone."

"What are you lookin' for in the dresser?" she asks, stepping closer and dripping all over me. She's trying to peek over my shoulder. She's such a shrimp that she's never taller than I am and never will be, except for when I'm on my knees, like I am right now, so I sag over to my right side to keep her from seeing the money.

"Remember? We're going to visit Mister McGinty tonight, so I'm lookin' for some spy clothes." When I'm attempting to sweet-talk her into something, I normally do my Glinda the Good Witch impression, because that gal has the nicest voice I ever heard, but I'm so off balance that I'm afraid I'm going to topple over at any second, and when I do, my sister will see what I'm trying to hide, and then I'm going to have to tell her what she did and that would be the worst thing to happen, so I end up sounding like the Wicked Witch of the West when I say, "You know how important cleanliness is next to godliness is to him. We can't go over there to return his medal if we're sinfully dirty, so get back into the tub right this minute or I'll have to—"

"You found the Pagan Baby money!" Birdie joyfully shouts when she knocks me down and snatches it outta the dresser drawer. "Like you and Zorro are always sayin'," she sticks her bare chest out and crows, "it's okay to take from the rich and the church is *very* rich and give to the poor and we are *very* poor." She waves the green wad in my face. "I'm gonna give it all to Mommy so . . . so we can keep our house that still smells like Daddy in the nooks and crannies and she can stop going out on dates with what's-his-name and . . . we can buy lots of food at the Red Owl and we won't have to run away!"

O, *Dios mio*, when she puts it like *that*, believe me, I am so *mucho* tempted.

Keeping this money *would* do everything Birdie said it would, and more, but sad to say, as wonderful as living a life of luxury on Easy St. sounds, my annoying conscience is giving me two thumbs down.

I stand and wrap my arms around my slippery sister the best I can and tell her, "I love you, Birdie Finley, and I am really, really, really, really proud of you for doin' such a good and kind charitable act that would really help us out." I am dying to ask how she pulled the caper off, but chances are, she's gone foggy about the details. "More than anything, I wish we *could* keep the money, but we can't." I try to come up with the easiest explanation that someone with her limited brain power might understand. "We gotta put ourselves in those pagan babies' shoes."

"Don't be so silly, Tessie," she says with one of her great belly laughs, which, believe me, is really something to behold when she's naked as a jaybird. "Babies don't wear shoes."

Poor kid.

"But those babies *do* live on the Dark Continent and they gotta dodge poison Pygmy darts and cannibals all day long under the sweltering sun," I say, "while Crucifix-waving missionaries chase them through the jungle hounding them about converting to Catholic, and . . . and if their parents don't agree to sign on the dotted line, they get rolled up in one of Missus Tate's patchwork quilts until they do. So in the long run, that makes those babies a *lot* worse off than we are, don'tcha think?"

Birdie doesn't take long to say, "Roger that," because even the owner of a brain that moves slower than an African tree sloth immediately understands what a disgustingly hopeless situation those babies are in.

Of course, the plan I've come up with is *way* too complicated for my not-very-smart and very forgetful sister to take in, so I just tell her the parts that I think she'll understand and remember. "So here's what we're gonna do," I say as I steer her out of the closet. "The both of us will get into the tub and after you show me some more Burl bubble beards, we'll get dressed and head downstairs. You can watch some more television while I heat up our suppers, and after that, we'll meet up with Charlie and go see Mister McGinty."

"Ship . . . ship . . . hurray!" she yells, which I 100% knew she would, because even though she is unpredictable in many, many, many, many ways, I can always count on her gigantic heart and her gigantic appetite to win out. She could never say no to the gummy brownie in the Swanson's TV dinner *and* spending time with Charlie and our good friend Mr. McGinty who will have windmill cookies and root beer at the ready, that's entirely too much deliciousness for my little tweetheart to resist.

21

THE ELEMENT OF SURPRISE

So far, everything is going according to plan.

Once Birdie and me were smelling more like Joy than week-old vase water, I hung a red towel out our bedroom window to let Charlie know that we need to meet with him at our house ASAP! And Gert must've called Louise to tell her what yummy dessert she wanted her to pick up at Meuer's Bakery for the meeting tonight, because when our telephone rang around ten times while we were eating—it took me a while to figure out that it wasn't coming out of the television set, because it hardly ever rings this time of night since bill collectors call during the daytime—it was our mother on the other end of the line letting me know that she would be going straight from work to the Pagan Baby meeting. She was about to tell me something else, something about "shenanigans," but then she had to hang up because a customer needed servicing.

5:43 p.m. The Mutual Admiration Society is sitting on our back porch steps, polishing off the last bit of chocolate ice cream that I found in the back of our freezer compartment after my sister scarfed down her TV dinner and most of mine.

When the three of us are watching and waiting for Gert Klement to come lumbering out of her house toward her Rambler car, I'm wondering if Charlie gets sadder when he looks at garages because his is where he lost his mom forever, but he probably wouldn't tell me because he's such a clam, and anyway, it would be bad timing to ask him now. We need to stay focused on our very important missions.

Because that hobo wig is really starting to smell worse than one of Louise's "gourmet" dishes, I changed my mind, and Charlie agrees with me, that instead of me returning the Pagan Baby money on a solo mission tonight, we should pick #2 on my list of ideas: Bring the stolen loot to Mr. McGinty's shack tonight and beg for his help. He is such a good egg, who understands that Birdie can't help who she is, and he wouldn't want her to get into trouble any more than I would, but on the other hand . . . because he is also awfully religious and there's that *Thou Shalt Not Steal* Commandment, Charlie might be 100% sure that Mr. McGinty will play along, but I'm only 95% sure.

5:47 p.m. After Gert slams shut the back door of her house and makes the short walk to her garage, she noses her white car down the driveway, switches on her headlights that spotlight The Mutual Admiration Society on our back porch, and shouts out of her car window, "I spoke to your mother, girls. She expects the two of you to be present and accounted for when we return from tonight's meeting."

"Roger that, Frank," Birdie shouts back at her.

Same way *I* put myself in Daddy's shoes, and the same way I tried to explain to Birdie about putting *herself* in the pagan babies' shoes, because I don't hardly believe anything that comes out of anybody's mouths, least of all Gert's, I need to make sure she really *is* going to the Pagan Baby meeting and not parking down the block and doubling back to watch and see if the Finley ghouls and their faithful sidekick,

Charlie "Cue Ball" Garfield, climb over the black iron cemetery fence or sneak down Keefe Ave. to do other shenanigans.

After I hand off the Sealtest carton to Birdie so she can lick what's left off the sides, I tell Charlie, "Be back in a jiff," and I run out to the curb to see if the Rambler's taillights disappear around the block. Once I'm sure the coast is clear, I rush back and give my partners in crime two thumbs up.

Charlie, acting like it's no big deal, waves the wrinkly brown paper sack that's got a for-emergencies-only P B and M for Birdie, and the stolen $209—Charlie is very good at arithmetic and he counted it twice—inside. "You want me to be in charge of this?" he asks.

FACT: I was surprised by how unsurprised he was when I told him that Birdie was the Pagan Baby money thief everybody in the parish would like to tar and feather.

PROOF: "*Most* thefts are committed by people who are in desperate need of funds," he said with a shrug.

5:50 p.m. After I tell my fiancé that, yes, the Sergeant of Arms of The Mutual Admiration Society should be the holder of the loot, him and Birdie and me make our way across our backyard under the cover of creeping darkness. We shimmy up the cemetery fence easy, which is a big relief, because it's getting harder by the minute to make out the pointy spears on top. As usual, the cemetery streetlights in this part of Holy Cross aren't doing their job. (The caretaker doesn't understand why no matter how many new lightbulbs he screws in, they still flicker, but I think I do. I'm pretty sure it's Daddy's way of talking to Birdie and me, maybe in Morris's Code, which I am intending to learn the second I get the chance.)

As we make our way through the tombstones toward the shack, Charlie asks me, "You remembered your flashlight, right?"

I wrestle my trusty Roy Rogers out of my back pocket, flick it on, and hand it to him. I left the rest of the snooping TOOLS OF THE TRADE in our Radio Flyer wagon, because I knew we'd already have enough on our hands keeping Birdie in line, and we can't be weighed down if she gets away from us. So my newest BE PREPARED plan has us stopping *back* at the garage to pick up the wagon that we'll need to take with us when we roam around the neighborhood to gather information for the dare after we give Mr. McGinty's medal back to him and figure out a way to return the stolen loot to St. Kate's.

Because the Finley sisters can't stay out past midnight anymore now that Louise is going to the Pagan Baby meeting and not staying out to all hours with her lousy boyfriend, we have to follow a strict timetable:

6:00 p.m.–7:00 p.m. Spend time with Mr. McGinty.

7:01 p.m.–8:00 p.m. Work on Kitten's dare.

8:01 p.m.–8:15 p.m. Try to get Charlie to pucker up again before Birdie and me have to race back from wherever we are so we can beat Louise home.

Now that we know that Sister Margaret Mary wasn't kidnapped, that means she left somewhere on purpose, so we should start by asking around the neighborhood to see if anybody saw her standing at a bus stop or walking down North Ave. When we were first trying to figure out why she was missing, one of Charlie's other ideas was that she left the sisterhood for good, so maybe we'll find out *ex*-Sister Margaret Mary has a new job. Who knows? She could even be working up at Lonnigan's, serving cocktails alongside Suzie "That French Slut" LaPelt. Because you can't see squat under their black habits, all the kids wonder if nuns *have* boobies or if they got chopped off the same day all their hair was when they became nuns. If our principal *does* have a bosom, it'd be pretty revolting to see it falling out of a skimpy white top the way Suzie's do, so just in case, we better also make a stop at Dalinsky's Drugstore and pick me up some Tums before we stop at the bar. (It'd be so great to see the rest of Suzie. Birdie and me really do miss her. She used to love it when the two of us would get up on the bar and sing the "Sisters" song for the customers.)

Those are all good ideas, but what I'm pinning a bushel basket of my hopes on is finding out some dirt at the Milky Way way before that. After I order us a strawberry Mercury malt with three straws, yeah, it's a long shot, but The Mutual Admiration Society just might overhear one of Kitten's snitches blabbing away to another one of Kitten's snitches about what was in the note Sister Margaret Mary left while they're waiting for a girl in a shiny skirt and alien antennae on her head to roller-skate out with red trays full of the out-of-this-world food.

"Watch your step, Tessie," Charlie whispers as we're tiptoeing past the stretch of Phantom Woods. Just like me and every other kid in the neighborhood, except for my sister, who I have tracked down in a tree a couple of times after a wild streak, the other love of my life is terrified that something or someone is going to reach out of those gnarled black trees and Grimm-ly eat us. (No joke!)

Once we make it past Mr. Gilgood's mausoleum that is no longer the scene of a crime, and the weeping willow tree where we were supposed to have our Mutual Admiration meeting this morning—we're close enough to the caretaker's house that we can see a light shining out of his window—Birdie comes to a sudden stop, cocks her head, and does #1 on the LOONY list: Hearing, seeing, and smelling stuff that nobody else can.

Charlie looks over at the woods—I can see the sweat break out on the top of his pretty lip by the light of my flashlight—and says to Birdie, "Whatever you're hearin' that we're not, please tell m . . . m . . . me it's not coming outta the woods."

Instead of answering him, Birdie, who *always* has got on her side what *Modern Detection* describes as "the element of surprise," breaks free of our hands and makes a run for it.

I don't bother yelling *Stop! Stop! Stop! Stop!* like I usually would when she pulls a stunt like this, because my fiancé and me both know there is 0% chance—he could probably speak "statistically" about this for a good hour—that almost-always-starving Birdie would stop peeling faster than a GI on KP duty toward ex–army sergeant Mr. McGinty's windmill cookies and Graf's root beer that he keeps stocked for us in his cupboard.

But what Charlie and me *are* curious about is why, instead of running straight for Mr. McGinty's front door, Birdie has scurried over to the side of his shack, to the lit window. And how come she's crouching below it, giving us the shhh sign, and raising and lowering her hand the way I do when I want her to get down on all fours?

We don't have time for this! We're on a tight schedule and it's already taken us fifteen minutes to get this far, but what choice do we have? Charlie, who knows good as me what can happen when we don't buckle under to my sister's demands, shrugs and says, "Ladies first."

When we reach Birdie, I lean my back against the shack and whisper to her, "What the hell?" Mr. McGinty would not like it at all if he caught us spying on him. He hates *Gotcha*s! and he's so dang jumpy he might bayonet us by accident, and I think he knows jiu jitsu, too.

What my sister is doing only gets clear when she slowly stands up to peek into the shack window, which is one of the only ones in the neighborhood, except for Lutheran taxidermist Mr. Johnson's basement one, that she can see into without me or Charlie piggybacking her or the soda crate raising her up a notch.

Oh, for godssakes.

I know what she's up to. My little dodo Bird has gotten her wires crossed and is mixing up the plans. "First, we go see Mister McGinty and give him back his medal and ask for his help getting the money you took back into the Pagan Baby collection box. Second, we go snooping and eavesdropping around the neighborhood for information about where Sister Margaret Mary took off to," is what I told her *four* times when we were eating the chocolate ice cream on our back porch.

I get a hold of the back of her shorts and take in a deep breath to pull her down and repeat the plan to her *again*, but my sister knocks my hand away and points frantically at Charlie and me and then points frantically to Mr. McGinty's open window, so what choice do we have? Time is ticking and we still have so much left to do tonight, it's best for all concerned if the future Mr. and Mrs. Charlie "Cue Ball" Garfield just get this over with and . . . and lo and behold!

I'm so surprised when I peek into the shack window to see the two of them sitting at the card table talking softly and smiling at one another that my tummy does a handstand, because it can't figure out which end is up, either!

But I 100% know now that I'm not, I repeat, *not* going to have to spend the next three days biting my nails while I try to honor Kitten's dare, but I also 100% know now that our dear and gentle caretaking friend is, I repeat *is*, going to be sent up the river.

Mr. Lynwood "My friends call me Woody and my enemies call me their worst nightmare" Bellflower would drum me out of the modern detecting business for what I'm about to do, but I can't stop myself.

When the guy who's always on alert for intruders swivels his head and sees The Mutual Admiration Society peeking in on him and his guest, I shout, "Holy shit on a shingle, Mister McGinty! You really *did* kidnap Sister Margaret Mary?!"

22

A STATISTICAL MIRACLE

"Come on in, kids," the caretaker of the cemetery says when he throws open the door of his shack. "We've been expecting you. After you help yourself to refreshments, please join us at the table."

Of course, my sister practically knocks him down on the way to the snacks sitting on the kitchen counter, and after she's snagged them, she plops down in one of the three folding chairs closest to the gal who has been the topic of my every thought and most of my conversations since Gert Klement told Birdie and me and Louise on our back porch this morning that a "terrible incident took place last night."

"What's cookin', good-lookin'?" an overfriendly and too-affectionate Birdie says to Sister Margaret Mary after she stuffed the bottom half of a windmill cookie in her mouth. (Please, God, please, I'm begging You, don't let my sister suddenly go old-timey or juicy smooch our principal's cheek or . . . or do anything else really weird, because as You know, this prickly employee of Yours has the power to keep her in the third grade forever.) "We been lookin' for you all day, isn't that right, Tessie?"

I'm still standing next to Charlie in the doorway of the shack, because I'm so shocked to see our principal that I'm opening and closing my mouth like Charlie McCarthy before Mr. Edgar Bergen supplies him with words. I know what should be coming out of my mouth is *That's right, Birdie, we have been looking for Sister Margaret Mary all day, good remembering*, but that's what a really great *Gotcha!* can do to a kid. Turn them into a dummy.

Charlie has developed a case of lockjaw, too, but Birdie is having no problem gabbing away with the gal who I barely recognize. She still looks like she swallowed a yardstick, but she isn't dressed in her nun's clothes. She's wearing one of Mr. McGinty's white Sunday shirts and a pair of the gray pants he puts on when he's working in the cemetery, and her feet are in floppy mukluks and not in those squishy black shoes she wears when she sneaks around the halls at school trying to catch kids skipping out. And the answer to the playground question "Do nuns have hair and boobies?" is yes. Sister M & M's hair is styled in a pixie cut and it's a color that's close to the same as Mr. McGinty's chestnut brown, and if she had a job at Lonnigan's serving schnapps to customers, believe me, this nun would make a ton of tips.

Because Sister doesn't have any ropes or chains keeping her in the folding chair she's sitting so straight-backed in, it doesn't look like she's a prisoner being held for ransom, so what in the heck *is* this nun doing here running her hand down Pyewacket's back and looking at Mr. McGinty with so much love beaming out of her windows to the soul?

Uh-oh.

Was I right when I wondered if the reason her initials of M. M. are etched on the back of the expensive St. Christopher medal along with J. M. is because they really *are* doing the "horizontal polka"? Are the two of them sitting here planning a secret honeymoon trip to Wisconsin Dells? Was that what Sister Margaret Mary was doing when Birdie and one of Kitten's snitches spotted her near the weeping willow tree earlier? Practicing her running away?

Sweating bullets but sick of beating the bushes for her all day, I screw up my courage and ask from the shack doorway, "Why were you running around the willow tree today, Sister?"

"Tessie, please join us. I'll bring you and Charlie your cookies and soda," Mr. McGinty says with little nudges that get us going in that direction, "and we'll answer all your questions."

I don't want to stare at Sister Margaret Mary when I pull out the folding chair on the other side of Birdie, but I can't help myself, and neither can Charlie when he sits on the other side of me.

After Mr. McGinty brings down the venetian blinds on the windows, which is a little suspicious, if you ask me, he sets the plates of cookies and glasses of root beer down in front of my fiancé and me, places his hands on our principal's shoulders, and says, "Children, I'd like you to meet my sister, Martha."

"Your . . . your . . . WHAT?!" I holler.

Charlie spews out, "Sister Margaret Mary is your sister?!" because this life-changing information has caught him off guard, too.

After our principal uses her napkin to dab at the mess Charlie made on the table when the soda came shooting out of his nose, she nods and tells him, "That's correct, Jasper. Jimmy and I are twins."

This is not a case of mistaken identity on her part.

Jasper is Charlie's baptized name. I don't call him that because before his mother suicided herself, he was so outgoing that his neighborhood nickname was Jasper "The Friendly Ghost" Garfield, and I don't think he wants to be reminded of those good old days any more than I want anyone reminding *me* of when everything was good with my world.

The gal born Martha McGinty smiles down at my cat purring in her lap, the little Siamese traitor, then turns toward me and says, "And in answer to your question, Theresa, I was running around the weeping willow earlier today because I was attempting to catch Pye in order to remove a large burr she had embedded in her fur."

I saw Pye streak out from under the willow when I was looking for Charlie on top of the cemetery hill earlier, and I also noticed that horrible burr she had matted in her fur when she and Charlie were sitting on his back porch looking for feathered friends together after Birdie and me made our leap of faith into his backyard, so she's not making that up.

"Twins are a statistical miracle!" my fiancé says, like a pig rolling in you-know-what.

Sister Margaret Mary looks at her brother across the table and says with a dazzling smile that I have never seen before, "Indeed they are."

I don't know, ya know?

They don't *look* like twins, except for how tall and strong they both are, and the fact that they got the same hair color, cow-brown eyes, and those great choppers. But I'm not stupid. I know there are those *other* kinds of twins that aren't identical. I can't remember what they're called now, but those kinds of twins are *always* very alike in their personalities. Johnny and Janie Mahlberg, who are in the seventh grade, both of them have collecting bugs as a hobby. Sixth-graders David and Donna Peabody, the two of them love to play tetherball and can finish each other's sentences. And look at the Bobsey twins! Nan and Bert, and Freddie and Flossie, they like to have adventures and sometimes solve mysteries. But other than having very religious personalities, what could the so-called McGinty "twins" have in common?

Q. Is it even humanly possible that our principal, who I can't imagine even *being* born, more like ascending from Hell with strict instructions from Satan to be her meanest to kids, is related to our good and dear friend, sweet and shy Mr. McGinty?

A. *It is certain.*

Q. Oh, yeah? Then how come nobody told me this before?

A. *Cannot predict now.*

"How come you never told me you had a twin sister before?" I blurt out to Mr. McGinty.

He must not be offended by my suspicious-sounding tone, because he smiles, and says so convincingly, "But I have, Tessie. I'm certain I mentioned it on the afternoon that you and Birdie helped me plant the lilac bushes near Mister Gilgood's mausoleum. When you told me they were your favorites, I distinctly remember telling you that my twin sister, Martha, loves them, too."

Birdie and me talk about so *many* things with him when he's working in the cemetery, and he's very soft-spoken, and I *can* get easily distracted by her, so maybe he *did* tell me he had a twin the day he was planting lilacs near the mausoleum and I just didn't catch it because the smell of lilacs almost puts me in a stupor, or maybe I really do need hearing aids, or maybe, for some unknown reason, him and his so-called sister are making this whole story up, and a few days from now I'll get a picture postcard from Wisconsin Dells with Babe the Blue Ox on the front.

"Now that we've answered your questions, why don't one of you start out by explaining to Martha and me," the caretaker says, "why you thought I'd kidnapped her?"

"Tessie heard someone yellin' last night, 'I'm warning you! Watch your step! You're treading on dangerous ground!'" Birdie jumps in and says. "And she also heard a bloody-murder scream and then she saw outta our bedroom window a tall, skinny guy who *wasn't* Mister Howard Howard 'cause he's short and he eats too many jelly donuts with his Jim sneak behind the Gilgood mausoleum with a limp body!"

I automatically correct her, but in a very impressed way, because I'm proud that she remembers almost to the word what she told our mother on our back porch this morning. "Mister Howard Howard eats too many jelly donuts with his joe."

"Roger that."

"And when Missus Klement told Tessie this morning that *you*"—Charlie points at our principal—"had disappeared, she assumed that you were the kidnapped murdered victim that she saw."

"Kidnapped *and* murdered?" Mr. McGinty says.

"Disappeared?" our principal says, also with a surprised, puzzled look. "But I left a note for Sister Prudence explaining that I was called away on an emergency and that I'd return the following day, which she would have certainly shared with the other sisters."

"But Sister Prudence didn't find your note right away," Charlie says. "So for a while today, *everybody* in the neighborhood, not just us, thought you had vanished."

The McGintys look at each other across the table like they had no idea that the parish had been in such an uproar.

"I can understand how you might misinterpret what you saw out of your bedroom window last night, Tessie," Mr. McGinty says, "but how could you believe that I'd commit a kidnapping and a murder?"

"'Cause . . . 'cause . . ."

Oh, boy.

That is what my English Gammy would call, if she was a detective, THE CASE OF THE STICKY WICKET. I *didn't* want to hurt my friend's feelings and I can tell that I have by how craggy his salt-map face is looking. "I went to the library a few weeks ago and Miss Peshong dropped this book in my wagon all about detecting and I learned that when it comes to solvin' crimes that I needed . . ." It's going to take too long to explain how I step-by-step reached this awful conclusion about him, but I *can* tell him how *Modern Detection* expects a gumshoe to have means, motive, and opportunity. "I couldn't figure out what your *motive* would be to do something like that, because you are a very nice, religious gentleman, but you are also tall and thin like the guy I thought I saw carrying what I thought was a murdered body last night, which you had the *opportunity* to do because you live here." I fan my arm around the shack. "And the means to commit that crime are your very strong grave-digging arms that could easily strangle a gal or stab them with your switchblade knife. And the icing was stuck on top of the cake when Birdie and me came over here this morning to look for evidence behind the Gilgood mausoleum and we found this."

Uh-oh.

It isn't in my pocket.

"Actually, *I* found this in the leaf pile behind Mr. Gilgood's mausoleum." Birdie opens up her hand to reveal his beloved medal with a minx of a grin. What a show-off! She must've pickpocketed it offa me when we were sitting so close together on our back porch eating the Sealtest ice cream.

Of course, Mr. McGinty says, "Oh! Wonderful!" and looks overjoyed beyond belief to get back his holy lucky medal, but I am about to find out that's not *only* because it kept him mostly safe during the war. Before he fastens it back where it belongs, he aims a sweet look across the table and says, "Martha gave it to me the day I shipped out."

"So *that's* why it's got your initials and hers on the back!" Charlie jumps out of his seat and shouts like he just found gold in them thar hills.

"Not 'cause the two of you are gonna get married and go on a honeymoon in Wisconsin Dells," I add on.

FACT: Mr. McGinty and Sister Margaret Mary really *are* twins.

PROOF: Their eyes pop wide and their jaws drop open at *exactly* the same time.

"Do you want to set the record straight or shall I, Jimmy?" our principal asks.

"Let me," he answers, which is only right. He is our good and dear friend and this nun is not either one. "Tessie, what you heard last night was me shouting a warning to Martha to watch her step because the lights in that part of the cemetery, as you know, have never worked properly, and she was dangerously close to falling into Mister Peterman's open grave. Unfortunately, I wasn't quick enough with my warning, and the screech you heard was the one she made when she lost her footing, tumbled into the hole, and knocked herself out."

Hmmm . . .

I am very, *very* good at recognizing people's voices, especially if I've heard them talk hundreds of times and they sound a lot like Mr. Ed "Velveeta" Herlihy, but I guess it *is* possible that I might not have recognized Mr. McGinty's voice last night at 12:07 a.m. I was so wrapped up in practicing my Miss America routine, and I have *never* heard our soft-spoken friend yell, not once, even when I have forgotten to give him my *woo . . . woo . . . whoot* whistle when I come across him in the cemetery and accidentally scare him half to death. From years of experience, I know that people can sound very different when they raise their voices. Butch Seeback goes from sounding like a sock puppet to a stuck pig, and Birdie can go from sounding like a cooing pigeon to a squawking chicken when she gets all worked up, and Charlie's father, who barely talks at all? I can hear him bear-growling at his boys all the way to our house when he has had entirely too much joy juice.

"So you pulled your sister out of the grave and then you carried her limp body over to the Gilgood m . . . m . . . mausoleum so you could revive her," Charlie says, like he is an expert on getting knocked out, which he might be from all the times he watched his father deck his dearly departed mother.

FACT: I am the *worst* gumshoe on the planet.

PROOF: The facts that Mr. McGinty just laid out at his card table.

In my defense, at least I got the description of the man right, and I was also correct when I thought that the screech I heard sounded familiar, but what about . . .

"Wait just a cotton-pickin' minute," I say, feeling a little more clearheaded now that I got those cookies and root beer in my tummy, and some of the answers to the mystery I've been trying to solve all day in my head. There's something fishy about Mr. McGinty's explanation. The timing is off. His sister is a nun, for crissakes. They lead very dull, holy lives. Every kid in the neighborhood knows that the lights go off at the convent at 10:00 p.m. sharp.

"What were you," I ask our principal, "doing over here at 12:07 a.m. when you're supposed to be fast asleep?"

"Martha needed to speak to me about an important matter that couldn't wait," Mr. McGinty answers for her. "She came to discuss—"

"The stolen Pagan Baby money," Sister Margaret Mary says as she wraps her hand around Birdie's hand, like she's her prisoner and she doesn't want her to escape. "I was in the church the evening Robin took the donations out of the collection box, Theresa."

Oh, no . . . no . . . no . . . no!

"I'd been so concerned about the report the building inspector would make to the city after he closed the school down," Sister Margaret Mary says. "I've found praying to the Blessed Mother to be especially soothing, so I'd come over to the church to say a rosary, and that's when I saw Robin." She looks across the table at her brother and when he gives her a reassuring smile, she brings her windows of the soul back to mine. "Aware of the close relationship that you and your sister enjoy with Jimmy, the very next morning I asked him his opinion about the best way to deal with the situation. He implored me to give it a little time, because he was certain that either you or your sister would return the stolen money, which I was more than willing to do."

"Until last night," Mr. McGinty says.

Sister M & M says, "Yes," and continues to tell us her side of the story. "I waited until I knew all the sisters would be sleeping, including Sister Mary Elizabeth, who suffers from a wretched case of insomnia, to call Jimmy and ask him to meet me at the mausoleum as soon as possible. I should have been more careful, but I was in such a rush and I was so worried about being seen that I was looking over my shoulder and didn't notice Mister Peterman's open grave until it was too late." She touches the side of her pixie cut and winces.

I think back to when Birdie and me were behind the Gilgood mausoleum and Mr. McGinty told us in his commanding army voice this morning, "I have a matter of the utmost importance to discuss with you and it shouldn't be put off until tonight." At the time, I was positive that he wanted to expert-interrogate me about what I'd seen out our bedroom window, which is why I yelled, "Bee!" so my sister and me could make our getaway to the top of the cemetery hill, in case he was thinking of snipping off our heads with his sharp gardening shears, but obviously, I was wrong.

"But *why* was it so important for Mister McGinty to talk to Tessie and Birdie ASAP about returning the money?" Charlie asks like the questioning interviewer that he is.

"Another excellent question, Jasper," Sister Margaret Mary says. "Time was of the essence as I'm afraid Missus Klement stopped by the parish office after last evening's knitting circle to tell Father Ted and me that she strongly suspected that one of the Finley sisters had stolen the collection money." My heart skips a beat just thinking of how hot that buttinsky was on my sister's trail. "Missus Klement also informed us that if the two hundred and nine dollars wasn't returned by the conclusion of tonight's Pagan Baby meeting, she would be obligated to take matters into her own hands. She threatened to call her dear friend the bishop, who would've swiftly informed the authorities, and I—"

"There is no need for anybody to contact the authorities," Charlie says, and when he slaps down on the card table the brown paper sack that's got the P B and M and stolen loot inside, it kinda makes me swoon off my chair a little, because he is being a knight in shining armor fighting off a dragon. "Every dollar of the stolen Pagan Baby m . . . m . . . money is present and accounted for. I counted it m . . . m . . . myself and you know how good I am at arithmetic."

I'd love to believe that getting the money back will be enough to smooth things over with her, but I don't. Paying penance for your sins is such a big deal around here. So I get down on my knees and beg Sister

Margaret Mary, "I know she's a terrible reader, but please . . . you gotta understand . . . Birdie . . ." I'm fighting back tears, but losing the battle. Daddy is going to be so disappointed in me for not taking tender loving care the way I vowed I would when I stepped into his shoes. "She only took the money 'cause our family needs dough really bad and Gert . . . Missus Klement is trying to talk our mother into sending us away to homes . . . so when you call the cops, *please,* you gotta tell them that it was *me* you saw stealin' the money out of the collection box instead of her."

Mr. McGinty helps me back up to my feet and into my chair, then takes out his neatly folded hankie from his gray shirt and passes it to me. "Tessie, no one is calling the police on your sister, isn't that right, Martha?"

After I wipe my eyes and blow my nose, I look over at the strictest nun I've ever met, expecting her to say something awful like, *Even though we're twins, I'm afraid I cannot agree with you, Jimmy. As her godfather, you have a spiritual responsibility to teach the child right from wrong and how will she ever learn if she doesn't suffer the consequences?* But much to my astonishment what she *actually* says is, "Calling the police under these circumstances"—she squeezes Birdie's hand again—"is completely out of the question."

When I start bawling all over again, this time from relief, Birdie and Charlie put their arms around me, and even Pyewacket jumps from where she's been lounging on Sister Margaret Mary's lap to stay for a few seconds on mine, before she leaps into Birdie's arms, because the Siamese cat loves her most of all.

But even all the nice "there, there-ing" from the two people I love most in the world and Pye's loud purring still doesn't 100% convince me that our principal who eyewitnessed the stealing of the money from the collection box at St. Kate's *won't* call the police station and turn Birdie in. I'm not like Birdie and Charlie. I'm no pushover. I need to know *why* she'd do something so nice, so I ask her, "Are you *sure* you're not going to turn her into the coppers?"

"Let me explain something to you, Tessie, that I think will help put your mind at ease," Mr. McGinty says. "Before Martha and I moved to this neighborhood, we were raised in a small town in northern Wisconsin by a father who"—he glances over at his sister—"well, let's just say he was not a forgiving man."

"What happened to your m . . . m . . . mother?" Charlie asks.

"She died while giving birth to Martha and me," Mr. McGinty tells him with lots of affection, because he knows why Charlie can't help but ask that question.

"And what about your daddy?" I, of course, need to know. "You said he *was* not a forgiving man."

"Father was killed in a lumberjacking accident many years ago," our principal says. And I might be imagining it, because it has been a long and jam-packed day and I don't trust my powers of observation anymore, but Sister Margaret Mary sure doesn't sound all that broken up about her daddy getting killed by a tree. "The only family Jimmy and I have left are each other." She picks up the brown paper bag off the table where Charlie smacked it down, peeks inside, I guess to make sure the Pagan Baby money really *is* in there and that we've haven't been snow-jobbing her. She doesn't pull out the wad of cash and start counting it, though. She pulls out the other something I put in the bag for Birdie before we came over for our visit that has turned out to be a *lot* more interesting than I could've guessed in a million years. "Oh, look, Jimmy! A peanut butter and marshmallow sandwich. Those were always our favorites, too."

She's looking pretty tenderly at the sandwich, so I'm starting to believe that she might not turn Birdie in to the cops, but because I'm still only about 75% sure of that, I'm going to bribe her the other 25% of the way. With two TV dinner suppers in her tummy and all the windmill cookies that my sister just ate, she shouldn't go starving in the near future, so I point to the P B and M and tell Sister Margaret Mary, "Go ahead and take it as a thank-you for not squealing Birdie out."

I elbow my sister to remind her to say thank you, too, because she forgets her manners about as often as she forgets everything else, but nobody's home. Just like I knew would happen, the second she started running her little hand down the back of the tan and black Siamese, the two of them boarded the Orient Express to parts unknown. (Joke!)

7:18 p.m. Mr. McGinty looks up at the clock hanging on the wall above the brown sofa that he must've slept on last night so his sister who had gotten knocked unconscious could be comfortable in his bed until she could get her wits about her again. "It's getting late," he says. "If you intend to return the money to the collection box before Gert Klement's deadline, Marty, you should leave soon."

With one more pat of Birdie's hand, Sister M & M a.k.a. Martha "Marty" McGinty says, "I'll just change," and then she excuses herself from the card table and disappears into her brother's bedroom, and when she does that, just for a second, that nun kind of reminds me of Clark Kent disappearing into a phone booth, because that's about how big our friend's bedroom is and also because it seems like our principal is being very super about not turning Birdie in.

While we wait for Sister Margaret Mary to come back, Charlie asks Mr. McGinty something that would be of big interest to a kid who keeps track of so many things and has a very unforgiving father of his own. "So who did you come to live with in the neighborhood after you got turned into an orphan?"

Maybe it's because he is such a private person, but it sure doesn't look at first like Mr. McGinty wants to tell him, but then he does. "Henry Michael Gilgood was my mother's brother," he finally says. "Marty's and my uncle. He took us in."

"Mister Gilgood in the mausoleum that you take such extra good care of? The guy who was the richest man in the whole neighborhood who lived in the airplane house?!" I practically shout, because hot damn!

If Mr. McGinty inherited everything in his uncle's Last Will and Testament because his sister is a nun who has taken a vow of poverty, that explains how Daddy's old friend could afford to buy the beautiful tombstone from Mr. Patrick Mullarkey & Sons whose business it is to carve cemetery markers with check #2315 because Louise couldn't afford to, and also how come he's got $201,789.05 keeping itself warm in the vault at the First Wisconsin Bank.

I never told him that I knew what he did for Daddy, and I'm *not* going to tell him now how I discovered his checkbook when I was looking for an envelope in his desk so I could send off for the cool booklet in the back of the Superman comics that would teach me "How to Become a Ventriloquist"—**Throw Your Voice! Fool teachers, friends and family**. 'Fessing up to digging through his private property, well, it *might* make him a little ticked off, but mostly it would embarrass the heck out of humble Mr. McGinty if he knew that I discovered what he'd done. He's not a bragger, he's more like Zorro. He likes to keep his mask on when he's doing charitable work.

"Yes, our uncle Henry is entombed in the mausoleum, Tessie," he says with the funniest look on his face. I can't really put my finger on it. Is it the missing sadness washing over him the way it washes over me? "I'm aware of his reputation around here," Mr. McGinty says, "but nothing could be further from the truth."

I wouldn't know because I never met Mr. Gilgood in the alive state, he was long gone before I was born. But the word around the neighborhood is that he was a very strange guy. A hermit. Different. Somebody also told me he was something called a "Homo" and I have no idea what old country that means he came from. All I know is that I've always thought the poor guy should've counted his lucky stars that he died before somebody in the neighborhood started talking about how they should get him sent away to a "home" for not fitting in around here.

"Uncle Henry was a wonderful man," Mr. McGinty says with a sweet, remembering smile on his face now. "Gentle and generous, soft-spoken, an outstanding photographer, a lover of opera and architecture, and a lifelong member of the Audubon Society. These are a few of his photos." He points over to the wall above his sofa at the beautiful framed pictures that I have always admired of woods and streams, and Birdie's and Charlie's favorite, three hummingbirds sipping nectar out of a flower.

Charlie, who's acting now like he's taking one of his surveys, asks Mr. McGinty the next question on his list, which happens to be something I've been wondering about, too, because of course, we're a match made in Heaven, so we are on the same wavelength, most of the time. "You told us you were waitin' for us and you had out our windmill cookies and root beer already when we got here. If time really was of the essence like Sister Margaret Mary said and it was so important to talk to Tessie about returning the Pagan Baby money ASAP, what if tonight turned out to be one of those nights that her and her sister and me didn't pay you a visit? What if we'd hung around the block and played kick the can instead, or did some snoop—" I kicked him under the table, because our religious godfather would not, I repeat *not* approve of the blackmailing part of The Mutual Admiration Society's business.

Mr. McGinty answers, "When I discovered the girls behind Uncle Henry's mausoleum this morning, Tessie couldn't get away from me fast enough, but Birdie wanted to stay and talk." He's referring to when I wanted to play it safer than sorrier because I thought he might be the kidnapping murderer and I feared for our lives. "Tessie *sister*-promised Birdie that they'd come back tonight for a visit, and where the girls go, you're never far behind, so I knew it was just a matter of time before the three of you would show up on my doorstep tonight."

"A *sister*-promise can never be broken, no matter what," drifting Birdie lowers her anchor and says. (Joke!) Or maybe she pulls her derailed brain into the train station and says that. (Also quite funny.)

Mr. McGinty grins at Birdie and says, "Speaking of sisters . . ." He looks over at his closed bedroom door and lowers his already soft voice. "I have a favor to ask of you, Tessie. I realize that Marty can be quite . . . quite . . ." Because he's such a good egg who follows the Golden Rule down to the letter, I think he's trying to come up with a nice way to say that his sister can be mean as hell. "In my experience, people often grow up to treat others the way they were treated as children even though they don't mean to." He gets this faraway, sad look on his face. "So I'm afraid my sister has a tendency to be a little—"

"Too strict and really bossy and whip-cracking," Charlie says.

"Yes," Mr. McGinty admits with a sigh. "She can be a stickler for rules and at times too hard on those who don't follow them, but as you saw tonight, her heart is in the right place." My guts are telling me that there is a *lot* more to the McGinty twins' story that I will have to drag out of him during one of our fishing trips. "So if you could just take it a little easier on her, kids, I'd appreciate it."

Well, long as she doesn't suddenly change her mind and become a stickler for the rule about turning thieves in to the police, I figure what the heck. I owe it to the guy who has been such a good caretaker, not only of the cemetery, but of Birdie and me and even Charlie. "I can't *sister*-promise you," I tell him, "but . . . as the president of The Mutual Admiration Society I have the authority to *regular*-promise that we'll all try and be a little nicer to her from here on out."

"Thank you for washing and ironing my habit, Jimmy," Sister Margaret Mary says when she returns from the bedroom looking like her usual scary self in black and white. "As you said, I best be leaving before the Pagan Baby meeting ends." She tucks the paper bag that's got the loot and the P B and M inside under her arm. "I wouldn't want to bump into Missus Klement while I'm returning the money."

Charlie, my little gentleman, picks up my Roy Rogers flashlight and says, "I was planning to stop by the church to say some prayers for my mother, it's her birthday on Saturday, so I would be happy to escort you, Sister. We don't want you to fall into another grave with the Pagan Baby money, because statistically speaking that would be very bad timing."

"And I have Mister Peterman to attend to," Mr. McGinty says, "but perhaps the Finley sisters would like to accompany you as well. It's a beautiful evening, and according to the weatherman, it might be the last one for quite a while."

I tug Daddy's Timex out of my shorts pocket.

7:25 p.m. I was hoping that Birdie and me would have enough time to swing by Lonnigan's Bar to visit with Suzie "That French Slut" LaPelt, but just like Mr. McGinty, we have a grave to attend to, and we can't do both if we want to get home before Louise does.

"Thanks for the offer, but we have a previous commitment," I say very politely to Mr. McGinty, then I turn to Sister Margaret Mary and, yes, this kind of sentimental sloppiness usually makes me want to throw up, but I hug the nun who is letting my partner in crime off the hook, and then I do the same to her twin brother, and, of course, so does my lovey-dovey sister. I really, really, really, really want to nuzzle Charlie, too, the way Birdie did, but being an innocent, she can get away with that sort of thing. I just wink at my one and only before I pick up my sister's hand and his "babies" take off at a run toward Daddy's tombstone to tell him about our day and our plans for tomorrow, because that's something we've done since we lost him, and we will keep doing it until the day when the good one of his daughters joins him on high and the other one of us takes a trip below . . . below . . . below.

Because even if he isn't here in body anymore, the Finley sisters know in a certain kind of way that nobody else can ever hope to understand, that our daddy has no trouble hearing us loud and clear. His death might've ambushed Birdie and me, kicked us over and over again where it hurts and will continue to do so, but, believe me, it will *never, ever* beat the love outta us. We are all for one and one for all forever and always.

23

A CONFESSION

11:55 p.m. Friday: As usual, I'm doing what I always do in the middle of the night. Slipping my hand under my sister's heinie every half hour to make sure she hasn't wet the bed, working on my lists, shadowboxing, practicing my impressions, a couple of sure-fire jokes that will get the crowd going, and the "Favorite Things" song that I'm going to perform for the talent portion of Miss America someday in honor of my father.

I'm also thinking how I really don't know if things could have gone more smoothly at the fish fry tonight, except for when Sister Margaret Mary got up to announce that our school was given a "clean bill of health." Termites had something to do with the basement steps collapsing under Tommy "Two-Ton" Thomkins, and it wasn't the dangerous kind of "gas" that building inspector Mr. Hopkins thought he smelled, but I was wrong, too. It wasn't Beans and Wienies Wednesday that was causing the awful stench in the school basement. The sulphur smell was coming out of janitor Mr. Wayne "Creeper" Carlson's little room. Turns out that just like everybody else around here, he has a hobby that makes his life worth living. Mr. Hopkins discovered Creeper's hard-boiled egg collection in a hole in the wall behind the incinerator. According to the gossip, the eggs that were found behind the Betty-Grable-loving-the-tractor-too-much calendar were beautifully decorated with the faces of movie stars.

FACT: Painting hard-boiled eggs is a normal hobby to have during Easter time, but it's a very weird way to spend your leisure hours during other parts of the year.

PROOF: I am definitely sending this story into *Ripley's Believe It or Not!*

After hearing the back-to-school news, I usually would've joined in the rumble, but considering what our principal did for Birdie, and that I regular-promised her brother that I would try to go easier on her, I did *not* pelt Sister Margaret Mary with potato pancakes after she made the announcement at the Friday Fish Fry tonight, so I did not get instantly expelled the way half of the juvenile delinquents did, including that maniac Butch Seeback, thank you, sweet Jesus.

Because I am working very hard to follow Mr. Lynwood "My friends call me Woody and my enemies call me their worst enemy" Bellflower's detecting directions to the letter, I reach under my pillow and pull out my detecting notebook and stubby pencil. In Chapter Seven of the best book ever written on the subject, he wrote, "Once an investigation has reached a conclusion, it is important to create a *case file*," so by the light of my Roy Rogers flashlight, I jot down most of everything that happened tonight.

FACT: I bumped into Kitten Jablonski in the little girls' room and after I stepped back far enough to make sure one of her pimples didn't parachute down to my face, I told her what Sister Margaret Mary wrote in the note Sister Prudence found, but not *why* she wrote it, because her hurrying over to the cemetery to talk to her brother about the stolen Pagan Baby collection money is none of Kitten's damn business. I just left it at, "Sister had an emergency situation to attend to."

PROOF: Of course, my confidential informant didn't apologize for daring me and putting me under so much pressure, because her saying she's sorry for anything, well, that's not one of her business policies. What she did was punch me in the arm and tell me, "I absolve you of the dare, Finley," and then she made sure that her snitch, Linda O'Brien, who *is* a slave to the nuns this week for telling her mother that she didn't know her ass from a hole in the ground the way Charlie said she was, told every single kid that passed in front of her in the cafeteria line to get two fish sticks slapped on their plates, "Finley completed the dare so lay offa her, and if ya say one word about this hairnet, you'll be eating your perch with a busted lip."

FACT: What's-his-name will *not* be coming around and beeping the ah-OO-ga horn of his souped-up Chevy every morning, or keeping our mother out late at night, not for a while at least, because I did #4 on this list:

JUST DESSERTS

1. Find out where the numbskull lives and smear black shoe polish on his Chevy's whitewalls.
2. Put a bag of burning dog doo-doo on his porch, ring the doorbell, and run.
3. Call him at his "alleged" job at the American Motors plant and use that impression you learned from watching gangster movies where wops are always threatening *their* enemies: *Dis is Three-Fingered Louie Galetti and you-a better stay away from that doll Louise Finley if you-a don' wanna be fitted for a cement raincoat, ya goomba.*
4. ~~Doctor up his food, *if* you ever get to meet him face-to-face.~~

PROOF: After all the folderol during THE CASE OF THE TROTS, if there is anything that Louise Finley does *not* want to be associated with it's a bad case of diarrhea, and I mixed up so many ground-up Ex-Lax pills into Leon Gallagher's tapioca pudding dessert when he was hypnotized by Louise's bouncing bosom that he got too pooped to participate the rest of the night. (Joke!) He didn't even make it to the little boys' room. (Ha . . . ha . . . ha . . . *Gotcha!*)

FACT: Louise doesn't need his "alleged" American Motors paycheck ASAP anymore, so she told Birdie and me that we can start calling her *Mom* again. She sang "Some Enchanted Evening"—hers and Daddy's song—the entire walk home from the fish fry, which I found a little annoying, but I guess it's better than having to listen to her sing the blues. (Birdie will take Louise up on her offer to call her Mom, but I won't. I think you need to have a really bad memory like my sister's if you want to forget and forgive somebody.)

PROOF: Louise had a very good reason to feel enchanted, because Mr. Fleming, the father of Mary Jane Fleming, who has been calling our mother every day from his desk at the First Wisconsin Bank to tell her that she better make a payment on our house or else, told Louise at the fish fry that a mysteriously large amount of dough turned up in her checking account late this afternoon, which should take care of matters.

FACT: I have already solved THE CASE OF THE MIRACULOUS MORTGAGE MONEY.

PROOF: Mr. James "Jimmy/Good Egg" McGinty got plenty of dough from his rich departed uncle to do as many charitable acts as he wants, and I'm pretty sure our godfather would really miss the Finley sisters if we had to move out of the neighborhood and into the poorhouse.

FACT: The Pagan Baby election has been called off and a winner declared, due to the niceness of *another* mysterious do-gooder who pleads the Fifth.

PROOF: Some genius kid waited until Gert Klement left to set up for the fish fry this afternoon, and then she stuck her weird sister in front of the Motorola television and her game shows and some Hershey's kisses that she found under her bed. She then rode her Schwinn bike up two streets to Kenfield's Five and Dime on North Ave. to buy the biggest piece of poster board she could find—she only paid for it because she couldn't stick it under her T-shirt without getting caught—then she five-fingered a thick black marker and a pair of red pom-poms and she rode a block over to Melman's Hardware. This is where she sliced open a bag of cement in aisle seven with her father's lucky Swiss Army Knife and scooped some of it into a brown paper bag. The last stop she made was at Dalinsky's Drugstore for more candy and Tums and Ex-Lax.

When the same smart kid finished her errands, she came home and refilled a bowl to the brim with Hershey's kisses and set it down in front of her sister, who was happily watching *The Price Is Right*. Then she popped into her garage and mixed up the cement in a coffee can and printed a *huge* sign with her left hand so no one would recognize her excellent handwriting. After that, once she made sure that nobody was around to wonder what the hell she was doing, she ran down the block.

She was not at all worried that she would get seen by Mrs. Nancy Tate. Due to her excellent investigative skills, she knew that gal was up at Rhonda's Beauty Parlor getting a permanent wave, when she stuck the sign in the hole she made in the Tate's front lawn, along with some of the cement to prevent easy removal:

ONE-TWO-THREE-FOUR!
DON'T BE A BIG FAT BORE!
GET YOUR POM-POMS OUT AND CHEER!
FOR THE HOOVER SALESMAN OF THE YEAR!
(MR. HORACE MERTZ MAKES EVENING HOUSE CALLS.)

Considering how strongly that kid feels about an eye for an eye, in her opinion, that patchwork-quilting, pagan-baby-torturing holy roller who slid her vicious little foot-long dog through her rumpus room window the night two snooping sisters spied her hoochie-coochie dancing for a vodka-on-the-rocks-swilling traveling vacuum cleaner salesman got off easy.

FACT: You should've heard some of the *other* slogans that kid came up with.

PROOF: WHORE also rhymes with FOUR.

After about a hundred of the busybodies who had seen the new advertising sign on her front lawn came up to Mrs. Nancy Tate at the fish fry to ask her why she was so nuts about Mr. Horace Mertz, my mother's opponent rushed right over to Gert Klement and told her that she changed her mind about running for treasurer and withdrew her name. (That same kid might've also paid two dollars to the loudest and most obnoxious kid in the church choir, baritone Bertie Buss, to follow Mrs. Nancy Tate around the cafeteria shaking those two red five and dime pom-poms while singing "Rockin' Robin," in case the gigantic poison-pen sign cemented into her front lawn wasn't enough to make that lame duck waddle out of the fish fry with her tail between her legs.) (Joke!)

FACT: I think Charlie is about ready to set a date.

PROOF: He kissed me longer this time on the cheek with his buttery lips on our walk back home from the fish fry.

FACT: Mrs. Gert Klement is *not* happy.

PROOF: Sure, she's glad that she got her Pagan Baby money back, but I could tell that she was crushed that she didn't get the chance to call the cops and get Birdie and me sent away to "homes," for now, anyway.

So all and all, as I lay here now next to my always-sweet-smelling, snoozing partner in crime, I'm thinking The Mutual Admiration Society did okay on our first kidnapping and murder case. Our investigation wasn't perfect, but from years of experience and all the time Birdie and me spend in Holy Cross, I have long suspected that not just the Finley sisters or my Charlie, but *nobody* gets those and-they-all-lived-happily-ever-after fairy-tale endings. We must all BE PREPARED to have a little Grimm mixed in. (No joke.)

Until Butch Seeback gets moved permanently to the juvie home after he commits some awful Ed Gein crime, I will always have to keep my eyes out for him, and my poor sister will probably always be a weird loonatic, and buttinsky and battle-ax Gert Klement will never bury her hatchet, and Louise will more than likely start dating what's-his-name again after his trotting clears up, and I will always miss Daddy with every beat of my heart, every breath, every lightning bolt, and every joke. Not a minute will go by in the day that I won't wonder how I'm going to live to the next minute without him, and every single night when I stand in front of our bedroom window, I will cry when I see the curve of his headstone under the cemetery's flickering streetlights.

On the other hand . . . like Daddy always told me when he was punching his bag and making our basement floor slippery with sweat, "No matter how bad things get, Tessie, you gotta always remember, come Hell or high water, a Finley never, *ever* throws in the towel."

So . . . in the *spirit* of things (Joke!) I already got my brand-new list ready and raring to go when the sun peeks through the cracks of my sister's and my bedroom window shade:

TO-DO

1. Take tender loving care of Birdie.
2. Make Gert Klement think her arteries are going as hard as her heart.
3. Practice your Miss America routine.
4. Learn how to swim.
5. Be a good dry-martini-making fiancée to Charlie.
6. Do not get caught blackmailing or spying.
7. Just *think* about making a real confession to Father Ted, before it's too late.
8. Stop at Bloomers for pink roses for Daddy.
9. Test Birdie again to make sure that she really *does* have ESP and her guessing every single one of those numbers that I was thinking of tonight wasn't half-Irish luck.
10. Beat Jenny Radtke to the top of the Finney Library Billy the Bookworm chart or just beat her.

11. Tell Birdie you found one of Louise's L&M cigarette butts at Daddy's pretend grave.
12. Learn Morris's Code.
13. Steal new Halloween costumes for Birdie and me from Kenfield's Five and Dime.
14. Go see Suzie "That French Slut" LaPelt at Lonnigan's so Birdie and me can sing the "Sisters" song on the bar and play the Arabian Nights pinball game and talk to her about Daddy, and as long as you're there, ask her for a demonstration of this ooo-la-la kissing you are hearing so much about.
15. Stay back after school on Monday and find Gracie Carver so you and Birdie can tell her all about what happened while she was gone. She will get such a kick out of it and laugh that relaxing Southern way.
16. Keep your eyes peeled for a dead body. Current second-place winner in the "Best Mourner" in the parish contest Mrs. Sophia Maniaci, who is a Sicilian—an especially vengeful type of Italian who everyone in the neighborhood knows you shouldn't cross—hissed out to the current first-place winner, Mrs. Ann Tracy, when she was leaving the fish fry, "*Il bacio della morte*," which is the kiss-of-death curse, so it shouldn't be long before The Mutual Admiration Society has another great-good-luck murder case on our hands.

The End

ACKNOWLEDGMENTS

Deepest thanks to the wondrous souls who make me laugh, crack the whip, swipe off my tears, and encourage me not to throw in the towel:

My forever-loved brilliant and hilarious son, Riley, my guiding light and muse. Casey, my daughter and best friend whose strength, intelligence, love, and sassiness are truly something to behold. Her husband, John-Michael, "Big Daddy," one in a million. And our gifts from on high, Charlie and Hadley, the grandest of babies, possessors of magic and the kindest hearts, who inspire us to be our best selves.

Kelli Martin, the charming and talented-beyond-words fairy godmother who waved her magic wand over the story. Should all writers be so lucky to work with an editor of her caliber and grace.

The Lake Union team, including copyeditor Deb Taber, proofreader Johanna Rosenbohm, and cover designer Rachel Adam, who provided me with the kind of publishing experience that I'd only dreamed of. It was a privilege to work with every single one of them.

My literary agent, Kim Witherspoon, whose insight has proved invaluable over the years.

Star authors who offered such lovely praise—Mary Kubica, Heather Gudenkauf, Cassie Selleck, and Barbara Claypole White—you are the bomb.

Dear friends Beth Hoffman, Fran "Elfie" Wagner, Bonnie Shimko, Emily Lewis, and Dr. Meagan Harris. I have been informed by sources that I'm currently not at liberty to discuss that they're all going to Heaven for reading early drafts.

Social media manager extraordinaire Susie Stangland, and Maddee and Jen at Xuni.com, who work wonders on the internet and beyond.

Love to Rebecca Winner for her continued generosity and kindness.

And to you, and all the readers who allow me to be part of their lives, I remain forever honored and grateful.

ABOUT THE AUTHOR

Photo © 2011 Megan McCormick/Shoot the Moon Photography

Lesley Kagen is an actress, voice-over talent, speaker, and award-winning *New York Times* bestselling author of eight novels, including *The Undertaking of Tess*. Her work has been translated into seven languages. A mother of two and grandmother of two, she lives in a hundred-year-old farmhouse in a small town in Wisconsin. Visit with her on Facebook and at her website, www.lesleykagen.com.